The Lord Is My Shepherd

THE LORD IS MY SHEPHERD

Book One

The Psalm 23 Mysteries

Debbie Viguié

Abingdon Press fiction
a novel approach to faith

Nashville, Tennessee

To my mother, Barbara Reynolds, who loves mysteries and has been one of my greatest supporters.

ACKNOWLEDGMENTS

I would like to thank Barbara Scott; she is a true superwoman and a fantastic editor. I'd also like to thank my agent, Beth Jusino, who believed in this series from the beginning. Thank you as well to my husband, Scott; my father, Richard; and both my grandmothers, Mildred and Mary. Thank you to my wonderful friend, Marissa Smeyne, and her family for all their help. Thank you also to the dear friends who listened patiently to me talk about this series: Ann Liotta, Juliette Cutts, and Calliope Collacott.

1

More than anything, Cindy Preston hated Mondays. As a kid Mondays meant that it was time to stop playing and go back to school. They were the day that her dad always left home on business trips, which he did a lot. On Mondays she had to take drama classes because her brother did, and anything he did she had to do too. She never got to act. Kyle always overshadowed her. Instead, she helped construct the stages he strutted around on.

As an adult, Mondays were even worse. Returning to any job wasn't pleasant after a weekend of freedom. But you could double that since she worked at a church, which meant Mondays were hell.

Of course, "hell" wasn't a word Cindy would use at church, unless she was talking literally about the place and its demonic denizens. She'd had a lifetime of paranoia pounded into her by her mother. "You don't curse at church. You don't fall asleep during the sermon. You don't look at boys. You don't wear slacks."

Cindy knew exactly what couldn't be done at church, but she always felt a little unsure about what you *could* do.

The first time a friend invited her to a Pentecostal service Cindy had spent the entire time telling people to put their hands down, because she was just sure you couldn't do that in church.

Cindy smiled grimly as she pulled into the parking lot of First Shepherd. She might not know what she could do at church, but she did know that in a pinch she could work there. Even if that meant she had to wear skirts and dresses every day. Slacks still didn't feel right in a sanctuary. She turned off the engine and leaned her head back for a minute, closing her eyes.

"God help me."

Cindy had never had a job that was so rewarding or half as exasperating. At any ordinary job you could leave on Friday, lock the door behind you, and come back on Monday morning and expect to find things where you left them. Not so much when you worked at a church.

Last Monday had been one of the worst days yet. They were preparing for Easter week, one of the busiest times of the year with extra services, programs, and special events. As if that hadn't been enough, the church's furnace had quit working, someone had broken a key off in the nursery room door lock, one of the women's bathrooms had flooded, and her binder of master calendars and room assignments had somehow found its way from her desk to the pulpit.

Cindy contemplated sitting in her car until everyone else showed up for work. An extra half hour of quiet sounded good, but she knew she couldn't sit there. The one advantage of arriving first was the chance to assess the damage before anyone else, especially Pastor Roy, showed up and freaked out.

Maybe if everything is quiet I can play a quick game of solitaire.

She got out of her car and walked toward the main gate that shut off the parking lot from the church buildings. With her left hand she slid a deck of cards out of her purse and shuffled them with one hand. She'd learned the trick in junior high, and it always calmed her down.

Please, God, let the soda machine not be empty.

Given that the high school youth group had a big outreach the night before, only God Himself could have left a can in the machine for her.

When she inserted her key in the gate's lock and twisted, it didn't click. Cindy stood for a moment, puzzled, before she pushed open the unlocked door.

"Somebody's in trouble," she muttered. Staff rarely forgot to lock the gate at night.

"Hello, anyone here?" she called as she stepped into the courtyard. No reply. She hesitated for a moment. The silence was always disturbing early in the morning, especially after the noise and clamor of Sunday services. She glanced around uneasily but didn't see anyone.

Cindy headed straight across the open breezeway toward the sanctuary, sticking to her normal routine. She shuffled the cards with her left hand faster and faster and prayed that the women's room wasn't flooded again. Without breaking stride, she scooped up a small piece of paper from the ground near the door and stuffed it in her coat pocket, intending to throw it away in the office.

She unlocked the sanctuary door, stepped inside, and moved along the wall toward the bank of light switches, which some "art-over-practicality" architect had discretely positioned beneath a portrait of Jesus twenty feet from the door. In the darkness her foot caught on something soft and out of place, and she crashed to the floor, smacking her elbows and one knee. Her cards flew from her hand, and she could hear them flutter down around her.

Now what? What had the youth group kids done to the sanctuary this time? Cindy scrambled to her feet only to feel her twisted knee give out from under her, and she fell against the wall. Her shaking hand reached out and caught the light switch. With a loud clunk, the overhead lights slowly came on, and she turned around to see what she had tripped over.

A man, wearing a long black coat, lay sprawled on the ground. Half a dozen of her cards had landed on him, but he didn't move. Cindy jumped backward, hand pressed to her chest.

"Oh! Sir, are you all right?"

As she approached him carefully, he still didn't move. Cindy bent down and shook his leg, like she had learned once in a first-aid class. *Did he have a heart attack?*

When he didn't move she took hold of his shoulder and rolled him onto his back. She gasped when her eyes met his vacant stare. One look at those eyes and she knew he was dead. She had seen that look before, eyes just like that, open and frozen. Then she saw the knife sticking out of his chest.

Cindy screamed and jumped backward, slamming into a pew. Her injured knee buckled, and she collapsed to the floor, still screaming.

The empty church sanctuary caught the sounds of her screams and bounced them around the high-ceiling room.

Her own voice was all she could hear. The body was the only thing she could see. The coppery smell of blood nearly overwhelmed her.

Something flashed in the open doorway six feet away. A dark figure seemed to fly across the threshold, landed next to her, and rolled to a stop on one knee. His eyes blazed like black flame, and his black hair framed the murderous face of a devil.

Cindy screamed louder and tried to push away from her position on the floor, but her hand slipped on the glossy surface of a playing card and she fell onto the man-devil's shoulder. He wrapped one arm around her waist, and with the other he pulled her head down to his chest. She struggled against him, but he held her so tightly she couldn't free herself.

I don't want to die! She pummeled him with her free fist.

Through the haze of terror that enveloped her, she heard him speak. "I'm Jeremiah, the rabbi from next door. You're safe."

Safe. Safe. The word rattled around in her brain until she finally remembered its meaning. No one is ever safe. She stopped screaming, but her body shook with gulping sobs. With her head pressed to his chest she could no longer see the body on the floor. She forced herself to take deep breaths.

The rabbi shifted slightly and let go of the back of her head. She heard him dialing three digits on a cell phone: 9-1-1.

"Yes, this is Jeremiah Silverman. I'm at the Presbyterian church on the corner of Main and Lincoln in Pine Springs. I'm in the sanctuary with a lady who just found a dead body here. Send the police. Yes. Yes. That's correct. Thank you."

"The police are on their way," he said still hanging on to his cell. His voice was calm and soothing.

She nodded.

"Are you okay? You're not hurt at all?" he asked.

"My arm hurts and my knees from when I tripped," Cindy said. She forced out each word through chattering teeth.

"I think you're okay. You're just in shock."

Of course she was in shock. She remembered how it felt. It was one of the only things she remembered about that day when she was fifteen and saw her first dead body.

"Let me help you up," Jeremiah said.

Some morbid part of her wanted to look at the body again, to reassure herself that it was no one she knew. The rest of her was quite sure she'd never forget what she had seen.

I'm going to be sick. She stumbled a few feet away from the rabbi.

"Hold on. Where are you going?"

"I need to get out of here," she said.

"I don't think that's a good idea. Wait until the police get here. In the meantime, this will keep you a little warmer." Jeremiah slipped his coat around her shoulders. "Put your arms into the sleeves."

"He's dead, right?" She knew the man was dead. Eyes didn't lie, and the dead man's eyes told her everything. Still, she needed to hear it, needed to know that she was right. Needed for someone else to acknowledge it.

"Yes, he's dead." Jeremiah's voice was calm and authoritative.

Cindy nodded. He put his arms around her, and she gladly leaned into him again. They slid to the floor against the back pew to wait for help.

2

JEREMIAH CONSIDERED QUESTIONING THE WOMAN ABOUT WHAT HAD happened, but realized he'd hear the story soon enough once the police showed up. He leaned back against the pew and held her. She had calmed down considerably, but he gently stroked her hair to soothe her.

He glanced over at the body: a man in his late forties, a black-handled Bowie knife sticking out of his chest, and playing cards fanned out around him. Whoever had stabbed the victim had used a lot of force to drive the weapon in that far. The blood that had spilled out onto his white shirt was dark and dried. He'd probably been dead for several hours before the girl found him.

Girl. He glanced down at her and smiled. She was old enough to be someone's mother. He guessed her age as close to thirty. Her long, light brown hair fanned out over his shoulder and chest. Her eyes were squeezed shut, but he remembered them as vivid green and wide with terror. He must have made quite a sight barreling through the door the way he did.

He had been the rabbi at the synagogue next door for almost two years and had seen her on many occasions in the parking lot, but he didn't know her name.

Jeremiah smiled grimly when the police arrived in less than five minutes. If his emergency call had been about a stolen car or a purse snatcher, they would have waited hours for the police, but mention "dead body" and watch them come running with sirens blasting.

Officers sealed off the area just in time. Outside the sanctuary Jeremiah could see several people he took to be other staff members showing up at the door for work. They had certainly gotten a lot more than they bargained for.

"Sir, could you and the lady step over here?" a detective asked, waving them toward a pew a little way from the body.

"We can move now," Jeremiah told the woman. "Are you ready?"

Cindy nodded, and he stood. She struggled for a moment, and he could see the bruises that had already formed on her knees and her right arm. He stooped down, put his hands under her arms, and pulled her into a standing position. She gave him a fleeting smile before her eyes fixed on the body. He grabbed her chin and gently pulled her head around to face him.

"Come over here with me," he said. He kept an arm around her and half-led, half-carried her over to the detective. Jeremiah lowered her into a pew and then sat beside her.

The detective took a seat in front of them and turned around. He passed a hand through his sandy blonde hair, and his sharp eyes looked her over before turning on Jeremiah.

"My name is Mark Walters," he said, addressing Jeremiah.

"Jeremiah Silverman. I'm the rabbi from the synagogue next door."

The detective nodded toward the woman. "I take it she found him?"

"Yes."

"Were you with her at the time?"

"No, I was getting out of my car when I heard her screaming. I ran over to see if I could help and found her on the floor next to him."

"A real Good Samaritan," the detective commented, not unkindly.

"Not quite. I'm Jewish."

The detective just blinked.

"Sorry, bad joke," Jeremiah said, mentally cursing. The last thing he needed was to anger the police. Neither he nor the synagogue needed that kind of attention, especially not with Passover about to start.

Mark stared hard at him for a moment and then nodded. "My wife makes jokes when she's scared or upset. I guess she's not the only one. Me, I find it hard to be funny when there's a dead man on the floor of a church and a killer on the loose."

"I'm sorry," Jeremiah said. "This is just a stressful way to start your day, you know?"

"That I do know," Mark agreed.

He turned his attention back to the woman who sat quietly, staring off into the distance. "I need to ask her a few questions."

Jeremiah put his arm around her shoulder, and she turned to look at him. "The detective has a couple of questions for you."

She seemed to wake up at that and blinked slowly, as though only now seeing him. She looked at the detective and cleared her throat. "Yes, of course," she said, her voice hoarse.

"I'll make this as quick as I can," the detective said. His tone was reassuring.

"Thank you."

"Your name?"

"Cindy Preston."

Cindy. It suits her, Jeremiah thought.

"Okay, Miss Preston, do you work here?"

She nodded. "I'm the secretary."

"The man on the floor, do you know who he is?"

"No," she said.

"Have you ever seen him before?"

"No."

"Okay, that's fine. You're doing fine," Mark assured her. "Can you tell me what happened this morning?"

"I fell over him." Tears streaked down her cheeks.

"You fell over him?" Mark asked.

She nodded.

"Okay, how about before you fell on him. What were you doing?"

"I unlocked the sanctuary."

"Is that part of your job?"

"Yes. I'm almost always here before everyone else, and I unlock the sanctuary and then the office and then any other rooms that are going to be used in the morning."

"So the sanctuary was locked this morning when you got here?"

She nodded and wiped at her eyes. "Yes. The main gate wasn't, though."

"You mean the gate out by the parking lot?" the detective asked.

She nodded.

Jeremiah and Mark exchanged a quick glance. Mark turned back to Cindy. "Is the main gate usually locked?"

"Yes. I mean, every once in a while the last person to leave forgets, but not often."

"So, the main gate was unlocked but the sanctuary was locked?"

"Yes."

"Okay. You unlocked the door and then what happened?"

"I tripped over him before I could reach the light switch," she said. "My cards went flying out of my hand."

"So, the playing cards are yours?" Mark asked.

"Yes. It's my lucky deck."

"Not so lucky today." Mark sounded grim. "So you fell, and your cards went flying. What next?"

"I got up and turned on the lights. I turned to see what I had tripped over, and there he was, lying face down."

"Face down?" Jeremiah asked before he could stop himself.

Mark glared a warning but didn't say anything.

"Yes. I thought maybe he'd fallen or had a heart attack or something. I asked if he was okay, and when he didn't answer, I grabbed his shoulder like they showed us in the first-aid class and rolled him onto his back. That's when I saw the . . . the . . . knife." She took a deep breath and bit her bottom lip.

"That's okay, ma'am. What happened after that?"

"I screamed, I think, and he came." Cindy turned to look at Jeremiah.

"I see," Mark said.

"I found her here on the floor beside him, and I called 9-1-1."

"Have you seen the victim before?"

Jeremiah shook his head. "No."

Jeremiah spied another officer checking out the crime scene. He watched the man walk the perimeter of the sanctuary; his eyes roamed over everything. In the background Jeremiah could hear Mark's droning voice, as he asked Cindy the same questions in three different ways. They trained police to do that. By asking the same questions, but varying the language and prompting for more and more detailed responses, they could often get more information out of witnesses than a simple narrative. They also could tell if a person was lying. It was hard not to slip up when being questioned like that. The second detective had made it almost all the way around the sanctuary when he stopped and bent down. The officer whistled low, and their detective turned to look.

"Miss, I'll be right back," Mark said and hurried to join his partner.

The two bent over to examine something on the floor. Because Jeremiah's line of sight was blocked, he couldn't see what they were looking at. When they stood up, though, he could read their lips.

The cards belong to the woman. She tripped over the body, and they went flying. Still, make sure you tag them all.

Done. You get anything solid from her?

Not yet. She seems clean, but she could just be a good actor.

Her car was still warm when officers arrived, and this guy's been dead for several hours.

She could have killed him last night and come back today.

I don't think so. The pastor says that she was at the hospital most of the night with one of the elderly members of the congregation who was dying.

We got a confirmation on that?

I'll call the hospital. I don't think we have anything to worry about with her. How about the guy?

Works next door. Heard her screaming and came to help.

Mark walked back toward them. The detective crouched down and touched Cindy's shoulder. In his hand he held a small plastic bag. Inside was a silver cross and chain encrusted with dried blood. Etched into the center of the cross was a lamb.

"Have you ever seen this before?" Mark asked.

She straightened slightly and nodded. "That's a Shepherd's Cross."

"What's a Shepherd's Cross?"

"The church gives them out to Shepherds. They're members who volunteer to visit the sick and the shut-ins."

"Like you?"

"No, I'm not a Shepherd, just a secretary."

"And just how many Shepherds are there?"

"Thirty."

"Is there any way to know which Shepherd lost this? Any distinguishing size or markings?"

She shook her head. "They're all identical. You don't think—"

"Is there anything else you can think of? Did you see anything unusual?"

"I don't think so."

Seeing the blood-covered cross had excited Cindy's interest, but Jeremiah could see she was about to cry again. If a Shepherd had been responsible for the murder, it would be devastating to her.

"I don't think she remembers much right now," Jeremiah offered. "She's still in shock."

Mark looked at him again with intense scrutiny. Even though it made him uncomfortable, Jeremiah knew how to sit quietly and stare back calmly.

"Okay," Mark relented. "Ma'am, is there a place we can reach you if we have any further questions?"

Cindy nodded and gave the detective her home phone number. Jeremiah then gave his to the detective as well.

"One last thing, did either of you touch anything?"

Jeremiah shook his head no. Cindy nodded.

"The door and the light and . . . him . . . when I rolled him onto his back. And, of course, my cards."

"Nothing else?"

"I don't think so," she said.

Mark turned back to Jeremiah. "We're done with her for now, so she might want to go home. We still need to question the rest of the church staff. She should consider taking a day or two off. I'll call later this week if I have more questions for either of you."

"But I can't take time off," she said. "This is Easter week, and there's so much to do."

"Cindy, you can call your pastor later today and make that decision with him, okay?" Jeremiah said.

"I suppose . . ."

Mark continued to stare at Jeremiah. "We're not done talking with the other people who work here yet. I can get one of the other officers to take her home."

"You probably need them here. I can run her home," Jeremiah said.

Mark gave him the ghost of a smile. "Thanks, Samaritan."

Jeremiah just nodded. He refused to let the detective bait him.

As she walked out of the sanctuary, Cindy took a deep breath of fresh air, which seemed to clear her head. A crowd of strangers stared and whispered as she passed by. She had never felt so on display. Pastor Roy was talking with a detective, but he smiled at her and gave a reassuring nod. She'd call him later. What a sight she must be! She still wore Jeremiah's coat, and he had his arm around her shoulders, half-pushing her toward the parking lot.

Only a short hedge separated the parking lots of the church and the synagogue. A small gap in the bushes close to the buildings allowed people to cross from one parking lot to the other. The dirt pathway was a testament to the unspoken accord the two congregations had shared for nearly thirty years. On Sunday mornings the church used the synagogue's lot for overflow parking. On Saturday mornings the synagogue did the same.

Jeremiah steered Cindy toward his car, an older black Mustang. She hesitated a moment. Was it safe to leave with him? After all, he was really a stranger to her. She glanced over her shoulder, but no one looked their way. Her coworkers would be occupied by the police for quite a while. Jeremiah opened the car door, and she allowed him to help her inside. Moments later they drove out of the lot.

"Right or left?" he asked.

"Right. Then right on Stanton," she said.

She looked at Jeremiah sideways. "I thought you were the murderer when I first saw you."

"Lucky for you I wasn't." He glanced at her and smiled.

"Yeah, lucky."

"It explains why you tried to get away from me, though."

"Sorry."

"Don't be. You were terrified, and I came out of nowhere. You seem better now."

"It helped to leave."

"Not surprising," he said. "Sometimes a little sunshine can chase the shadows away."

"I like that."

He turned onto Stanton Street. "Now where?"

"Turn right at the signal," she told him, forcing her eyes back to the road.

He nodded and slowed as he made the turn. "You're the church secretary?"

"Yes."

"So basically you run the church?"

She laughed, and the sound surprised her. "I'm not sure that the pastor would agree with you."

"Then he's an idiot."

"I wouldn't say that," she said.

"I would. Marie, the secretary at the synagogue, is like the field marshal. She schedules meetings and events, makes sure everyone knows what they're doing every day, keeps the staff informed of what's going on, listens to everybody's problems and tries to solve them all."

"That pretty much sums up my job. So, what is it you do at the synagogue? I think you probably said, but I don't remember much of the last hour."

"I'm the rabbi."

"Oh!"

He laughed. "It's really not that impressive. I just try to help people like you do. Then once a week or so I get up and make a speech."

"You're being modest."

"Am I?"

She nodded. "I've attended synagogue a couple of times, and I know there's a lot more to it than that."

"Really? You better tell me so I can expand my job description."

Cindy wished she had a witty response, but at the moment, she felt as if her brain were fogged like a windshield on a cold day. Instead, she just stared out the front window.

"It's left on this next street, second house on the right," she said.

He pulled up outside her tiny yellow house with white trim. She stepped out of the car and felt a chill run up her spine. For a moment she had an image of walking into her home and tripping over another dead body.

Cindy jumped as Jeremiah's hand descended on her shoulder. She hadn't even realized that he had gotten out of the car.

"I'll walk you inside," he said matter-of-factly.

"Thank you." She took a deep breath and walked up to the front door, pulling her keys from her purse.

"Wait!" he whispered.

She stopped. Something in the tone of his voice commanded obedience. She turned and stared at him. His eyes were no longer deep and gentle but blazing, and his jaw was set.

"What is it?" Fear washed over her.

"The door."

Slowly, she turned and looked. It stood ajar. Not much, just a crack, but it had been opened. Blood drained from her face. When she heard footsteps, she grabbed Jeremiah's arm. Someone was in her house!

3

WHAT DO WE DO?" CINDY'S VOICE QUIVERED.

"You're not expecting anyone?" Jeremiah asked.

She shook her head no and fixed eyes dilated wide with fear on him. *I should call the police*, he thought. It was probably just a common burglar, but the timing was suspicious, and it could be the murderer.

He could hear one person moving around in the room just inside the door. If there was anyone else in the house he couldn't hear them. He crept closer to the door, squatting down slightly and presenting his right shoulder toward the house. Just as he reached the door he could hear the intruder start to whistle.

Staying well to the side, he motioned for Cindy to get behind him. Her breathing came fast and loud. He pushed open the door. A man stood in the hallway. He shouted as the door opened, and Cindy screamed.

Jeremiah could see both of the man's hands, and they were empty. He vaulted through the doorway and reached the stranger in two bounds. He shrank back from Jeremiah and raised his hands to ward him off. Jeremiah grabbed the

24

man by the shoulder and stopped short before slamming his head into the wall.

"Mr. Grey!" he heard Cindy cry. "What are you doing here?"

"You know him?" Jeremiah asked, without looking at her.

"Yes, he owns the house."

Jeremiah released him and took a step back but kept his eyes trained on the other man's face.

"Cindy, what's going on here?" Mr. Grey demanded.

"I'm so sorry, Mr. Grey. We saw the open door and thought you were a burglar."

The older man's countenance relaxed. "I'm sorry I frightened you. I'm here to do the maintenance on the air conditioning."

"What maintenance?" she asked.

"I'm checking it before summer gets here to make sure the ducts are clean. I left a message on your answering machine last week."

"I didn't get it," Cindy said. "I'm sorry. Harold Grey, this is Jeremiah, the rabbi at the synagogue next door to First Shepherd."

"Rabbi," Harold said, offering his hand.

Jeremiah shook it warily, still not liking the situation. He noticed that after the initial surprise Harold wasn't looking either him or Cindy in the eyes.

"Mr. Grey, sorry if we scared you," Jeremiah said.

"That's all right. I figured I would just slip in and check out the system while Cindy was at work so I wouldn't have to bother her. Speaking of which, is everything okay, Cindy?"

"A man was killed at the church, and Cindy found his body this morning," Jeremiah said.

Harold jumped slightly. "Killed! That's terrible! Was it a church member?"

"No," Cindy said. "I'm sorry, the police sent me home after they took my statement. The rabbi was kind enough to drive me," she said.

All the blood drained from her face, and she started to rock slightly. Jeremiah jumped forward just in time to catch her as she began to slump.

"She's fainted. Help me," he told Harold.

Together they carried her to the couch. Harold headed for the kitchen and returned with a cold, wet cloth, which Jeremiah used to bathe her face before putting it around the back of her neck.

Cindy's eyes fluttered open. "What happened?"

"You fainted, but you're fine," Jeremiah said.

"Is there anything I can do?" Harold asked.

"No, I've got it," Jeremiah said.

"I should probably go then. I was just about to leave when you two arrived. Cindy, is there anything I can get you?"

"No, thank you. I'm sorry, Mr. Grey."

He patted her hand. "Just try and get some rest. We'll talk later."

Jeremiah saw the older man to the door and closed it behind him. Alone, he turned and looked at Cindy. "I'm just going to take a look around and make sure there are no other surprises."

"Thank you," she said with a voice full of relief.

From where he stood he could see all of the living room and the kitchen. He headed for the hallway and discovered two bedrooms and a bathroom. One bedroom looked like it was used as an office, with a filing cabinet, a desk, and chair.

He moved over to the computer. The computer was off. He opened the closet and spotted a couple of board games and a few boxes labeled "crafts."

From there he entered Cindy's bedroom. A bed, chest of drawers, and a dresser filled the small space. On the nightstand lay a Bible and a couple of other books that looked like they were retold fairy tales. Everything in the room reflected a pale shade of green. Only shoes and clothes filled her closet. Satisfied that nothing seemed out of place he returned to the living room.

Cindy sat up straight on the couch and looked much better. "Thank you for being my hero again."

He smiled. "You know us heroes—never satisfied with rescuing the damsel once. As long as she's in danger we have to keep rescuing her."

"This damsel is extremely grateful. Thank you, Rabbi."

"Jeremiah, please, Ms. Preston."

"Call me Cindy."

He smiled. "You have a nice place here."

"Thanks. Mr. Grey rents it cheap to staff members. I could never afford it otherwise."

"How are you doing?"

"Better," she said. "I've never seen a murder victim before."

"I know," he answered.

"I'm sorry. First murder, first unknown person in my house, first time fainting. You've really caught me at my best today." Cindy shook her head.

"I think you've handled it pretty well, considering," he said. It was time for him to go, but he found himself delaying. He wasn't sure if it was out of concern for her or curiosity about the murder.

"I just keep going over it in my head, you know?" she said. "I mean, who would want to kill that guy and in the church? It makes no sense."

"I'm sure it made perfect sense to the murderer." He smiled warmly.

"Probably. It's just, I usually feel safe in the sanctuary and now I don't feel safe. Do you know what I mean?"

"I grew up in Israel. Sometimes safety seemed like a luxury," he said.

"I had no idea. That must have been hard with all the violence."

He shrugged. "When a place is home and it is all you know, you don't stop to think about how it could be different."

"You must have left when you were young."

"Why do you think so?" he asked, letting himself smile at her.

"You sound American. I would have thought you grew up around here."

"Thank you. Are you going to be okay?"

"I think so. I just wish I knew why that guy was killed."

"You would feel better if there was a real reason, and it wasn't just some random act?" he asked.

"Much. I know that probably sounds lame. I'm just not a big fan of randomness."

"Well, I wouldn't worry about it. I'm sure the police will figure out who did this and why," Jeremiah answered.

"The door was locked. I know it was. There aren't many people who have a key to the sanctuary. How did he get in there?"

"Maybe the killer let him in."

He regretted saying it as she turned pale.

"There was a youth rally last night," she muttered.

"Would the kids have been in the sanctuary?"

"No, it should have been locked before they got there last night."

"Hopefully, by the time you get back to work they will have caught this killer." He edged toward the door. "You should put some antiseptic and bandages on your knees."

"Thanks. How long have you been a rabbi?" she asked.

He smiled. "Two years. Speaking of which, I should get back before my secretary decides I'm what all the commotion is about."

Cindy smiled wanly. "We can't have that."

"Yes, when she gets going—" He let an exaggerated eye roll say the rest for him.

"Thank you again. For everything."

"Don't worry about it. Us religious types have to stick together."

"Interesting way of looking at it."

He shrugged, fished a card out of his pocket, and put it on the kitchen table. "Here's a card with my office and home phone numbers. Please, don't give it to any members of my congregation."

"Trying to avoid three a.m. phone calls from neurotic parishioners?" she asked, standing.

He nodded. "A year ago I changed my home number and now I only give it out discreetly."

"I'll guard your secret," she said.

"Somehow I think you will. Remember, call if you need me."

"I will," she promised.

———⊷⊷⊷———

Two minutes after Jeremiah left Cindy regretted his absence. Her house was too quiet, yet every time a sound interrupted the silence, she jumped out of her skin. Her lunch bag sat on the kitchen table where she had forgotten it, next to the crossword puzzle she'd printed out from her online paper subscription. She'd ultimately skipped breakfast and the crossword so she could get to work early and deal with any messes. *I had no idea what kind of mess I would find.*

She glanced at the clock on the microwave and realized with a start that it was still well before noon. Maybe a shower would rinse all the horror of the morning away. She briefly contemplated burning her clothes, but since the navy skirt and jacket were one of her few matched sets, she decided to wash them instead.

Once she made up her mind, Cindy changed quickly and pulled on her fluffiest bathrobe. As she loaded the washer, she automatically checked her jacket pockets. Her fingers brushed against cold metal, and she pulled out one of her cross necklaces. She had rushed out of the house that morning before putting it on.

She stared at it for a moment in surprise, having forgotten all about it. She thought about the cross that the detective had shown her. Why had there been a Shepherd's cross covered in blood? The answer seemed obvious, but she didn't want to come to terms with it. At least not yet. There could be an innocent explanation. There were only thirty Shepherds, and the police were probably well on their way to tracking down the owner. Best to leave it all to them. In her other pocket she found the crumpled piece of paper she had picked up earlier.

The phone rang, and she jumped. She dropped the necklace and the paper on the shelf above the washer and rushed to her bedroom. She sat down on the bed before picking up the phone.

"Hello?" she asked, hoping that she sounded calmer than she felt.

"Cindy, this is Pastor Roy. Did you make it home all right?"

"Yes. Thank you for calling."

"Is Rabbi Silverman still there?"

"No, he just left."

"Do you need me to send somebody over? The police have finished questioning Geanie and Ralph."

"No, I think I'm okay. I could probably come in this afternoon."

"You shouldn't have to do that. Stay home."

"Thank you," she said, relieved. She wasn't up to going back there yet.

"If you could tell me where to find the Maundy Thursday program on your computer, I can pass that along to Geanie and she can make a couple of changes before we print it out."

It was Easter week and with a special service Thursday evening, a prayer service Friday at noon, and events all weekend it was not a good time for her not to be there. She took a deep breath. "Why don't you have Geanie call me, and I can walk her through it."

"Good idea," the pastor said. He sounded relieved. "You take as much time as you need. We'll manage here."

He might as well have said what Cindy already knew. *Everyone's panicking because we don't know what to do.* She closed her eyes and gritted her teeth in frustration. "I'll be back tomorrow."

"Now, really, that's not necessary."

"I'll be there."

"Great! I'll have Geanie call you in a little bit."

"Okay. Call if you need anything else."

"You betcha."

She hung up and stared at the phone. It would be good for her to go back to work in the morning. *Get back on the horse*, that's what her father would say.

The phone rang again almost immediately. It was Geanie, and Cindy told her where to find all the files on her computer that she would need. Geanie hung up without asking how she was.

Cindy held the phone for a moment and then dialed her parents. After the third ring her mother picked up.

"Hi, Mom."

"Cindy, dear. I thought it was your brother calling. His plane landed an hour ago in Belize, and he said he'd call when he reached the hotel."

"No, it's just me. So, Kyle's in Belize?"

"Yes, he's filming a new travel show this month. You know, I just don't know how he finds the time to fit it all in," her mom gushed.

"Yeah, he's a superman." Cindy stood up and closed her bedroom door. On the back of it hung a dartboard with a large, glossy picture of a blonde man in an explorer's vest. She pulled the darts out of the picture and sat back down on the bed.

"Did you get Kyle's *TV Guide* article I mailed you?"

"Yes, Mom, I got it." Cindy threw a dart at her brother's picture.

"Doesn't he just look wonderful?"

"Yeah, Mom. Thanks, I really needed a new picture of him." Cindy tossed a second dart that pierced one of her brother's pearly white teeth. "Is Dad back from Iraq yet?"

"Not until Wednesday. Then he's off again on Tuesday. I swear sometimes it feels like I live alone."

Cindy's father worked for an engineering firm that was rebuilding infrastructure in Iraq. He always joked that he was part of the war clean-up crew.

"So, what's new with you, dear?" her mother asked.

"I found a dead man at the church this morning. He'd been murdered."

"Honey, that's terrible!" her mom said, all attention finally focused on her. "Are you okay?"

"Yeah. I fell over him, and I'm a bit bruised, but I'm mostly just upset."

"Were you close to him?"

"I tripped on him. I ended up on the floor right next to him," Cindy said.

"No, I meant personally. Did you know him very well?"

"No, he was a stranger."

"Well, that's a relief."

"Yeah."

"Do the police have any leads?"

"I'm not sure."

"Well, I wouldn't worry, dear. They'll find the killer. You know, one time when your father . . ."

Cindy zoned out and didn't hear the rest of what her mom had to say. A few minutes later she said good-bye and hung up.

After showering and puttering around the house for awhile, it was after one when Cindy stopped to eat her lunch.

It still sat on the table next to the crossword she hadn't had time to work on that morning. She picked up a pen, needing something other than dead bodies to think about while she ate.

One Across. Utensil. Five letters. She grimaced as she filled in the letters for "knife." *That's okay, you're fine. Everything is just fine.*

The phone rang, and she jumped again.

"Hi, it's Geanie," the woman said when Cindy picked up the phone.

"Hi, Geanie. What is it now?"

"The Women of Faith want to know if they can use the Fireside Room Tuesday night for their meeting instead of the Round Room."

"When it comes to the Fireside Room—"

"Just say no. I know. I was just checking."

"The Digging for the Truth class is meeting there Tuesday night."

"Thanks."

"Geanie, is everything else going okay over there?"

"Yeah. The police left about a half hour ago. They've got the sanctuary cordoned off with that yellow police tape, like you see on TV."

"How long do they plan on blocking it off?" Cindy asked. "It's Easter week, and we need to use the sanctuary."

"I'm not sure, I heard Roy talking to them about it, but I don't know what they told him."

"Well, call if you need anything else."

"Thanks, I will."

Cindy hung up and returned to her sandwich and the crossword. *One Down. _____ Instinct. Six letters, begins with a K.* She wrote down "killer" and just stared at the word for a minute. Her kitchen window rattled, and she looked up to see a man staring in at her.

⚬⚬⚬

Jeremiah found it nearly impossible to concentrate after returning to work. Marie, his secretary, walked into his office without knocking. He sighed and sat back as she frowned at him over the top of her gold spectacles. Her short brown hair was brushed back from her face.

"You're not eating enough," she pronounced.

He shook his head and forced a smile. "Marie, you say that about everyone. Honestly, you don't have to worry about me. I have a mother."

"Some mother if she lets you go around all skin and bones."

"Marie—"

"I'm only saying," she said with a shrug. "Lots going on next door today."

He smiled. The stack of papers in her hand was just an excuse. Marie knew he knew what was going on, and it was killing her. He coughed and took the stack of papers from her, flipping casually through a dozen phone messages, none of them important. He could tell her curiosity was only growing more intense.

"Was there anything else, Marie?" he asked, looking up finally.

"So, are you going to tell me or not?" she asked.

"You mean about the murder next door?" he asked.

"Murder! I knew it! I said to Ruth that there were too many police over there for it to be anything else. So, who was murdered?" She settled down in the chair across from him.

He laced his fingers behind his head and leaned back as she leaned forward.

"Nobody at the church seems to know him."

"A stranger, huh? What was he, trespassing on church property? Did he attack somebody? Did the pastor shoot him?"

He stared up at the ceiling so as not to laugh. Marie should have considered a job in journalism the way she could ask questions.

"They don't know who he was or who killed him. He was found this morning in the locked sanctuary, stabbed to death."

She sat back in her chair with a small, triumphant sigh. "Then it had to be one of the Gentiles who did it."

"Marie, I think you're the only one who still uses that word."

"Who do you think did it?" she asked, ignoring him.

"I don't know." He shook his head.

"It had to be an inside job, someone who had keys to the sanctuary."

"Or someone who could pick a lock," he said, half to himself.

"How many lock pickers work at churches, or even attend them for that matter?"

"I don't know, Marie. You just might be surprised."

She harrumphed as she rose to her feet. "By the way," she said as she got to the doorway, "Ms. Goldsmith is on line two."

He dove for the phone. Ms. Goldsmith would not be amused that she had been left holding so long. He needed a good talk with Marie about that.

"Ms. Goldsmith, so good to hear from you. No, we're all fine here. No, the police are actually right next door at the church. No, no one here needs an attorney, but I will pass along your generous offer. Thank you. Good-bye."

After hanging up he closed and locked his door. He needed some time to think, and he needed a little privacy. He considered going home but dismissed the idea. The best place to hear everything that was going on was at the synagogue. If there was anything most churchgoers loved more than God, it was good gossip, and that extended to both Jew and Gentile. He could only imagine what the pastor next door was going through. If Marie had received several phone calls already, the lines next door had to be completely tied up. No, the gossip would be spreading, and it wouldn't take long to spread across ecumenical lines right into his office.

The practical side of his nature told him not to involve himself anymore than he already had. He should thank Yahweh that it had happened next door instead of in the synagogue. That was the kind of attention the church didn't need. *And I certainly don't need it either*, he thought, tipping back in his chair.

It was a big week. Wednesday night was the beginning of Passover. The first two nights were marked by celebratory feasts. Jeremiah smiled grimly. He had received a stack of invitations from his congregation to dine at their homes for the first night. This year, though, he was far wiser. Last year he had caused quite an uproar by choosing a home to dine in each of the first two nights. He'd been a new rabbi and naïve despite his thirty-three years. He had no idea how political temple life was at that point. The jockeying for position to gain his attendance this year had been even fiercer. He was not one to forget past mistakes, though.

This year all members and their families were invited to celebrate the first night's feast together at the synagogue's multipurpose room. Marie had been quick to point out the potential pitfalls in that plan. If seating was on a first-come, first-served basis then people would be showing up in the morning to get good table position at the front close to Jeremiah. If seating was assigned, then the favoritism problem of the year before would rear its ugly head. Jeremiah prided himself on the solution. The head of each attending family was given a raffle ticket. Numbers would be drawn randomly and tables assigned that way. No favoritism, no politics. At least, that's what he hoped. For the second night he would join Marie's family. It made sense, and few people could argue with that decision.

The one drawback with the plan was that the next few days were going to be very busy for everyone. He glanced at his watch. It was almost time to meet with the committee that had graciously agreed to plan and prepare the meal.

With a sigh he got up and left. Marie glanced up at him as he passed her on his way out of the office.

"They're meeting in the multipurpose room," she offered.

"Thanks."

Detective Mark Walters hated Easter. While most people were busy celebrating life and resurrection, all he could see was death and destruction. Of course, he saw death every day. It was brutal, ugly, and part of the world. Resurrection, on the other hand, he had never seen. In his view those kinds of miracles, if they ever had happened, were part of a long ago past.

He sat in his car in the church parking lot as he dictated his notes, thoughts, impressions, even his plans for dinner, into his digital recorder. Back at the office he would plug it into his computer and let his computer type it all up for him. Then he'd edit his report and call Francesco's for reservations.

Mark let his eyes drift from the church to the synagogue next door. "And run a background check on Jeremiah Silverman, rabbi, just for good measure," he said. He shut off the recorder and yawned as he started the car.

He had been up half the night investigating another murder at a park about three miles away. A man by the name of Miguel Jesus Olivera had been found dead on an ivory-colored donkey on Palm Avenue, one of the streets bordering the park.

"It's gotta be some kind of political statement," Keenan, one of the other detectives, had surmised.

Mark knew better, though. The religious significance of a donkey on Palm Avenue the Sunday before Easter had not been lost on him. The discovery that the dead guy's middle name was Jesus had clinched it. That significance and a few well-chosen words had gotten the editor of the local paper to sit on the story for twenty-four hours. Now there was a second murder to deal with, this one actually inside a church. It smelled to him like a wacko with a big-time hatred for religious types. Either that or someone who hated Easter as much as he did. Either way, it wasn't good, and Easter was still a long way off.

4

CINDY LEAPED UP FROM THE TABLE AND GRABBED THE PHONE TO DIAL 9-1-1 before she recognized the man staring in her window. Heart slamming against her ribcage, she put down the phone and opened up the front door.

"Oliver, you scared me!"

"Sorry, I heard you were home, but I knocked and nobody answered." Oliver Johnson was a tall man in his mid-forties. He had been going to First Shepherd for the last couple of years and had been a Shepherd for the last six months. A terrible suspicion formed in her mind as she remembered the sight of the bloody Shepherd's Cross the detective had shown her.

She shook her head firmly. There was no way Oliver Johnson was a cold-blooded killer. Still, a shiver went up her spine, and she rubbed her arms to warm herself.

"What brings you here, Oliver?" she asked as he stepped inside.

"My job, unfortunately."

She motioned him toward the couch, and he took a seat. "I don't understand." Oliver was a reporter for the *Pine Springs Gazette*. He covered human interest and community affairs.

"Well, when the reports came in about the church this morning, my editor assigned me to the story."

"But you don't cover crime," she said.

"No, but the editor remembered that I'm a member at First Shepherd, and he wanted me to work with the crime reporter on this story."

"So, this isn't a social call." She sat down on the couch.

"I'm afraid not. I'm sorry. I know you probably just want to be alone right now. I know I would if I were in your shoes."

"That's okay. You're just doing your job. I guess you heard that I was the one who found the body."

"Yes, I was so sorry to hear that." He moved closer, eyes fixed intently on her.

"It was terrible," she confided.

"I can believe it. I realize talking about it is probably the last thing you want to do right now, but anything you could tell me would be helpful."

Cindy didn't like being interviewed. She rarely knew what to say, and it always came out sounding so boring. She forced herself to take a deep breath. At least this wasn't a job interview. If she messed up, Oliver's story would just be less interesting. Cindy told Oliver how she had found the body and how Jeremiah had called the police. Oliver listened and scribbled furiously on his notepad. It went better than she had expected. She pretended that she was telling Oliver, the concerned parishioner, the story, rather than Oliver, the newspaper reporter. She even found that it was a relief to tell someone the story now that she was calmer and could do so in a more normal fashion.

"You're very brave," he said softly.

"Not me. I was terrified. I was actually relieved when you showed up. Being here alone isn't really making me feel any better. I've been jumping at my own shadow."

"You'll never know how sorry I am that this had to happen to someone as sweet as you."

"Thanks," she said. *Sweet. I hate it when people call me that. It's like "nice." What do they mean? Sweet . . . nice. You might as well be describing a piece of chocolate or a sunny afternoon.*

Oliver was speaking again, and she tuned back in. "Can I ask you just a couple more questions?"

"Sure."

"Do they know yet who the man was?"

Cindy shook her head. *The dead man with the eyes. That's all he was.* "You'll probably have to ask the police. I'd never seen him before and neither had Pastor Roy."

"Okay. Did the police say if they had any suspects?"

"I don't know. I'm sorry." *Again, I'm the clueless loser. Nancy Drew would already have the entire case solved if she'd tripped on a dead body at church. But then Nancy also took so many risks, just like Lisa used to.*

"That's fine. One more question. Did you see anything else out of the ordinary? Maybe the police found something strange?"

"Not that I know of," she said. "I was pretty out of it, though. Hopefully, they can be more helpful. Hopefully, they've already found the guy who did this." *And how many more times can I say "hopefully"? No wonder Kyle's the one with a television travel show, and I'm the one answering phones at a church.*

"Yes, I hope they have someone behind bars right now so we can all put this behind us," Oliver said fervently.

"Is there anything else?"

"No, I think that pretty much does it. I'll call you if I need anything more, if that's okay."

"That's fine." *Fine. Fine. I may as well have said "nice,"* she thought, completely disgusted.

He stood to go. "Keep your chin up. I'll be praying for you, especially tonight. Only happy dreams for you, I hope."

"Thank you."

"It's just a terrible start to Easter week, you know. First the guy in the park and now this."

"What guy in the park?"

Oliver turned red and dropped his eyes. "Sorry. I'm not supposed to say anything."

And that was exactly the wrong thing to say to get Cindy to back off. "Oliver, tell me, what do you know?" She put as much pleading into her voice as she could. If he knew something that would help her make sense of what had happened, then he wasn't leaving without telling her.

"A jogger found a guy on Palm Avenue, next to the park. He was dead and sitting on a donkey."

"Dead on a donkey on Palm Sunday on Palm Avenue?" she asked.

"Yes. Police asked the editor to keep it quiet for a day while they try and figure it out."

"A man was killed in mimicry of Jesus' entry into Jerusalem, and the police want to keep it quiet?"

"Wouldn't you if you were them? I mean, that's pretty crazy, right? They don't want people to get scared."

"It's a little late for that," she said grimly.

"Are you okay?"

43

"No, but I am a little better. Now I know that the guy in the church wasn't killed at random." She opened the door for Oliver. "Good luck with the article."

"Thanks," he said, a bewildered look on his face as he left.

Cindy leaned against the door for a moment and breathed deeply. As relief flooded her, she had the sudden urge to leave the house but realized that her car was still sitting in the church parking lot.

She grabbed her purse and keys and locked the door behind her. The church was less than two miles away. The air was warm, and birds were singing. Spring had arrived in Pine Springs with all its promise of new life. Birds feathered their nests. New leaves had popped out on all the trees, and tulips bloomed in bright bouquets. With so much around her alive and green, it helped to drive away the images of death that plagued her mind.

By the time she was halfway to the church, she resolved to walk to work more often. The air and the exercise were good for her, and they definitely did a lot to brighten her mood. It was safer than driving too. Lots of people died in cars every day.

When the church came into view she saw the janitor, Ralph, and Drake, one of the church members, standing on the front lawn. Two of the three crosses the church had put up the Friday before to celebrate Easter were standing, but the third lay on the ground.

"What's going on?" Cindy asked as she walked up.

"Hey, Cindy." Drake gave her a quick hug. "You okay?"

She nodded.

"One of the crosses fell over a couple of hours ago. A gust of wind caught it just right and over she went," Ralph said. "Drake is helping me put it back up."

"We need to anchor all three of them deeper in the ground and brace them," Drake said. "By the time we're finished they should stand through a hurricane."

"That's better than I can say for the buildings," Ralph said with a short laugh.

"With you two on the job I'm sure they'll withstand anything," Cindy said.

"Yeah, now just give me a hammer and some nails and let me reconstruct these buildings," Drake said.

"Wait, here you go." Ralph handed Drake a hammer and three nails.

Drake looked at them and then at one of the two standing crosses. "Hey, can you put me up for the night?" he wisecracked, waving the nails at the cross.

"Very funny, Drake. I think we've all heard that one a million times," Cindy said.

"But never in such dramatic fashion."

It felt good to joke around with Ralph and Drake. Maybe she should have stayed at work and not gone home earlier.

"You guys are nuts," she said.

"You know what they say, you don't have to be crazy to work here, but it helps," Ralph said.

"Tell me about it." Geanie emerged from the office.

"Hey, Geanie, how are you doing?" Cindy looked at her quizzically.

Geanie was known for her particularly outlandish clothes. Today, though, she had dressed in a short, black-velvet skirt, a plain black tank top, and pink flats with no nylons. Her blond hair was pulled back in a ponytail, and she wore no makeup.

"Better now that you're here. You just saved me from calling you with a gazillion more questions." She grabbed Cindy's arm and pulled her back toward the buildings.

"I'm trying to understand your look today. I hate to admit it, but I don't get it."

"I had a whole goth thing going on this morning. Got here and somehow it seemed way inappropriate. I ditched the black boots and fishnets. I had these pink shoes in my desk from a couple of months ago. I took off the overshirt I had on and scrubbed off all the makeup. I figured the last thing anyone needed was to see me walking around looking dead."

"Probably a good choice." Though Cindy had seen Geanie in a goth outfit before, and she had looked very much alive compared to the man who had been stabbed in the sanctuary.

Geanie was the church's graphic artist and all-around computer whiz. When she first started working for the church, she had revamped all of their publications, from Sunday bulletins to monthly newsletters and everything in between. If it could be printed, odds were it had her finger-prints on it. Perhaps because of her talent and her endearing quirkiness, she was given a lot of free rein.

"So, what did you need to ask me?"

"Roy still can't get me a schedule for the Maundy Thursday service."

"Have you tried asking Gus?" Gus was the minister of drama and choir for the church. For Thursday night he had planned a big program with a play and a lot of singing to celebrate the Last Supper.

"Yes, and he gave me the order of service for the parts he's doing, but he has no idea what Roy has planned for the rest of the evening. Is there going to be a sermon? Opening greeting? An invitation? Offering?"

"I see the problem," Cindy said with a sigh.

"It would be a lot easier if Roy and Gus would just work this out together and then let the rest of us know what's going on."

"Yeah, but that's not likely to happen."

"Tell me about it. I'm surprised they can stand on the podium together Sunday mornings."

It was no secret that the two men didn't get along, or at least it wasn't a secret to the staff. There did seem to be many in the congregation who were blissfully unaware of the tension between the two.

"When do you have to print the programs?"

"I wanted to print them this afternoon, but even if you could pry what I need to know out of Roy, I can't get it ready to print until sometime tomorrow now."

"I know you like to get these things done early, but between you and me, when is your drop-dead day?"

"Wednesday afternoon. The team is coming in Thursday to print the newsletter."

"I forgot it was newsletter week," Cindy said.

"I wish I could."

"If I have it all to you tomorrow at three o'clock can you make it work?"

Geanie nodded. "It's going to be tight, though."

"But we'll make it."

"As long as the copiers don't die on us like last Easter," Geanie said glumly.

"We resurrected them, though."

"Yeah, but you had to drive two hours to L.A. for that one part when they couldn't send a repairman. And then we all had to stay until nearly midnight printing and collating."

"Don't remind me," Cindy said. "Let's just pray extra hard for all the office equipment this week."

"Printer, don't fail me now," Geanie said, smiling for the first time.

"Amen."

"So, what else can I do for you?"

"Harold is trying to schedule a meeting the Sunday after Easter for the Shepherds but none of the available rooms are big enough, and I'm not sure if any of the other groups can be moved."

"Where did the Shepherds hold their last meeting?" Cindy tried to remember.

"He said they've had scheduling problems for the last couple of months so they've been meeting at his house. They met Saturday, but he wants to resolve the scheduling issues so they can just meet here after services."

"I'll take a look and see who I can move to another room," Cindy said. "Then I'll go talk to Roy about getting you a schedule for Thursday night."

"That would be awesome."

As it turned out, Pastor Roy's afternoon was booked solid with meetings. Cindy only managed to pop in for a minute and ask him to write out the order of service for her. He told her he would have it on her desk by the morning. Before she could ask him anything else or bring up the morning's events with him, his four o'clock appointment arrived.

For the next little while she worked on finding a room for the Shepherds to meet in, without much success. She was starting to feel edgy and realized the police detective had probably been right about taking some time off. The work would all be waiting for her in the morning. She wasn't sure, though, that she was ready to face her empty house alone.

"Geanie, what are your plans this evening?" she asked as she walked by her desk.

Geanie looked up from her computer. "My new boy-friend is taking me out to dinner to celebrate our one-week anniversary," She giggled.

"A week. Wow, what a milestone," Cindy teased.

Geanie blushed. "He's really romantic."

"Obviously. Have fun."

"Thanks."

Cindy looked at the clock. There was still about fifteen minutes left in the workday, but technically she shouldn't even be there. "I think I'll get out of here early."

"See you tomorrow," Geanie said.

Cindy left the office and walked toward the parking lot. A chill raced up her spine as she passed the closed doors to the sanctuary. The yellow police tape looked menacing against the glass and brick of the building. She forced her-self to look away. After she passed through the main gate she looked at her car and knew she wasn't ready to go home. She still needed to be with people, but everyone she could think of already had plans for the evening.

She hesitated a moment and then walked through the hedge and headed for the main building of the synagogue. Fortunately, the office was well marked with an overhead sign, and the door was open. Cindy walked in and looked around.

Behind a large desk sat a woman in her late forties. She stared at Cindy with open curiosity. The nameplate on her desk said *Marie Henson*.

"Hi, are you Marie?" Cindy asked.

"Yes, may I help you?"

"I'm Cindy. I work at the church next door. I was just wandering if Rabbi Silverman was in?"

Marie cocked her head to the side and stared at her as though she were sizing up Cindy. "He is, but I'm not sure he's taking visitors at the moment."

"I can wait while you ask him," Cindy offered, determined not be intimidated by the whole secretary-restricting-access-to-her-boss thing.

"I'll be back in a minute." Marie stood up and walked to the back of the office. She knocked on a door and then poked her head in. After a couple of moments she stepped back and opened the door wide. "He'll see you," she said as she took her seat.

"Thank you."

Cindy walked around Marie's desk and into Jeremiah's office. She closed the door behind her. He stood up to shake her hand across the desk. "Come in and take a seat."

She settled into the chair across from him as he sat back down. His formality threw her slightly off.

"I'm surprised to see you again so soon."

"I decided to drop by and thank you again for all you did for me this morning," she said, suddenly feeling very foolish. She fidgeted with her hands, wishing she had a deck of cards she could manipulate.

"That's very considerate. Shouldn't you be home resting, though?"

She shrugged. "I came to get my car and got caught up in the Easter crunch."

He nodded. "It's like that over here for Passover. If I have to answer one more question about Wednesday night's Seder, I'm going to quit."

She smiled. "That would be a great loss to your congregation."

"It might be worth it if it taught them to listen the first time. Do you think there's any hope of that?"

"Not a chance."

"Then I should probably get out of here so I won't have to quit in vain."

Her eyes fell on the newspaper open on his desk to the crossword puzzle. "You do the crosswords too?" she asked.

"Yes, it helps my vocabulary. Today's is pretty hard, though. I always know I'm in for a rough time when I can't fill in the first one."

"One across is easy. It's 'knife,'" she said.

He glanced down. "No, I don't think that's possible."

"Sure it is. I was working on it at home before I came over. It's 'knife,' I'm certain of it."

"Not unless I've been misspelling 'knife.' One across is only four letters."

"What?" she asked.

He handed it to her, and she looked at the puzzle. "This isn't the same puzzle as mine. Is this today's paper?"

"Yes."

"Then how can that be?"

"They might be different papers. This is the Gazette, which one do you get?"

"The Gazette. Online version, not print. But they use the same crossword for each. They always run the same one."

"Apparently not today," he said.

She looked at the small print below the puzzle. "Daily crossword provided by Ink and Paper Games." She handed the paper back to him. "That's weird. All I can say is welcome to Monday."

He laughed out loud. "Kind of makes you anxious about Tuesday, doesn't it?"

"I should say so. Although I've never met the Tuesday yet that was as bad as a Monday."

"You might have a point there, especially this week. Tonight I have to clean my kitchen and throw away anything that has yeast in it before Passover begins," he said. "I must admit, I never look forward to that. What do you have planned?"

She shrugged. "I'm not sure. I'm not really ready to go back home. It's too quiet there."

"I understand. You look a lot better than you did earlier, though."

"I feel better," she confessed. She leaned closer. "Because now I know, it wasn't random."

He started. "How do you know?" he asked.

"The police are keeping it out of the papers for now, but they found a dead guy last night, sitting on a donkey on Palm Avenue."

"Palm Sunday, the 'triumphal entry' of Jesus into Jerusalem a week before his death, riding on a donkey?"

"Exactly," she said.

"Coincidence?"

"I don't believe that." She studied his face for a moment. "And neither do you."

"Well played," he said, a sly smile slipping across his face. "No, I'm not much of a believer in coincidence."

"So, what do we do?"

He laughed. "We let the police handle it."

She flushed. Of course that was what they should do. What had she been thinking to even ask something like that? But something else tugged at her. Something that made her wildly uncomfortable.

"I think you're feeling so involved because you found the body. If it had been one of your coworkers who found it, you'd probably be able to let it go more easily," he suggested.

"But I *am* the one who found the body. What if that means something, like maybe God wants me to find the killer?" She couldn't believe the words coming out of her mouth. Every fiber of her being screamed that it was too dangerous and that it was best to look away.

"Or maybe since you are the first one to the church every-day, it was not God, but the killer who wanted you to find the body," he countered.

A shiver ran up her spine, and she felt a sick, twisting sensation in her gut. "But why would somebody want that?"

He shrugged. "No reason that I know of. So, two bodies not a coincidence, but you finding the second one probably is."

She nodded. "I can buy that. The alternative is too creepy."

Jeremiah leaned back in his chair, his face blank and his eyes veiled. "So, why are you sharing all of this with me?"

She already knew the answer. It was because somehow she believed that he would understand, whereas her coworkers would not. Out loud she said, "Because you were there."

Now she could feel him studying her, trying to read her expression. If they had been playing cards she would have done her best to give him nothing. They weren't, though, and she needed him to trust her because she needed someone to talk to about it all. So she let her emotions spill onto her face without trying to censor them.

After a moment he nodded, almost imperceptibly, and she let her relief show.

"In the spirit of avoiding home, can I buy my hero a cup of coffee?" she asked. *Smooth, real smooth. Knowing my luck he'll think I'm hitting on him. Awkward.*

He hesitated, and she resisted the urge to crack her knuckles.

"That sounds really good," he said at last. "But it's going to take me several hours to clean tonight, and I need to get started."

"Some other time then," she said, trying to hide her disappointment.

"Of course, if you really feel the need to get away from your house and do something nice for the hero," he said with a grin, "I could use some help cleaning out my kitchen."

She started laughing, and after a moment he joined in. "Well, that's the strangest offer I've ever had."

"Did I mention I hate cleaning out the kitchen? Come on, it'll be fun. I'll even buy us some pizza."

"Pizza. That's a good Jewish food to start Passover with," she said still laughing.

"Not at all. Pizza is a tradition. Jewish people can't eat anything with yeast in it during Passover. I always like to celebrate the last day or two before Passover and the first day after Passover with pizza."

"Okay, if you buy the pizza, I'll help clean your kitchen."

"Wonderful. Let me just get my coat, and we can leave."

It was then that she remembered they'd only met a few hours before. She didn't even visit the homes of guys she dated until at least the fifth date, when she was sure they weren't psychos. Still, these were extenuating circumstances. She doubted that Jeremiah would have come to her rescue if he'd been a psycho killer. Another thought occurred to her, though.

"You sure it'll be okay? I mean, you're the rabbi, and I wouldn't want to create some kind of scandal for you."

"You think we need a chaperone?"

She rolled her eyes at him. "Don't tease. I've known some pastors who were really touchy about having women over to their houses when no one else was there."

He smiled at her. "You don't know my synagogue very well. It's a scandal even when I don't have women over to my home." He stood up and crossed to a coat rack in the far corner where he retrieved the jacket that he had put around her earlier that morning. As he put it on she was glad to see that it looked no worse for wear.

"After you," he said, opening the door for her.

She walked out, and he locked his office door before leading her past Marie's desk. "I'm leaving now, Marie. I'll be home this evening if you need to get hold of me."

Marie stared at Cindy through narrowed eyes, and she couldn't help but feel that the other woman disapproved of her.

Once they reached the parking lot, she commented, "I don't think Marie likes me."

He laughed. "All of the good Jewish mothers have been trying to set up the rabbi with their single daughters. She could tell you were single, and she probably didn't like it one bit."

"That's what I was talking about," Cindy said, suddenly uncomfortable. She had already been involved in one church scandal, and that was enough for any Monday.

"It's fine. Thanks to this morning everyone has better things to gossip about. Shall we just take my car? I can drop you back here later," Jeremiah asked.

"Sure."

Ten minutes later he pulled up outside his house. Once inside he called out for a pizza. Cindy noticed he even had the number memorized. Kind of sad.

"Pizza should be here in about forty minutes," he told her when he'd hung up. "Would you like the grand tour?"

"Why not."

"Okay, let's start here in the living room."

As she turned slowly her eyes almost popped out of her head. "Rabbi," she said, "I think you've been holding out on me."

5

Standing in the middle of Jeremiah's living room, Cindy pointed to the single bookshelf. "Emily Dickenson, Robert Frost, Shakespeare's Sonnets. I would not have taken you for the poetry type."

He smiled. "And what type would you have taken me for?"

It was a good question, and it reminded her that she was standing in the house of a man she barely knew. She fought the sudden urge to run for the door. Strangers weren't safe. Still, he wasn't a complete stranger. He was her rescuer, the one who had come running when she screamed.

What if it's because he's the killer, a voice whispered in her head.

No, that couldn't be. Jeremiah would have had no way to access the church sanctuary. Since the dead man had no connection with the church, it had to have been his killer that unlocked the sanctuary. She shivered and wrapped her arms around herself. No, it couldn't have been Jeremiah. He just wasn't the killer type. Still, that didn't mean she was even remotely sure what type of person he was.

She forced herself to relax and she shrugged. "Don't know yet."

"Let me know when you figure it out."

He gave her a quick tour of the rest of the house. It was spartan, with very little in the way of furniture and decorations. Like her house it had two bedrooms, and like her, Jeremiah used one of them as an office and the other as his bedroom.

She excused herself to the bathroom and took the opportunity to splash cold water on her face in an effort to pull herself together. It had been a long day, and her nerves were shot. She stared at herself in the mirror and took a deep breath.

Pull yourself together, Cindy. Jeremiah is no killer. Besides, there was no way he could have gotten into that sanctuary last night.

Unless someone else left it unlocked.

She gritted her teeth in frustration. Resolutely, she left the bathroom and returned to the kitchen where Jeremiah had flung open the cupboards. "So, is tomorrow the beginning of Passover?"

He shook his head. "Passover starts Wednesday night. Normally, you clean the night before, but the first night's Seder is being held at the synagogue, and I have to help clean there tomorrow night. That means my house has to be cleaned tonight."

"Okay, what do we do? You have to get rid of everything with yeast in it, right?"

He smiled at her. "Yes, but it doesn't stop there. Anything that swells when placed in water for seven minutes. So, anything that has yeast, rice, beans, and corn has to go."

"Are you kidding?"

"I never joke about Passover."

She pulled a box of spaghetti out of the cupboard. "So this just gets tossed?"

"Yes, unless there's something you want it all goes in the trash."

"There's a homeless shelter that a lot of the local churches support. I'd be happy to box up whatever you don't want and take it over tomorrow."

"Sounds like an excellent idea."

He disappeared into his office and came back a minute later with a medium-sized box. She put the spaghetti inside while he reached for a package of leek soup.

"What's wrong with that?"

"You'll find that most packaged foods contain soy or corn."

"I had no idea," she said.

"Ashkenazim have stricter rules about food that has to be purged before Passover."

"Ashkenazim?"

"Jewish people from northern Europe, mostly Germany and Russia," he explained. "Others, Sephardim, can eat rice and beans during Passover."

"Wow, deprived by genetics," she burst out before she could stop herself.

He stared at her, surprise clear on his face. She winced and was about to apologize when he burst out laughing. She joined in, and it was a moment before either of them regained some composure.

"You want to know the worst part?" Jeremiah asked.

"Tell me."

"It passes through the mother. My first cousin, his mother was Sephardim. We tried to have Passover at their house once when I was five, and it was a total disaster." Cindy laughed again. "My mother wouldn't let us eat anything, because it might have been tainted."

"Stop," she begged, wiping the tears from her eyes.

"That's what she said every time my dad tried to sneak food when she wasn't looking."

"That's perfect," she said.

"That was the worst holiday meal."

"I've got a better one."

"Prove it."

"When I was eight my grandmother convinced us all to have Easter dinner at her sister's house."

"And?"

"Her sister was a wiccan. She insisted we all had to participate in some spring ritual of hers. She made us stand around the dinner table chanting. She had this ceremonial knife, and it was passed from person to person. My dad got it, and I don't know what came over him, but he stabbed the ham with it. My aunt starting yelling. My brother jumped up and down, screaming 'Dad, it's resurrecting, it's resurrecting!' There we were, my aunt yelling at all of us, and my dad stabbing the ham over and over. She kicked us out of the house, and we had to eat Easter dinner at McDonald's."

"You win," Jeremiah conceded.

"Thank you."

"I can just see your dad and the ham," Jeremiah said, snatching up a knife from the carving block and pantomiming stabbing the food box with it.

His smile was broad, and the muscles in his arm flexed as he wielded the knife. Cindy laughed, as much at him as from the memory.

He's strong enough to have driven that knife into the dead man. The thought came unbidden, and she instantly stopped laughing. She took a step backward, almost involuntarily.

Jeremiah caught the movement and looked at her for a moment before lowering the knife. "Maybe it's not a good day to discuss stabbing things," he said, his voice suddenly serious.

She nodded and watched as he put the knife away. He flashed her a grim smile, and she returned her attention to the cabinet. The doorbell rang.

"Pizza," Jeremiah said, sounding relieved.

They ate mostly in silence and returned quickly to the work at hand. Half an hour later Jeremiah carried a box of food to his car and came back with a look of satisfaction on his face.

"Now, the hard part," he said.

She raised an eyebrow.

"Cleaning."

Mark sat at his desk, leafing through papers. His partner, Paul, walked over and pulled up a chair. "Where are we?"

Mark shook his head. "The victim's name was Ryan Bellig from Raleigh, North Carolina."

"What was he doing out here?"

"I don't know. I contacted his employer. He was on vacation, due back the end of the week. He never told anyone there what his plans were. I did find out that he was a churchgoer, First Presbyterian."

"The church he was found in is Presbyterian. Maybe he attended services yesterday. Every time my in-laws travel they attend services at a church where they're traveling."

"I thought about that," Mark admitted. "But none of the church staff recognized him."

Paul shrugged. "Maybe he kept a low profile."

Mark shook his head. "I spoke to his pastor at First Presbyterian in Raleigh. He said Ryan used to be a regular attendee, but he hadn't gone to services in three years. It seems his wife and daughter were murdered, and the killer was never found. After that, he stopped going to church."

"And now *he's* murdered and in a church. There's irony for you."

"Tell me about it."

"So, the question is, why here, why now?"

Mark leaned back in his chair. "His boss said this is his first extended vacation in years. He's taken the occasional long weekend, but that's it. I contacted the Raleigh police and asked to see the file on his wife and daughter."

"You think whoever killed his family waited three years for him to leave the state, followed him, and finished him off?" Paul asked.

Mark shrugged. "Right now I don't know what to think. How are we doing on the donkey guy?"

"He has no family in the area, and we've ruled out friends. They were all at a church gathering Sunday night when he was killed."

"Don't tell me."

"Yeah, you're going to love this. He didn't go to First Shepherd, but his friends do."

Mark groaned. "Two murders connected, albeit loosely, to the same church."

"Yeah."

Mark stood. "I'm going home to get some sleep. I have a feeling tomorrow's going to be a long day."

∞

"I won't blame you if you want to go home now," Jeremiah said.

Cindy looked pale, but resolute as she shook her head. "I said I'd help, I'll help."

He handed her some gloves and a sponge. "Okay, we'll start here in the kitchen. Everything that food might have touched, or the steam from cooking food, has to be thoroughly purified."

"And by purification you mean what exactly?"

"It depends on what it is. Some things get immersed in boiling water, some things are passed through fire, and some things, like the light switches, can just be wiped down with ammonia."

"You've got to be kidding!"

"I never—"

"I know, you never joke about Passover. Where do you want me to start?"

"How about the light switches and the doorknobs throughout the house. Everything has to be cleaned, not just the kitchen."

"Wow."

"I even have to check my clothes and make sure there are no crumbs anywhere, including the pockets."

"I could never be Jewish."

"Why's that?"

"It's too much work."

He smiled.

They worked for a little while in silence. He glanced over at her from time to time. It had been foolish to invite this woman into his home, to spend more time with her and possibly incite her curiosity. For someone who was trying hard to stay out of the whole murder mess he was doing a terrible job of it.

After he finished cleaning the oven he taped it closed since he had no intention of using it during Passover. He did the same with several cabinets. Finally, they both ended up at the sink, wringing out sponges at the same time.

"This is going to take forever," she said.

He smiled. "It would be much worse if I was actually having a Seder here."

"I can't imagine what you're going to have to do at the synagogue tomorrow night!"

"Care to volunteer?"

"No, thank you," she said with a laugh. "Two nights of this, and I'll be the one they find dead . . . of exhaustion."

He knew it was hard for her to joke about what she had seen that morning, but the fact that she was trying was a good sign.

"How do you think that guy got into the sanctuary?" he asked.

She stopped and looked up at him. "You know, I've been thinking about that. There's no way he was killed while the church was open and then someone accidentally locked him in. The lights were off. It's pitch dark in there regardless of the time of day."

"Which is why you tripped over him and didn't see him in the dark," Jeremiah filled in.

"Exactly. If it happened last night, the light would have had to be on in the sanctuary for the killer to even see him, let alone stab him to death."

"Unless you're dealing with a blind killer."

She looked uncertain for a minute and then shook her head. "No, there are no blind people who are in any way associated with the church."

"Okay, let's assume for now our killer was sighted."

"Then he'd have to have seen what he was doing, which means the light would have been on when he killed him."

"But the light was off this morning."

"Yes." Cindy moved to stand directly in front of him, eyes quickening with thought. "Whenever you lock up the sanctuary, it's standard to turn the lights on for a minute just to make sure no one's in there praying, or asleep, or —"

"And if whoever locked the door had the light on, they would have seen the body and called the police."

"Exactly," Cindy said.

"Which means, that whoever killed him turned off the lights and locked the door."

"Which means," Cindy continued. "The killer definitely had to have a key to the church."

"Unless someone had a key stolen and hasn't bothered to report it, the killer goes to the church," Jeremiah said, staring intently at her.

"The killer is either on staff or one of the ministry leaders," Cindy finished.

They both stood for a moment in silence, staring at each other.

"Oh no," she whispered as realization set in. "I know the killer."

Looking at her stricken expression and panic-filled eyes, Jeremiah knew she wouldn't rest easy until the killer had been caught.

He put a hand on her shoulder and steered her toward the dining table. She sat down, and he got them both some ice water. He grabbed a pad of paper and a pen and put them down on the table.

"Okay, Cindy, let's just think this through logically."

"How?"

"Which staff members have keys?"

"All ten of us."

"Okay, who?"

She took a deep breath. "There's me, Pastor Roy, Associate Pastor Jake, Wildman—"

"Wildman?"

"Pastor Wyman. He's the youth pastor."

"Kids nicknamed him?"

"I believe the name actually came from seminary."

Jeremiah shook his head. "Okay, who else?"

"Geanie the graphic designer, the janitor Ralph, Danielle the children's pastor, Gus the music minister, Loretta the organist, and Sylvia the business manager."

"Okay," he said, looking at the list. "I think it's safe to eliminate you."

She smiled. "That's very generous of you."

He shrugged. "I'm that type of guy. Okay, so let's also put down here the ministry leaders that have keys."

"Drake Stryker, head of the men's ministry. Jesse Raybourne is head of the women's ministry. The last would be Harold Grey; he's the head usher."

Jeremiah added the names to the list and stared hard at the last one. "Harold Grey, your landlord?"

"Yes, that's right."

He thought of the bloody cross on the floor of the sanctuary. "Would any of these people have a Shepherd's cross?"

She nodded. "Harold's a Shepherd."

"Anyone else on this list?"

"No."

He looked up at her and saw the moment when what she had said sunk in. Her eyes widened. "No, not Harold! I can't believe that."

Jeremiah shrugged. "Maybe his cross just happened to be in the wrong place at the wrong time."

"Or someone's trying to frame him."

"Could be." He didn't believe it, though.

She looked like she was about to cry. He stood up from the table. "The police probably have a suspect in custody. Let's not worry until we know more. How about I drive you back to your car so you can go home?"

She bolted up from the table. "No!"

He looked at her quizzically.

"Howard has a key to my house."

"We have no reason to believe he means you any harm," he said, and then paused. Grey had been in the house when they arrived and had seemed nervous the entire time. What had he been doing there? Had he really been checking on the air-conditioner?

He looked at Cindy and could practically taste her fear. Safety was a big deal for her, perhaps more than for anyone he'd ever met. Slowly he nodded. "Okay, you should probably check into a hotel for the night."

Cindy walked into her room at the Ramada Inn. She bolted the door behind her and breathed a sigh of relief. She didn't have anything with her because she hadn't wanted to go home to pack. Jeremiah had dropped her at her car and then followed her to the hotel to make sure she was okay. They had said goodnight in the lobby.

She crossed over to the window and looked down on the street. A church and a few businesses were scattered on the other side of the road. One church had a large, blazing cross on the front of it. It was situated next door to a strip mall where a check cashing place flashed its open sign next to a laundromat that was closed.

After she pulled the curtains to shut out the world, she undressed in the darkness and gratefully slipped between clean sheets. She prayed for safety and for the police to catch the murderer.

As she tried to fall asleep she couldn't block the image of the murdered man from her mind. She shivered as it played again and again in her memory. Then she thought of Jeremiah, swooping in to save her like some avenging angel. Although, she had to admit, she had thought him a demon when she first saw him.

She wondered why he had moved to America and resolved to ask him later. *If I even see him again.* They weren't even friends. It was unlikely Jeremiah would want to continue with their rescuer/rescuee relationship.

Cindy flipped onto her side and pounded her pillow into submission. She didn't normally like hotels. Only a thin bit of wood separated her from countless strangers. She always felt so exposed sleeping in a hotel, and she had no idea how Kyle did it as part of his job. Then again, they had always been opposites.

She turned to her other side, trying not to think about her brother. From where she lay she could see the door of the room. In the dim light she stared at the doorknob, and half a dozen times she started up, thinking she saw it move.

"Stop being an idiot," she told herself. She forced herself to close her eyes even as her mind tried to figure out how many hotel workers had a key to her room. There were probably as many keys to her room as there were to the church sanctuary.

Please, God, let it not be Harold. She couldn't cope if it was. He had a key to her house. If she found out he was a murderer, she was sure she would never feel safe in any house she rented.

She finally drifted to sleep. Her dreams were filled with dark figures that lurked in the shadows, wanting to hurt her. Mocking laughter filled her nightmares, and someone chased her, a key ring jangling on his belt.

He stood in the shadows, watching. It wasn't quite time, but he could wait. Just a little longer. He stared intently at the building. The neon sign blazed out, identifying and distinguishing the small shop from the buildings on either side. "CHECKS CASHED" it screamed for all the world to see. A young woman, her frail arms shaking from the effort, pushed open the barred door and staggered outside. Tears streamed down her cheeks. She deserved better, and so did the other wretched examples of humanity that passed through its doors every day. It was time to put an end to it.

He moved toward the door and pulled it open, the bell chiming as he stepped inside. The owner stood behind the counter, cold eyes sweeping over him, sizing him up.

"What can I do for you this evening, sir?"

"The question is what can *I* do for society?"

⸎

Mark stood in the middle of a sea of glass and wood shards and for a moment believed he had stumbled into a war zone. He walked slowly into the building, glass crunching beneath his shoes, and looked around. What once had been a long counter had been hacked to pieces with an axe and the remnants scattered through the room, out the door, and onto the street outside. Every fixture had been destroyed. Even the fluorescent lights had been shattered. Illumination came from some portable lights the uniformed officers had set up. Money had been flung around the room, and he noted that much of it was covered in blood.

He thought briefly of the scene at the church, where the secretary's cards had landed on and around the body. Only here, there was no body. He turned as Paul walked up beside him.

"Unhappy customer?"

Mark shook his head slowly. "Angry customer kills the guy, runs off. Thief kills the guy, robs the till, runs off. This is different. The killer systematically destroyed everything in here and didn't take anything."

"Except the body," Paul pointed out.

"Have you found it yet?"

Paul shook his head. "No, just the blood."

Mark looked up at the wall where the words *Get Out!* had been written in blood in foot-tall letters.

He took a deep breath. "This is . . . something else."

"What?"

Mark continued to stare at the letters. "It's almost like a command or a warning."

"To whom?"

Mark shook his head slowly. "The panic button was never pushed?"

"No, the guy must not have had time," Paul said. "There was never any alarm sounded."

Mark took another look around and then walked outside, needing some fresh air to clear his head. He glanced at his watch. It was nearly two in the morning. The call had come in just after midnight from a driver who had been using the parking lot to turn around and had noticed that the doors were hanging off their hinges. He had already been questioned and sent on his way.

The detective walked the parking lot, looking for something, *anything* that would give him a clue. His thoughts turned back to the blood inside. There had to be a body. Why would the killer have taken it with him, though?

It didn't seem right. The killer must have left the body somewhere; they just hadn't found it yet. He turned to go back inside, and his eyes fell on the building next door. It was a small church with an electric cross glowing on its front. A sick feeling twisted his gut, and he walked slowly toward it.

Something fluttered on the lawn. He approached, and in the light from the electric cross he looked down. A table, a twin to the one that was smashed up in the store, lay flipped upside down. Lying spread-eagled on it was the body he had been looking for. The man's eyes were frozen wide in terror. His throat had been slit. The victim's shirt had been ripped open to expose deep furrows that had been cut into his chest. Bloody dollar bills were clenched tight in each fist.

"Paul!" Mark shouted.

Moments later his partner stood next to him. The other detective whistled low.

"Looks like we found our body," Mark said grimly. There was something familiar about it all, something he felt he was missing. Paul bent down to take a closer look.

"So, why leave Mr. Moneybags on the church lawn?"

"Good question," Mark said.

"Wild week. Three murders so far."

"And the week's only getting started."

"At this rate imagine how bad it's going to be by Easter," Paul said. Mark swore to himself. "What is it?"

"Easter week. Someone's recreating Easter week."

"What do you mean?"

"First, the guy on the donkey—the triumphal entry of Jesus into Jerusalem. The next thing he did was drive the money changers from the temple."

"That's what this is?" Paul asked.

"Yeah, think about it. Money changers took advantage of people who didn't have much choice. These check-cashing places charge insane fees and prey on people who are down on their luck, those who don't have bank accounts, or need quick loans."

"Yeah, they make it nearly impossible for people to survive while at the same time earning the gratitude of those who need their services," Paul said.

"Exactly. The whole driving-the-money-changers-from-the-temple thing. Jesus smashed up their tables and equipment."

"Just like inside," Paul noted.

"And he drove them out with a whip."

"And this guy has certainly been worked over with a whip," Paul said, indicating the lacerations on the man's chest.

"Sick. Two events of Easter week have already been recreated."

"What about the guy in the church? What did he represent?" Paul asked. "I mean, aside from the location, there was nothing unusual about that one. Nothing like this or the donkey guy."

Mark shook his head slowly. "You got me."

"Maybe we should talk to somebody who might know."

"I think you're right." He looked back down at the dead man. "We've got to catch this guy before he kills again."

Paul gestured to the building across the street. "I'll head over in a little bit and find out from the management which of the rooms facing this direction are occupied tonight."

"Maybe somebody saw or heard something," Mark agreed. "At least, let's hope so."

6

Cindy awoke to a knock on the door of her room. She glanced at the clock on the nightstand and saw that it was just after six-thirty.

"Just a minute!" she called.

She got up, threw her clothes on, and opened the door with a yawn. There in the hallway stood the detective from the day before. He looked almost as surprised to see her as she was to see him.

"Well, Ms. Preston, funny seeing you here. Where's your Good Samaritan?" he asked, glancing over her shoulder.

"Not here, if that's what your suggesting," she said, flushing angrily.

"May I come in?"

She stepped back, and he walked inside. He headed straight for the window and threw open the curtains, making a clucking sound as he did so.

She stepped away from the door, but left it open. She had no desire to be closed in with the man, even if he was a detective. Questions crowded her brain as she tried to figure out what he was doing here.

"Interesting view," he noted.

"The church looked nice," she said.

"Not as nice as it was."

Curious, she stepped forward, but he turned and faced her, and she stopped halfway to the window.

"So, you checked in here last night?"

"Yes."

"What time?"

"Around eight-thirty."

"Did you look out this window?"

"Yes, why?"

He ignored her question and pushed on. "Did you see anything unusual?"

"No."

"Did you hear anything unusual last night?"

"No, what's going on?"

"See for yourself," he said, motioning to the window.

Cindy approached, keeping one eye on him. Finally, she reached the window and looked down. There were half a dozen squad cars in the street in front of the church and the check-cashing place. Police officers were walking around the area and talking to people. Then she saw the body on the lawn being loaded into a black bag.

She jumped backwards with a cry and nearly collided with the detective. He put a hand on her arm.

"Now are you sure you didn't see or hear anything last night?"

"Nothing," she said, shaking her head.

"Then perhaps you'd like to explain why you were staying here last night, and why there's a killer running around who likes to leave bodies where you'll see them?

Tears streamed down her face. "I don't know."

"Why didn't you sleep at home last night?" he demanded.

"I was too scared."

"Of what?"

She turned to look at him. "Jeremiah and I were talking about it last night, and I realized that the only Shepherd who has a key to the sanctuary is Harold Grey. He's my landlord. He has a key to my house, and he was in there yesterday when I left the church in the morning."

He glared at her and said through gritted teeth, "What part of 'call me if you think of anything' didn't you understand?"

She started to cry in earnest. "It couldn't be Harold; he's a sweet man."

"Yet, you were so afraid that you felt the need to check into a hotel for the night. And now, right beneath your nose, someone else has been murdered."

Cindy pulled away and sat down on the bed, burying her face in her hands. It was all too terrible to believe. Could both bodies really have been left for her to see? Who would do something like that?

"Cindy, do you have any enemies?"

She looked up at him. "No."

"Are you sure?"

"Positive."

"Then what can you tell me about this Harold Grey?"

"He's been a member of the church for years and years. He's retired. He's the head usher, which is why he has a key to the sanctuary, and he's a Shepherd. He owns a couple of houses in the area, and I'm renting one. Yesterday, when Jeremiah drove me home, he was in the house when we got there. He said he was checking out the air-conditioner before the heat starts. He said he'd left me a message on my answering machine about it the week before."

"Did he?" he prompted.

"No, not that I ever heard."

"Do you ever find yourself on Palm Avenue on Sundays?"

"I guess. I'm not sure. Are you talking about the guy on the donkey?"

"How did you hear about that?" he asked.

"Oliver works for the newspaper. He came to my house yesterday to interview me about the body in the church. He let it slip, but I don't think he was supposed to."

"You got that right," he growled. The detective took a deep breath. "Okay, so the Palm Sunday guy. Now this one, the money changer thrown out of the temple."

"Really?" she asked.

"Yeah. No question about that."

"That's terrible!"

"Someone is sending a message. Do you have any idea what part of the Easter week story the body in the church could represent?"

She thought about it for a long minute. Nothing about the man or the way he'd been found or the place rang any bells. "No, I'm sorry."

"Does the name Miguel Jesus Olivera mean anything to you?"

"No, I don't know a Miguel."

"How about Jason Schneider or Ryan Bellig?"

She shook her head. "Are these the men who were killed?"

He didn't answer, but instead flipped through his notebook. "Is there anything more you want to tell me about Harold Grey?"

"I can't think of anything."

"Okay. I need you to not leave town until I clear you to do so."

"Why?" she burst out.

"Also, if you plan on staying here again tonight, I'd suggest changing rooms. We'll be in touch."

As he left the room, she found herself more bewildered and frightened than before. After locking the door she grabbed her cell phone. A moment later she remembered that Jeremiah's card was still sitting on her kitchen table. Why hadn't she bothered to program the number in when she had the chance?

If she went home and changed clothes, she could get his number. She shivered, not sure she was ready to go back home. *Ten minutes, that's all it will take to get in, change clothes, and get out.*

Forcing herself to take a deep breath, she grabbed her purse and her keys, and headed for the lobby, where she checked out of the room. If Harold was the killer, the police would surely arrest him within hours. If he wasn't, then she had nothing to fear from staying at home.

Unless the killer really is targeting me, and it's someone other than Harold.

She tried to push the thought from her mind. The killing had been random. There was no way the killer could have known she had checked into the hotel the night before. The only person who knew that was Jeremiah. Her heart skipped a beat for a moment but she reminded herself that he couldn't be responsible for the dead man in the church.

Soon she arrived home and sat in her car, building up courage. The house looked normal. Finally, she forced herself out of the car and when she went to the front door she discovered it was locked. *Just like I left it. But then so was the sanctuary.*

She opened the door with a hand that shook and stepped hesitantly inside. It only took a moment before she screamed.

Unable to sleep well because of worrying about Cindy, Jeremiah rolled out of bed. She should have been perfectly safe in the hotel. Still he went through his morning ritual, cursing himself for not having gotten her cell phone number. He was just about to leave the house and head over to the hotel to check on her when the phone rang.

"Help me!"

He recognized the voice as Cindy's. "Where are you?"

"My house! Someone's been here."

"Did you call 9-1-1?"

"Yes."

"I'll be right over."

He slammed down the receiver and raced out the door. Ten minutes later his Mustang screeched to a stop outside her house. She was sitting on the front porch but jumped to her feet when he got out of his car. She ran to him and threw her arms around his neck. He held her tightly, feeling the shudders that rippled through her body.

A minute later he heard a car pull up. He stepped away from her and turned to see Detective Mark Walters. The detective walked up and looked him over. "Rabbi."

"Detective."

"I figured you'd turn up sometime today."

Jeremiah had no idea what he meant by the remark. He glanced at Cindy, who looked pale.

"Good morning, *again*, Miss Preston," Mark said.

"Again?" Jeremiah asked before he could help himself.

Mark smiled wryly. "Yes, Miss Preston and I just finished a long conversation not half an hour ago."

"What happened?" Jeremiah asked, feeling more protective of Cindy than he would have liked.

"I'll let her fill you in later . . . after she fills me in on the here and now."

Jeremiah and Mark both turned toward Cindy. "I came home to change clothes before work. The front door was locked, but when I walked inside I could tell someone had broken in," she explained.

"Did you touch anything?" Mark asked.

"The door and the phone."

"Okay, show me."

Cindy led the way to the front door, with Mark right behind her and Jeremiah trailing. The rabbi's thoughts churned.

Inside, books and papers had been flung about the room. The cushions had been pulled off the couch and one of them unzipped, its foam exposed. Her television, DVD player, and stereo were undisturbed.

Mark moved slowly through the living room, asking questions. Jeremiah glanced toward the kitchen and saw that the drawers were all open, but only one kitchen cabinet was ajar.

Jeremiah walked back toward Cindy's office. Her computer seemed untouched, as did her filing cabinet. The window remained closed and locked.

He continued on to Cindy's bedroom and paused in the doorway. Her end table drawer was on the bed, its contents spilled beside it. On the other side of the bed her jewelry box had been dumped. Half a dozen different cross necklaces had been placed in a pile separate from the rest, which was spread out on her comforter. The window in the room was also closed and locked.

He returned to the living room.

"—looking for something," Mark was saying. "And, whatever it was, he didn't want you to know. That's why he only unzipped one pillow instead of shredding all three of them. It was meant to throw us off."

"What was he looking for?" Cindy asked.

"I think I know," Jeremiah said.

They both turned toward him, and he led them back to her bedroom. Cindy cried out and moved toward her jewelry, but Jeremiah put a hand on her shoulder to restrain her. Mark pushed past them, walked around the bed, and then saw what Jeremiah had seen.

His eyes glittered. "He doesn't know we found the Shepherd's cross."

Jeremiah nodded. "He's hoping Cindy picked it up."

"Which means our killer searched the scene when he realized it was missing, knew she was the first person there yesterday, and came looking for it," Mark said.

"And whoever he was, he didn't break in here," Jeremiah said softly.

"No. He tried to cover his tracks, but he couldn't help locking the door behind him. What kind of person does that?" Mark asked.

"Someone with an interest in the safety of the property," Cindy said, face ashen. "Harold, my landlord."

"Not only did he know you weren't here last night so he could break in and look through your stuff, he knew where to stage the next murder for your benefit," Mark confirmed.

"Next murder? What are you talking about?" Jeremiah asked.

"Your girlfriend can fill you in later."

Out of the corner of his eye Jeremiah saw Cindy turn crimson. He kept his cool and just stared at Mark.

"I'm not his girlfriend," Cindy spit out.

Mark held Jeremiah's gaze for a moment before turning back to her. "What's important now is that we go find Harold and ask him a few questions."

"But he's such a nice man," Cindy protested weakly.

"Some of the worst people you've ever met masquerade as the nicest," Mark said.

"Could you please call me and tell me what happens?" she asked. "I'm not going to feel safe until this murderer is caught."

Mark gave a noncommittal shrug and then turned to the door. Jeremiah moved, inserting himself casually between the detective and the exit. "She needs to know if you have a suspect in custody," he said softly.

"Calm down, Rabbi. I'll give her a call later today."

"Thank you," Jeremiah said. He moved so the detective could leave.

Mark nodded. "Don't touch anything. In fact, the two of you need to leave now. Forensics will be here in a few minutes to sweep for prints." He pulled his cell phone from his belt and left.

Cindy collapsed onto one of the chairs at her kitchen table. Jeremiah stood for a moment, listening as Mark talked to another officer.

"Yeah, break-in. Looks like the killer was trying to get that cross back. No. She thinks it could be her landlord. Yeah, Harold Grey. Yeah. Meet me there. It's time we asked Mr. Grey some questions."

Jeremiah and Cindy left the house a minute later. She looked up at him with tired eyes.

"How did you sleep?" he asked.

"Great until the police came to my room," she said.

"Yeah, about that—"

"Condensed version?"

"No, I want to hear the whole thing."

⸺◦⟨∞⟩◦⸺

When Mark met Paul outside Harold Grey's home, he hoped they could put an end to the killing spree. A man in his early sixties answered the door.

"Harold Grey?" Paul asked.

"Yes."

"Sir, we're detectives," Mark informed him, flashing his badge. "Do you mind if we come in and ask you a couple of questions?"

"Not at all," he said and ushered them inside. They took seats in the living room, and Mark took a moment to study the man before him. He didn't seem like a serial killer, but appearances could be deceiving. And with the stakes as high as they were, they couldn't risk letting the killer go free.

"A body was found at First Shepherd yesterday," Mark said.

Harold nodded. "I heard. Terrible business."

"Where were you Sunday evening?" Mark asked.

"At a play in Los Angeles with my wife. We're season ticket holders."

"And what time did you leave?" Paul jumped in.

"A couple of minutes after ten."

"Can you prove that?" Paul pushed.

Harold nodded. "Why? Wait, I'm not a suspect, am I?"

"We're talking to everyone who had access to the sanctuary," Mark said, unwilling to divulge more than that. They would check out Grey's story, but he had a sinking sensation in the pit of his stomach. Harold Grey wasn't their guy. Still, they had to be sure.

"You're a Shepherd at the church, is that true?" Mark asked.

"Yes," Harold said, looking puzzled.

"Do you mind showing us the cross?"

Harold pulled it out from underneath his shirt and then slipped the chain over his head and handed it to them. Mark took it and stared at it for several seconds.

"Sir, it is my understanding that there is no way to tell the Shepherd's crosses apart," Mark said at last.

"Ordinarily that's true, but I can assure you this cross is mine."

"How?" Paul asked.

"Turn it over," Harold instructed.

When he did Mark saw the engraving and read aloud. "The First Shepherd of First Shepherd."

Harold beamed. "When they started up the program five years ago, I was the first volunteer to go through the training. They gave me that cross special because of it."

Reluctantly, Mark returned it. He exchanged a grim glance with Paul. They were back to square one.

Cindy hunched over her keyboard at work. She was beyond caring if anyone caught her surfing the Web when she should be working. She typed in the name "Ryan Bellig" in the search box on Google and held her breath, expecting thousands of entries to come up. A second later the search came back with just under a hundred hits, most of them with highlighted words like "tragedy," "violent death," and "latest in a string of grisly murders." She clicked on the latter one and followed the link to a newspaper article that was three years old.

On the left hand side she saw a picture of a man in a dark suit, a tear rolling down his cheek. She stopped and stared. It was the man from the sanctuary floor, when he was still alive. His eyes were filled with pain but so wondrously alive. Her eyes dropped to the caption beneath the photograph: *Ryan Bellig at the funeral of his wife and daughter, the latest victims of the Passion Week Killer.*

Passion Week Killer! She was staring so intently that she didn't see Danielle walk up to her desk until the other woman put a hand on her shoulder. Cindy jumped. *It's not good to zone out like that; it's not safe.*

"Are you okay?" Danielle asked in the voice she usually reserved for the children.

Cindy started to say she was fine, but stopped. It wasn't true, and she was in no mood to pretend. "Actually, I'm not okay at all."

Danielle's eyes widened. "I know this has been a trying time for us all."

"More for me than for most," Cindy said.

Danielle patted her shoulder, her watery blue eyes perplexed. "Maybe you should consider speaking with someone to help you feel better."

"What will help is to catch this psychopath," Cindy said, through gritted teeth. "Then maybe I can sleep at home without people trying to break in."

"Someone broke into your house?" Danielle looked shocked.

"Yes."

"But why?"

Cindy was about to tell her about the cross but stopped short. If Harold wasn't the killer, then she didn't want to alert the killer to the fact that she knew what he was looking for. One thing was for certain at First Shepherd. If you wanted the whole church to know something, the fastest way was to tell Danielle.

"I don't know, but there have been more murders," Cindy said. At least that wasn't confidential.

"How terrible!"

"Yes," Cindy said, relieved that someone else was giving it the weight it deserved.

"I really do think you should see someone."

"I don't need to talk to a shrink or a pastor or a therapist because I've seen people killed," Cindy growled. *Seen people killed.* She took a deep breath. But she hadn't seen anyone killed, not in a long, long time. She had just seen the bodies. *Big difference. Easy there. I'm not fifteen, and Danielle's not my mother.*

"I'll manage," Cindy forced out and somehow managed a small smile. She had been crazy to think she could tell someone how she really felt. "Is there something I can help you with, Danielle?"

The children's minister brightened and handed her a piece of paper. "Here's what the kids are doing for Easter services."

Cindy took the paper and felt rage building inside her. "Geanie is the one who needs this, not me."

"I figured you could just give it to Geanie for me."

Cindy thought about shoving it back in her face. Danielle had come through the back door and had walked right past Geanie's desk in order to get to Cindy. It was no secret that the two disliked each other. Geanie usually managed to stay professional, but Danielle wouldn't even acknowledge Geanie's presence in the room, let alone talk to her. Cindy turned pointedly and stared at Geanie who just rolled her eyes and shrugged.

"Sure, I can give it to her," Cindy said, stifling the urge to turn the piece of paper into an airplane.

"Thanks, dear, and you make sure and see someone about those problems of yours."

Danielle turned and sailed out of the office, head held high and humming to herself.

"Would you like to bring it to me, or shall I come to you?" Geanie asked.

"Tell you what," Cindy said. She crumpled the paper into a ball and tossed it at Geanie's head.

The other girl caught it and laughed. "Nice one."

Cindy shared a brief smile with her before returning to the computer, eager to know more about the Passion Week Killer.

7

MARK WALKED INTO THE CHURCH AT FIRST SHEPHERD AND MADE A BEE-line for Cindy's desk. She stared intently at her computer screen and didn't seem to notice when he stopped in front of her. He waited a moment and then cleared his throat.

"I'm surprised to see you here."

She jumped and turned to look at him with startled eyes. "Detective! Sorry, just lost in thought."

"So I noticed."

"I couldn't stay home, not with so much to do here and everything how it is there."

He shrugged. He didn't really care what her motivation was.

"What can I do for you?" she asked.

"Yesterday I asked your pastor to pull together a list of all the church's Shepherds for me. I'm here to pick it up. I also need to ask him a few questions."

She raised one eyebrow and picked up the phone. "Roy, Detective Walters is here to see you. He also wants to know if you have the Shepherd list available for him. Okay, I'll send him in."

She hung up the phone. "I'll have a list with names and addresses ready for you by the time you're done with your meeting."

"Thanks. I assume that means he didn't have it ready?"

She rolled her eyes. "I assume the fact that you need it means Harold's not the killer?"

"We can't rule anyone out for sure at this point, but I'm fairly certain it's not him."

She slumped. "I'm relieved and also really frightened now."

"I think that's a pretty normal response. So, where I can find the pastor?"

"Roy's office is right over there. Go on in," she said, pointing to a door in the far wall.

A moment later he walked into the head pastor's office. It was a cozy room lined with bookshelves. A black leather sofa sat against one wall. Mark chose one of the matching chairs in front of Roy's desk. He guessed the pastor to be about sixty, with tanned skin and close-cropped grey hair. Probably a golfer. The pastor's smile revealed bright, white teeth. A bleach job.

"Good to see you again," Roy said, extending his hand.

Mark shook it. "Most people feel they can go a lifetime without seeing me again."

Roy looked confused for a moment and then the smile returned to his face. "Sorry, habit. So, what can I do for you? You wanted a list of the Shepherds, right? I'll see what I can do about getting that to you."

"Don't worry about it," Mark said.

"Okay."

"I'd like to ask you a few questions, though."

"Go ahead."

"Is there any event in the Bible during Easter week that could be symbolized by the presence of the dead man in your sanctuary?"

"For starters, it wasn't called Easter week back then, of course."

Mark wondered if hitting a pastor would buy him a ticket on the express train to hell. He forced a smile. "Of course not, but you get my meaning."

"Well, I just want to be precise."

"I'm looking for something a little less precise and a little more symbolic."

"Dangerous ground to traverse, indeed," Roy said, forming his fingers into a steeple. "Take the whole 'eye for an eye' debate. Is it literal; is it figurative? The problems that can be had, the headaches, over a lack of precision."

"Are you serious?"

"Very serious." Roy met his eyes.

Mark cleared his throat. "Okay, then, could you tell me what the next event in Easter week is, traditionally, as we understand it, not necessarily in actuality."

"I don't know what you mean," Roy said.

Mark stared at him. Could the pastor really be that dense? Or was he just one of those guys who never liked to be nailed down and so never made any clear statements? He had dealt with that type before, and he didn't have the time or patience to deal with Roy. He stood abruptly. "Thanks for your time, pastor."

"Anytime. Glad to help." Roy smiled with those bleached-white teeth.

The detective resisted the urge to slam the door behind him. Back in the main office Cindy held a paper aloft without even turning around to see him.

"That was fast." Mark moved to take it from her.

"You want something done around a church, you just have to know the right people to ask," she said with a smile.

"So, this is all the Shepherds?"

"Yes. Although it's still hard to think it could be one of them."

"The one thing I've learned as a police officer is that nobody really knows anybody else."

"That's depressing."

"That's the truth."

He looked up from the list and studied her for a moment. "How much do you know about the Bible?" he asked.

She laughed and gestured to her surroundings. "What do you think?"

"I think you avoided the question."

"Okay, fair enough. I'd say I have an average level of knowledge given my position and background."

"I'll pretend for a moment that your answer is more real than your last one," he said.

"Thanks."

"Can I ask you a couple of questions?"

"Sure."

He glanced around. Another woman sat at a desk a few feet away, one fist twisted in her hair and the other propping up her chin while she read. Somebody else was using the copier behind the partition. "Can we talk somewhere a little more private?"

Cindy nodded and stood. "Geanie, I'll be back in a few."

"Okay," the other woman said, without looking up from what she was reading on her desk.

They headed for the front door, but before they got there, it swung open and Harold stepped inside. The older gentleman nodded to Mark before turning to Cindy.

"Cindy, I've got a problem."

"What is it, Harold?"

"I'm here to set up for tomorrow's prayer service, and I realized my key to the sanctuary is missing."

"Missing?" Mark and Cindy asked at the same time.

"Yes." Harold held up his key ring. "I always keep it here next to my house key, and it's gone. I don't know what could have happened to it."

"When did you use it last?" Mark asked.

"The Sunday before last. I opened the sanctuary in the morning."

"But not two days ago?" Mark pressed.

"No, pastor beat me here. The alarm didn't go off, and I overslept."

"I'll open the sanctuary for you," Cindy said, returning to her desk for her keys.

The three of them walked through the narthex, and Cindy unlocked the sanctuary. She hesitated for a moment before stepping inside to turn on the lights.

"Thanks," Harold said.

"Mr. Grey, are you going to be here a while? I'd like to talk with you about your missing key," Mark said.

"Sure, I'll be here for at least an hour or so."

"Great."

He turned back to Cindy. "Where can we talk?"

She led him to another part of the building, unlocked another door, and ushered him into a Sunday school room. She grimaced in apology as he eyed the tiny plastic chairs. She perched on one, and he followed suit.

"Is there any possible religious symbolism for the guy you found in the church?" he asked.

"You mean like the Palm Sunday murder and the money changer thing?"

"Yeah, exactly like that."

"I haven't been able to come up with anything, and I've really tried."

He stared hard at her.

She crossed her arms. "Look, it's impossible to think of anything else when I know there's a killer running around loose."

He sighed. "I can understand that."

"I did find something, though, that might connect it all."

"What?" He leaned forward and tried not to feel ridiculous sitting in a kindergartner's chair.

"Ryan Bellig was from Raleigh, North Carolina."

"Yeah, and?"

"His wife and daughter were killed a couple of years ago."

"I know that."

"Did you hear they were killed by the Passion Week Killer, a serial killer who was never caught and who was killing his victims in imitation of events of Easter week?"

"Are you kidding me?"

She sat back, looking satisfied. "No."

"And just how did you come by your information?"

"I Googled his name and the old news articles came up."

Mark swore, and she colored slightly. He lurched out of his seat.

"Where are you going?"

"To call my partner and tell him to get in touch with Raleigh police. Then I'll talk to Harold about his missing key."

"Ask him if he saw it after Saturday afternoon."

"And why is that?"

"Last Saturday there was a Shepherds meeting here at the church. If a Shepherd really did kill Ryan on Sunday, then he probably stole the key from Harold on Saturday."

———

After the detective left, Cindy barely got any work done. After a dozen crises over rooms, Easter preparations, and misplacing the master-calendar binder twice, Geanie took over. Depressed, Cindy trudged out to the parking lot and climbed into her car.

She glanced with longing at Jeremiah's Mustang in the neighboring parking lot but knew he was busy with cleaning the Synagogue in preparation for Passover. She thought about offering to help, but from the number of cars in the parking lot it looked like he had all the help he could use. Besides, the last thing anyone needed was a Gentile girl asking questions, messing things up, and generally making everyone feel uncomfortable.

Cindy had no idea what to do. She didn't feel safe at church. She didn't feel safe going home. She didn't even feel safe returning to the hotel. Again, she glanced at Jeremiah's car. The only times she had felt safe since the nightmare started were when she was with him. *Wow! I'm pathetic.*

After a deep breath, she started the car. On a whim she drove downtown, trying to think up an excuse to buy something. She found a parking spot next to her favorite dress shop and wandered inside. Twenty minutes later she left, frustrated, empty-handed, and just as lost and frightened as she had been before.

Just face it, you're afraid to be alone.

She glanced into the window of the beauty salon next to the dress shop. She pushed open the door and went in. For fifteen dollars she could get a manicure while she decided what she wanted to do next.

The woman behind the counter glanced up with an apologetic smile. "I'm sorry, we're just closing."

"Oh," Cindy said.

"Would you like to come back tomorrow? I could squeeze you in during the lunch hour."

Cindy felt like an idiot. She didn't need a manicure. She didn't even really want one. Still, she found herself nodding because it was easier than figuring out what she wanted to tell the woman about why she never intended to come back.

"Your name?"

"Cindy Preston."

"Okay, Cindy. I have you down for twelve-fifteen tomorrow then."

Cindy nodded, backed out the door, and headed for her Focus. *I'll call and cancel in the morning.*

Before she could start the engine she saw Oliver walking out of one of the shops. She popped back out of her seat. "Oliver!"

He jumped and then turned and saw her. He nodded and waved. She locked her door and walked over to him. "Hey, how did the article turn out?"

"Good, thanks."

"How is everything else?"

"Okay. It's a crazy week, you know?" He shifted his weight from foot to foot.

"Tell me about it!"

"Are you okay?"

"No, not really."

"I'm very, very sorry to hear that."

"Me too. Hey, do you want to grab some dinner with me? I really need the company," she admitted.

"Um . . . sure. Why not?" he said with a faint smile.

"Great," she said, relief washing over her.

"Got anywhere in mind?"

"Anywhere, everywhere."

"You ever been to Rigatoni's?"

"The Italian place at the end of the block?"

"Yeah, we can walk there. Shall we?"

"Sure." She fell into step beside him.

"So, what's wrong?" he asked.

"I'm afraid to go back home."

"Why?"

"The murderer broke into my house."

Oliver tripped, but caught himself with a hand on a light pole. "That's terrible! Are you okay?"

"I'm fine. I wasn't home. Of course, now I'm too scared to go home."

He stopped and turned to look at her. "Cindy, you can't live your life afraid. Trust me, it's a terrible burden and one you shouldn't have to carry. I think you need to face your fear, go home, reclaim your territory, and do whatever you have to so that you feel safe there again."

He was right, and she knew it, but how could she explain to him just how terrifying that was? "After dinner?"

"After dinner," he agreed, relaxing and turning to continue toward the restaurant.

Jeremiah was gratified that almost thirty people showed up to help clean and purify the kitchen and the hall where they'd eat for the first night of Passover. Marie had brought her entire family to help.

When they were all gathered Jeremiah said a blessing. He followed it up with brief instructions.

"Marie has the master checklist of everything that needs to be done. Get your assignment from her, and when you've completed it, return to her for inspection, check off, and reassignment. Remember, we're here to get this done and done right. Please be reverent, reflect on the meaning of Passover, and work as quietly as possible so as not to disturb your neighbor's meditations. We must do our best in this effort. Still, I don't think it would offend the Most High if we tried to be done by ten-thirty. So, let's get to work!"

Everyone dutifully lined up in front of Marie, who gave out orders gleefully. He got in line as well, but Samuel Schuller approached him.

"Rabbi, may I speak with you for a moment?"

"Of course, Samuel," Jeremiah said, escorting him to the side. "What is it?"

"Our neighbors, who are Protestant, have often expressed interest in our religion and our holidays and rituals."

"Excellent," Jeremiah said. "I can think of no one better suited to provide them with understanding." He placed his hand on the other man's shoulder.

Samuel smiled at the compliment and then continued. "My wife and I have discussed inviting them into our home to partake of the second night's Seder with us."

"That is admirable. I know that is a common custom in some parts of this country."

"I have heard that too. It is a first for us, and I was wondering if you had any words of wisdom, Rabbi?"

In many ways Samuel's question represented the hardest part of Jeremiah's role of rabbi. He could answer questions about the Scriptures, traditions, rituals, and related things. Samuel, though, was asking for his personal opinion on something he had no firsthand knowledge of. He took a deep breath. Samuel was a deeply religious man, whose beliefs and sympathies were much more closely aligned with Orthodox viewpoint.

"Samuel, in this case I believe that pleasing Adonai and being a good host require the same measure of care from you. Share with your neighbors ahead of time what it is they can expect from the dinner. Also ask them, in respect of your traditions, that they carefully examine their clothes and make sure they are clean and that they bring nothing with them that might have touched food at their home. Then, you do not risk tainting your table or embarrassing your guests."

"Thank you, Rabbi," Samuel beamed. "That is excellent advice."

"I'm glad I could help."

Together they moved back to the line, and soon Jeremiah had been instructed by Marie to purify the floors in the hall and then to purify and set up the tables.

Cindy savored her chicken fettuccine alfredo to the fullest. It was incredible how good food could taste when you were really focused on it, or really trying to avoid something else.

Oliver was pleasant company, and she found herself gradually relaxing as they ate and talked. She started to wonder why he wasn't married. He was too old for her, but it was a habit she had picked up from her mother who constantly speculated on what kept bachelors bachelors.

It was a silly exercise, but she enjoyed focusing on something so mundane, so familiar.

"It's amazing how much better you feel on a full stomach, isn't it?" Oliver asked, as he slurped down the last bite of his spaghetti.

"It's so true," Cindy agreed.

"Feeling ready to face your house?"

She shook her head. "Not quite that brave yet."

"What's it going to take? Ice cream?"

"I won't feel safe until whoever did this is locked up," Cindy admitted.

"Really?"

She nodded.

"Surely, the police are close to making an arrest."

"I hope so. I don't think my nerves can take this much longer," she said.

"Do they have any suspects?"

"Is that the journalist speaking?" she teased.

"Nope, the concerned friend and fellow church member. Come on, we've known each other three years."

"That long?"

"Yeah, three years this month. You were one of the first people I met at First Shepherd. You helped me feel at home.

Safe. Let me help you feel safe at your home. I can help you work through this."

She looked into his eyes and wished she could tell him. She shouldn't, though. Not only was he a journalist, but he was also a Shepherd. Which meant he was a suspect. On the other hand, that meant he was going to know what the police knew soon enough. *I guess Mark didn't get to his name on the list yet.* "There are a few possibilities."

"Anyone I know?"

"Yeah, people we all know." Sadness nearly over-whelmed her.

He stared at her for a long minute. When he spoke again his voice was softer. "Cindy, why did someone break into your apartment?"

"The police think he was looking for something."

"Did they say what?"

She didn't want to lie to him and tell him no but she couldn't very well come out and tell him what the murderer had been looking for. She bit her lip. "I don't want to talk about it."

"That's okay," he said. "You don't have to. I just know that it helps to talk about these things."

"I don't think that's always true," Cindy said.

"Why not?"

Because some things never stop hurting no matter how much or how little you talk about them, she thought. She took a shaky breath. *I'm not fifteen anymore. No one can make me talk if I don't want to.* "Sometimes talking about the bad things doesn't make them better, it just makes them more a part of your life."

He reached across the table and grasped her hand. She jumped slightly, but then she looked into his eyes and felt his genuine compassion. It was one of the characteristics of a good Shepherd.

"We're not talking about the break-in anymore, are we?"

"I don't want to talk about it," she whispered.

"I think you do or you wouldn't have gone there."

He was right. She knew he was. It had just been a really long time since she had tried to talk about it with anyone.

"My, uh, sister—" Her voice cracked, and she started to shake. "When I was a kid, Lisa—" She could feel the tears start to slide down her cheeks.

"It's okay to talk about it. You don't have to be alone right now, Cindy."

"There was an accident."

"She was hurt?" he guessed.

Cindy nodded.

"She died?"

"Yes."

They sat for a moment in silence while she fought to control the pain and fear that the memory invoked. Finally, she squashed her emotions, and she felt like she could breathe again.

"Sorry," she mumbled.

"Never be sorry for feeling that way. What you suffered was great, and those who have not been in your shoes can never truly understand. But you do need to learn to live in spite of it. I didn't know your sister, but I do know if she loved you, she'd want that for you. Did she love you, Cindy?"

"Yes."

"Then that is what you need to carry in you, that love, that bond. Not the horror."

She wiped her eyes with a napkin. It was funny. All the time her parents had made her spend with therapists when she was a kid had never been so meaningful as these few quiet minutes with Oliver.

"Thank you."

"You're welcome." He squeezed her hand tightly and then released it.

"How did you know?"

He turned his face away, and she saw the muscles working in his jaw. When he spoke his voice was rough with emotion. "Years ago, a girl I cared for very much killed herself."

"I'm so sorry."

He turned back to her, and tears glistened in his eyes. "So am I. In a weird way it led me to my first newspaper job in Austin. I was running from the pain, and I know that's not a good way to live. It was such a senseless death, and I was young and selfish. But it taught me to see the pain others feel. Now, I try to help when I can."

"Well, you've helped me."

"Yeah?"

"Yeah. I'm going home to face my fears."

"Right now?" he asked.

She shook her head. "After ice cream."

"After ice cream," he agreed with a smile.

8

Filth and disease, they were everywhere. No one knew anything about cleansing, about purity, about being whole and blameless. They played at it. *Forgive me, Father, for I have sinned. I purified the house for Passover by cleaning the light switches with ammonia to glorify Adonai. God doesn't care what I do as long as I believe in him. I kill the infidels in the name of Allah even though I am no different than they. My soul is so pure I will not harm the creatures who are poisoning my child's drinking water. I worship Mother Earth as long as she stays out of my pristine, concrete high rise.*

What did they know of God, or his cleansing fire? What did they know of sacrifice, repentance? They tried so hard to scrub the evil from their souls, pretending it was never there. And look at the people they put their trust in, leaders more corrupt, more black-hearted than they knew or guessed. *They believe him to be a holy man. Fools!*

They were all sinners, every one. He stood in the shadows and waited with no illusions. Like all others he had fallen short of the glory of God. He had fallen so very, very far. Unlike them, though, he didn't feel the need to hide it like some secret shame.

First, the woman arrived, unlocked the front door, but left the closed sign in the window. Then, a few minutes later, the man walked quickly, looking constantly over his shoulder. He ducked inside the door, ashamed to be seen, wanting to hide. Just like a cockroach in the pale light of morning. *But I see him, and he cannot hide.*

He waited a moment, but the woman did not return to lock the door. Foolish. He finally slipped from the shadows and entered the door himself. There the two were, the man engaged in his secret shame, that which he would not share with his friends in the light of day. Such a simple, intimate thing with a significance neither dreamed of. They were unworthy, but they would have to do.

"Hello," Mark said, answering his phone. He glanced at his watch. It was just past eight in the morning. That meant he'd only slept about three hours. He had been up late pouring over everything he could get his hands on about the Passion Week Killer from Raleigh.

"A couple of bodies were found at Glamour Girl, the beauty parlor on Fifth Street," Paul said.

"I'll see you in fifteen." Mark hung up, relieved that it wasn't another religiously themed murder. Maybe they'd make it through Wednesday without one. It would be nice.

When he arrived the crime-scene photographer worked the far end of the room, and Paul talked to a distraught blonde woman, the owner it seemed. She smoked and waved her arm wildly, sending the toxic fumes through the air. Mark covered his mouth to avoid sucking it in. He walked toward the photographer.

"Hey, Jack."

"Hey."

Mark turned to look at the bodies. A man wearing a dark suit sat in the chair, his eyes frozen wide in terror. His throat had been cut. His bare feet were immersed in one of the pedicure tubs filled with blood. Beside the tub lay a woman with long, dark hair that fanned out around her on the floor. Her throat had also been slit. Each of her hands held one of the man's ankles.

He stood for a moment, taking it in. Paul joined him, and together they stared at the crime scene. "His name is William O. Carruthers."

"What does the "O" stand for?" Mark asked.

"Ollie. She's Mary Gomez."

"It figures."

"Why?"

"She's washing his feet," Mark said quietly.

"Yeah, so?"

"There's a story in the Bible about a woman who washed Jesus' feet and wiped them dry with her hair."

"During the week leading up to his death?"

Mark nodded. He passed his hand over his eyes. Any lingering doubt evaporated. "We're dealing with a serial killer. And I'm pretty sure this is an old game for him."

"I was hoping you weren't going to say that."

"Yeah, well, I'm saying it."

"How many more events of Easter week are we looking at?" Paul asked.

"A lot. The Garden of Gethsemane, arrest, trial, execution on the cross, Resurrection," Mark said.

"What comes next?"

"Tomorrow's Thursday. I think we're about to see an escalation."

"Like what?"

"Like the Last Supper," Mark said. "Jesus and his twelve disciples."

Paul swore under his breath.

"How far down the list of Shepherds did you get yesterday?"

"About half. All of them had their crosses. All of them had alibis for Sunday night."

"I'm not liking this," Mark said. "We've got to move faster."

"You still think the church killing is related?"

"Yeah, I think Ryan Bellig came looking for the man who killed his wife and daughter. And I think he found him."

"Too bad it didn't work out so well for Ryan. It would have saved the rest of us a lot of grief."

Mark grunted. "I found the hotel where Ryan was staying. Let's go check it out when we're done here, then we can split up the remaining Shepherds. Somebody on that list has got to be missing a cross."

Mark knelt down to get a better look at the woman. "What's the story here? Owner came to open up and found them?"

"Yes. Apparently Mary came in early some days, by appointment, to handle some of the male clientele who didn't want to come during regular business hours."

"Didn't want people to know they got manicures and pedicures?"

"Apparently. Weird."

"Lots of high-end corporate types do the manicure thing, part of that whole 'polished' look," Mark said. "I know a guy in the D.A.'s office who does, though he'd deny it."

"She's getting me a list of all Mary's other male clients and any others that had reason to know about this little routine."

"So our victim opened up shop, and the killer came right in?"

"Looks as though."

"Tell the owner I'd like to see her appointment schedule for two weeks in either direction, just to be sure."

"Already done."

"And?" Mark asked, looking up.

Paul shook his head. "You're not going to believe who's scheduled to come in today at twelve-fifteen."

"Our friendly, neighborhood church secretary?"

"Bingo."

Mark stood up. "You know, I really think the killer is performing for her."

"She's fast becoming the one constant in this mess. Only flaw in that theory is that she didn't witness donkey guy."

"Accident, oversight perhaps? Or maybe she didn't catch his attention until the church."

"What about Raleigh? Was he performing there for anybody in particular?"

"Not that I can tell. I'm going to call in the F.B.I. and see if we can get some help with this, especially since it looks like the same guy might be operating in a second state."

"Get them to check out their files and see if it might go further back," Paul suggested.

"Good idea. You know, maybe we'll get lucky. The woman washing the man's feet were the last bodies they found in Raleigh."

"He quit mid-week?"

"Yeah."

Paul stared at him intently. "I take it you don't think he's going to stop after this one, though?"

Mark shook his head. I can't explain it, but I have a feeling this guy's just getting started."

On Wednesday morning Cindy timed her arrival at the church so she was not the first one there. There was no way she was going to risk stumbling across another dead body when she was alone. She glanced over at the adjacent parking lot and sighed with relief when she saw Jeremiah's car. It made her feel better, knowing that he was nearby. After all, she hadn't been completely alone on Monday. He had been close enough to hear her screams and come to her rescue.

Inside the office everyone was jumping. Staff and key ministry leaders dashed back and forth, tending to last-minute details as they readied for prayer services. They'd already had two early in the morning, but the large one was scheduled for noon.

Geanie arrived at Cindy's desk and offered her a soda. The assistant sported a white shirt, short plaid skirt, and white knee-high socks with Mary Jane shoes.

Cindy took the can. "I'm not going to like this, am I?"

"*I* don't like this. You should be bringing me soda." Geanie crossed her arms.

"I like the look, but you do remember we're a Protestant denomination, right? As in *protesting* the Catholic church."

Geanie flipped a braid over her shoulder. "Be nice, it's the most churchy thing I own, and you know it."

"Fair enough. What's the problem?"

"The problem is Royus."

Cindy groaned. That was code for a Roy-Gus disagreement that affected everyone else. "What happened?"

"Roy decided this morning that he wants to cut the first thirty minutes of the Thursday night performance and preach a sermon about the events leading up to the crucifixion instead of showing them."

Cindy cringed, knowing how hard Gus, the actors, and the rest of the creative team had worked on the play. "And what was Gus's response?"

"He declared that he wants to cut the sermon Sunday morning about the Resurrection in favor of doing an interpretive dance about it."

"And?" Cindy asked.

"Both sides have dug in deep and are now firmly entrenched."

Cindy wondered if it was too late to go back to bed.

"I'll see what I can do," she promised Geanie.

"Thank you."

"You said your drop-dead deadline for Thursday's program was this afternoon?"

"Yeah. Two o'clock. And tell the gentlemen if they can't reach an agreement by then, that I will decide what's going to happen on Thursday. And assure them that neither of them will like it."

"I don't blame you, Geanie."

"Then don't try to stop me," she warned.

"You'll have resolution by two o'clock."

Cindy took ten minutes and personally delivered the ultimatum to both men. When she returned to the office, a stranger waited in the chair in front of her desk.

"The prayer service isn't until noon." She forced a smile.

The man stood. He had sandy hair and light-colored eyes and was only slightly taller than her. "I'm not here for the service. I was supposed to meet a friend of mine. I think maybe I got the time mixed up."

"Who are you meeting?" she asked.

"Oliver Johnson."

"I don't think he's here right now. He'll probably show up for the noon service, though. You're welcome to stay."

"I wish I could, but I've got an appointment then. Could you do me a favor?"

"What is it?"

"If you see him, could you tell him Karl stopped by? Tell him I'm sorry I missed him, but I'll catch him later."

"Sure."

"Thanks, ma'am, I appreciate it."

Cindy kept the smile plastered on her face as Karl left, even though she wanted to wring his neck for calling her ma'am. She sat down and stared at the mound of paperwork on her desk. More than anything, she wished she could just do some research instead. She had braved her house the night before but had been too freaked out to search online for more info on psycho killers with a taste for the religious.

Two hours later she sent email reminders to both Roy and Gus that they needed to make a decision about the Thursday program or suffer Geanie's wrath. Finished, she returned to the stack of papers that, if anything, seemed to grow rather than shrink.

When she glanced at the clock again it was noon. She could hear the muted sounds of the organ and considered spending her lunch hour in the prayer service. Then it struck her that she hadn't canceled her appointment with the manicurist. She reached for the phone and tried in vain to recall the name of the shop. She glanced over at Geanie, but the other woman was on the phone.

She stood up, deciding she might as well go. It had been a long time since she had a manicure, and it would be rude to cancel so close to her appointment even if she could remember the name of the shop to get the phone number.

It took her ten minutes to drive to Fifth Street. As soon as she turned down it, she realized she should have canceled. She recognized the yellow police tape from halfway down the block. *Just keep driving. You don't want to know.* When she got close to the shop, though, she swung into a parking space.

She got out of the car and approached the beauty salon. Policemen were everywhere, and two techs carried out a body bag.

"I took the liberty of canceling your appointment for you."

She spun around and saw Mark standing behind her. "This is insane. I've never even been inside this shop before yesterday evening. I came as they were closing, and they made an appointment for me today."

"You mean, this isn't part of your normal routine?" Mark asked, growing noticeably paler.

"No, why?"

"Cindy, I think you'd better come with me."

"Why?"

He stepped forward and grabbed her arm, eyes darting all around. "Because I'm pretty sure the killer's watching you," he whispered.

She gasped and then allowed herself to be pulled along to his car. She slid into the front seat and didn't bother asking where they were going as she took in what he'd said. It seemed preposterous, but even she couldn't deny the string of coincidences.

Mark started the car and drove off.

"Why me?" she asked after a minute.

"I don't know. Something about you has caught his attention, though, I'm sure of it."

"Who is he?"

"We don't know yet, but we're trying to find him as fast as we can."

"How do I know you're not the killer?"

"You don't," he said, glancing at her. "For that matter, you don't know the rabbi isn't either."

"Jeremiah?"

"Yes, Jeremiah. There are a few things about him that just don't add up."

"Like what?" she asked.

He didn't say anything.

"He's a kind man, a rabbi. How could you think that of him?" she asked.

"I'm a cop, how can you think it of me?"

"You're more accustomed to violence."

"He grew up in Israel."

"You're familiar with weapons."

"He served in the Israeli military. All citizens do over there."

"That doesn't make him a killer."

"It doesn't make him a boy scout, either."

"What about the Shepherds?" Cindy asked.

"We're fast running out of suspects in that area."

"Where are you taking me?" she asked.

"Somewhere safe while we figure this out."

"But I still don't understand. Why me? Why pick some random church secretary to torment?"

He glanced at her. "Maybe something about you set him off. Maybe you remind him of someone. Or maybe it's not random at all."

"But I've never done anything to anybody." Fear nearly choked her.

"Okay, then let's think. If no one has a beef with you, what about with your family?"

"My brother's a travel show host for the Escape Channel. He kayaks, bungee jumps, that sort of thing."

"Kyle Preston? Kyle Preston's your brother?"

"I see you've heard of him." She gritted her teeth.

"I'm a huge fan. Could you get me his autograph?"

"Can we please not talk about my brother!"

"Okay, okay." Mark took a deep breath. "What about your parents, what do they do?"

"My mom runs the household, and my dad's an engineer. He's currently helping build infrastructure in Iraq."

Mark nearly crashed the car. After he regained control he glanced at her. "Are you kidding me? This could be some nut-job terrorist taking revenge on daddy?"

Cindy took a deep breath. "A nut-job terrorist wouldn't bother with the Christian symbolism and wouldn't have done a practice run in Raleigh."

"You're right, sorry."

"None of this makes sense." She slammed her fist into the seat.

"Not everything in life makes sense."

"I'm not okay with that."

"I don't care if you're okay with that, it's the truth," he said. "If it helps I'm sure this all makes perfect sense to this guy."

"If it even is a guy," Cindy said in frustration. She turned to look out the window. Somewhere out there a killer waited, watched. *Can he see me now?*

They drove for a minute in silence. The more time Cindy spent alone inside her own head, though, the more terrified she became. Finally, she couldn't take it anymore.

"What happened back at the salon?"

"Two people were found dead. There was a man sitting in one of the chairs and a woman washing his feet."

She shuddered and felt sick inside. "He's making a mockery of Easter."

"Strange as this might sound, I'm not sure that's true. If he were mocking it, I would think there would be some perversion, or, at least, inversion of the events. Like the man would have been washing the woman's feet, or something like that."

"I guess."

She found herself staring hard at the cars that drove past. "I didn't see any murders connected with the Passion Week Killer that went beyond Wednesday," she said. "Is it possible this is as far as he goes?"

"Possible, but we can't afford to take that chance, especially before we have any real knowledge about the crime pattern in Raleigh and what or who might have triggered an end."

"You mean was he performing there for somebody?" she asked.

"That's one of the things we're hoping to find out."

"Is it possible that Raleigh wasn't the first time?"

He shook his head. "No word on that yet. We're still trying to get hold of the lead detective from back then, and hopefully, she can shed some light on things."

She closed her eyes and leaned her head back, wishing answers would come faster. "This all looks so much simpler on Scooby Doo."

"My wife loves that show. Are you a Freddie girl or a Shaggy girl?"

"Freddie. Definitely Freddie."

"My wife likes Shaggy. She has a thing for the lost puppy look."

"It explains a lot."

"Was that a crack?"

"Sorry," Cindy said, opening her eyes. "Reflex."

Mark smiled. "It's cool. Let me guess, Kyle was a pain to have as a brother."

"Good guess," Cindy said, laughing despite herself. "So, what now?"

"Is there anything significant between the feet washing and the Last Supper?" he asked.

"No, I don't think so. I mean, some preaching, maybe some miracles, but nothing that stands out."

"I didn't think so, either."

"We should talk to Gus, the music minister. He's spent the last couple of years working on the play they're performing. They did it last year as well. It's really quite good. He did tons of research—wanted his Easter pageant to be the best retelling ever."

"One civilian in the middle of this is more than I can handle," Mark said. "Every instinct I have says to keep you as far out of this as possible."

"A little hard when the killer keeps insisting on dragging me into it."

"Tell me about it."

"What do you think this is all building toward?" Cindy asked.

"I don't know. That's what scares me," he admitted.

"Imagine how I feel."

"I'm trying not to. If I have to imagine how anyone is thinking or feeling I'd rather it was the killer so I have a chance of catching this psycho."

She glanced around and recognized the neighborhood they were driving through. "Where are we going?" she asked.

"Nowhere at the moment, just driving, why?"

"One of the Shepherds, Joseph, lives up here. Have you interviewed him yet?"

"No, but he's on my list for this afternoon."

"He lives up there." Cindy pointed to the top of the hill. "He has a really old mansion and all this land. He often hosts picnics for the church in his backyard."

She saw Mark check his watch. "Mind if we pay him a little visit right now?"

"No."

A minute later they parked in the roundabout in front of Joseph's door. Mark made Cindy stay in the car, and she was glad to do so. She didn't believe for a minute that Joseph could be the killer, but she'd rather err on the side of caution.

She watched through the windshield as Joseph came to the door. After a minute the two men disappeared inside. They were gone long enough that she started to worry. Just when she was eyeing the police radio, though, they reappeared.

"Not him," Mark said as he got back into the car.

"At least you can cross him off your list," Cindy said.

"Yeah, him and his dogs."

"He shows dogs."

"You think? I saw enough trophies on the mantel to choke a horse."

"Rumor has it he buried a couple of his dogs in the old family cemetery behind the house."

"More power to him. Some guys race cars, and apparently, some show dogs. All I care is that he has an alibi that checks out and still has his Shepherd's cross."

9

JEREMIAH WENT FOR A WALK TO GET SOME AIR. A LONG NIGHT stretched before him. Volunteers were already hard at work in the kitchen preparing for the Seder. He glanced into the neighboring parking lot but didn't see Cindy's car. He couldn't help but wonder how she had fared the night before. He had thought about calling when he left the synagogue but decided against it in case she was actually asleep.

A car pulled into the church parking lot, but it wasn't hers. He continued to walk, breathing in deeply. A minute later he heard her voice, and he turned to see her getting out of the car. Mark exited the driver's side, and Jeremiah was instantly alert. Why was she in the detective's car, and what were they doing at the church?

He took a step forward. *Not your problem. Be glad she's turning to the proper authorities for help. You don't need to get involved.*

But he was involved, as much as he hated to admit it. He cut through the hedge and arrived next to her. "Is everything okay?"

She turned frightened eyes on him and for a moment he could swear that she looked like she was afraid of him.

He took a step back, and she blinked. The look faded. He glanced toward Mark and was surprised to note that the detective had a hand on his gun.

Jeremiah raised his hands shoulder high and took another step back. "What's happening here?"

"Two more people were killed," Cindy said.

After another glance at the detective, Jeremiah slowly lowered his hands to his sides. "And you were there?"

"After the fact," Mark said.

"He thinks someone is doing this for my benefit," Cindy said, tears welling in the corners of her eyes.

Jeremiah shook his head. It made no sense. Who would want to torment a woman like Cindy?

"What's the plan?" he asked Mark.

"The plan is to let the professionals handle it. I can't baby-sit you and her both, so do me a favor and stay out of it."

Do as he says. This isn't your fight. Not your friend, not your responsibility. He turned to Cindy "What are you doing here?"

"I needed to take care of a couple of things." She dropped her glance and scurried toward the office.

"This is how you baby-sit?" Jeremiah said.

Mark glared at him before hurrying after her. Jeremiah couldn't help himself; he followed too. He had no idea what had happened earlier, but from their actions, it couldn't have been good.

They were almost at the office when a man exited, heading away from them.

"Oliver!" Cindy called.

The man turned toward her, his body language guarded. "Hey, Cindy."

She walked toward him. "Thank you again for dinner last night."

"You were okay going home then?" Oliver asked.

Jeremiah eyed him with suspicion.

"Yes, thank you," Cindy said, all smiles.

Mark cocked his head to the side, also sizing up Oliver. "Oliver Johnson?"

"Yes."

"You're a Shepherd here at the church?"

Oliver nodded. "Can I help you?"

"I'm sorry," Cindy apologized. "Oliver, this is Detective Mark Walters. He's investigating the murder. Oliver is a reporter," she explained. "And this is Rabbi Jeremiah Silverman from next door."

"Detective, Rabbi," Oliver said, nodding to each of them.

"Mr. Johnson, where were you Sunday evening?"

"Doing visitation at the hospital."

"That's right!" Cindy exclaimed. "I saw you there."

Oliver smiled, but it didn't reach his eyes.

"And are you wearing your Shepherd's cross?" Mark asked.

"No, I usually keep it in my dresser at home." Oliver's eyes blinked rapidly.

Liar, Jeremiah thought. It took all of his will power not to call him on it. The reporter hadn't lied about visiting the hospital though.

"I'm going to want to see it," Mark said.

"Okay, do you mind if I ask why?"

"It's just part of the investigation. I'll be in touch a little later."

"Let me give you my card," Oliver volunteered, reaching for his wallet.

"I've got your contact information," Mark said.

"I'll take a card," Jeremiah said, striving to make his tone friendly. He pulled one of his own out of his wallet, one of the ones without any of his personal information, and exchanged with the reporter, noting the softness of the other's hands. *He's never worked with his hands; he's used to making a living with his mind, thinking on his feet.*

"Since we're being so formal, I'm not sure I have your number, Cindy," Oliver said.

Cindy flushed to her roots. "I'm in the church directory."

Odd time to flirt with her, Jeremiah thought.

Oliver grinned at her.

"I almost forgot to tell you," Cindy said. "Your friend stopped by the office earlier. Said he mixed up the time he was supposed to meet you."

"Did he leave his name?" Oliver asked.

"Karl. He said to tell you he'd catch you later."

All the color drained from Oliver's face. "Thank you," he murmured and then turned and walked away quickly.

Jeremiah shook his head. "That was—"

"—interesting." Mark completed his thought.

Cindy turned to look at them. "What?"

"What happened last night?" Mark asked.

"We bumped into each other downtown and ended up having dinner together at Rigatoni's."

"A date?" Mark pushed.

"No, we just had dinner. We talked."

Mark's phone rang and he answered it. "Yeah, yeah, on my way."

"One of the Shepherds, Jack Randolph, is on the run. I've got to go." He headed for the parking lot.

"What about baby-sitting?" Jeremiah called after him.

"Looks like you just got yourself another job, Samaritan!"

Jeremiah bit his tongue and turned to Cindy. "You know Jack Randolph?"

"Not very well. He's a professor, I think. No family that I know of."

"Well, hopefully, this is the end of it. Now, what do you need to do here? I'd feel better if we got you somewhere safer."

"I'll just be five minutes. How about I meet you at your car?"

He didn't like it, but he grudgingly agreed.

Cindy stepped inside the office, and Geanie pounced on her, eyes blazing. "Do you know what time it is?"

"Um, no?"

"Deadline time. And not a word from Roy or Gus."

"Then go ahead and make up the order of service the way you want to. That's what you told them you'd do."

"Really?" Geanie asked, eyes wide. "I've got your permission?"

"For what it's worth, you've got my permission."

Geanie did a little hop.

"Just one thing," Cindy continued. "I need to go now. You're in charge for the rest of the afternoon."

Geanie snapped a salute and sailed back to her desk. Cindy shook her head, wondering what havoc she had just unleashed. The deed was done, though, and it served Roy and Gus right.

Cindy shut down her computer, locked her desk, and headed for the door. Instead of marching straight to the parking lot, though, she found herself detouring to the sanctuary. She hadn't stepped foot inside since Monday morning.

The door stood open and half the lights were on. She walked inside, hesitantly at first, but then more boldly. She walked about halfway down an aisle and then sat down on a pew. She bowed her head and prayed that the police would catch the killer before he harmed anyone else. Finished, she stood, turned toward the back of the church, and saw a dark lump lying on the pew three rows back.

She took a step closer, and as soon as she realized it was a man she screamed. Seconds later Jeremiah sailed to her side. She realized he must have been closer than his car. Together they stared for a moment at the body in horror.

"I'm telling you that's a scream," the man said, suddenly sitting up and causing them both to jump back.

Cindy sagged against Jeremiah in relief. "Harry, you know you're not supposed to sleep in here," she told the homeless man.

Harry rubbed his face. "I didn't mean to sleep in here. I came for the service. And that preacher man just droned on so long I got a bit drowsy. And then you were screaming."

Out of the corner of her eye she could tell Jeremiah could hardly contain his laughter.

"Harry, you frightened me."

"You know I don't mean to frighten folks."

"I know, Harry. Service is over, though. It's time to go."

He got up and shuffled towards the door, and they followed him out. Jeremiah turned off the lights, and Cindy locked the door behind them.

"Can you get to the shelter all right, Harry?"

The old man nodded, and she felt sorry for him. Harry was a fixture in the neighborhood and a regular at the shelter down the street. She glanced up at Jeremiah, who regarded him through narrowed eyes.

"I still need to get that box of canned goods out of my trunk," he said quietly. "In all the craziness yesterday, it never got done."

"Would it be okay if we took it over now and dropped Harry off?" she asked.

He nodded.

The drive over was short and some volunteers happily came and emptied Jeremiah's trunk. Harry pulled a paper out of his pocket with great ceremony and handed it to Cindy.

"What's this?" she asked.

"I found it crumpled on the floor of the church. I figured I should throw it away, but maybe you want it for something."

"Thank you, Harry," she said. She took it and a quick glance at the paper revealed it to be a program from earlier in the day. She shoved it in her pocket.

A minute later she and Jeremiah were back in the car. "Where to now?" he asked her.

"I'd like to get my car back. It's parked downtown."

"Fair enough," he said.

They drove for a moment in silence.

"So, what happened this morning?" Jeremiah asked at last.

"Two people were killed in a beauty salon. The woman was posed washing the man's feet."

"Two murders instead of one?"

"I know. Escalation, huh?" she said. "I mean, it's not like he didn't have the opportunity before. The guy on the donkey, there could have been other dead people there, putting the palm fronds down or something. He's raising the stakes."

She clenched and unclenched her hands in her lap, wishing she had something to do with them. She needed to remember to put a different deck of cards in her purse so she'd have something to fidget with.

"No telling what he has in mind," Jeremiah said quietly.

She glanced over at him. "So, is it true that in Israel military service is mandatory for everyone, men and women?"

"Yes, although, any Arabs living in the country are exempt."

"So if you're Jewish you serve. No exceptions?"

He smiled. "Exceptions are made for people with mental impairments and physical disabilities. Also, exceptions are made for those pursuing some types of religious education and training."

Like a rabbi, she thought. "Oh. That's a convenient out."

"Yes, it is. Why do you ask?"

"Just something I heard, and I was curious about it," she said, trying her best to sound casual.

She felt somewhat relieved. It was stupid, but what the detective had said about the killer being anyone, even Jeremiah, had spooked her. It seemed hard to picture a sweet guy like him even carrying a weapon.

"Do you mind if I stop at home for a minute first? I want to pick up my suit for tonight's dinner so I'll have it with me."

"That's fine," she said. "How go the plans for tonight?"

He smiled. "Complicated. Fortunately, I have many eager volunteers willing to shoulder part of the responsibility."

Cindy laughed. "Sometimes it can take more effort to supervise the volunteers than it would to do their job."

"I have noticed that that seems to be true, particularly around holidays."

They pulled up outside his house. "Come in. It will only take me a minute."

She slid out of the car and followed him inside. She walked around his living room, and again her eyes fell on the bookshelf of poetry. Then she took a close look at the sparse furnishings and the paintings on the wall.

"I think I know your secret, Rabbi," she said.

"Really, and what would that be?" he asked, emerging from his bedroom with a garment bag.

"This is just like my house. You're renting this from a member of the synagogue. I'd be willing to bet nothing in this room, from the poetry to that hideous painting to that ancient video player, is yours."

"Very perceptive," he said.

She shrugged. "It's obvious. I should have realized that last time I was here." She pointed to the poetry. "These aren't your books."

"No, they're not," he admitted.

"It's amazing how most of the time we don't see what's right under our noses."

By the time Mark arrived on the scene, officers had already cornered Randolph in his home where he had fled after being approached at the university. Something felt off to Mark. He didn't see the guy they were hunting being stupid enough to stop off at home to pack a few things on his way out of town.

"What's going on?" he asked Paul.

His partner rolled his eyes. "He keeps shouting that he doesn't want to lose his job."

"He's crazy if he thinks that's the worst that can happen to him," a uniformed officer said.

Mark took a deep breath. "Any sign of a weapon?" The officer shook his head. "Okay, get me a vest."

"What are you doing?" Paul asked as the officer hurried off.

"Playing a hunch."

"Gambling with your life."

"You honestly think we've got a serial killer trapped in there?"

Paul sighed. The officer returned with the bulletproof vest, and Mark strapped it on.

"Don't do anything stupid," Paul cautioned.

"I think we passed stupid on Monday," Mark said. He walked slowly toward the door of the house, hands at shoulder height.

"Can't lose my job," he heard someone moaning inside as he got closer.

"Mr. Randolph?" Mark shouted.

There was silence for a minute and then the man inside the house shouted, "Go away!"

"I can't do that, Mr. Randolph. I need to come in and talk with you, just for a few minutes."

"No!"

"Please, Mr. Randolph. There's a lot of worried people out here who don't want anyone to get hurt."

"I never hurt anybody!"

"Well, we can talk about that when you let me inside." Mark moved to stand next to the door.

"I can't lose my job! I don't want to do anything else. I can't do anything else!"

"We can talk about that too."

"Really?"

"Sure. Just let me come inside, Mr. Randolph."

The door opened slowly. Mark glanced out at the street and saw half a dozen weapons drawn. He stepped around the door and saw a middle-aged man wearing jeans, a shirt and striped tie. He was short with thinning hair and a bit of stubble on his face. His eyes were wild, desperate, and for a moment Mark wondered if he had made a terrible mistake.

Then Randolph turned and sank down on a chair in the living room, his head in his hands, and rocked back and forth. Mark eased inside, leaving the front door open. He positioned himself so the shooters outside would have a clear shot at Randolph, and he would be out of the line of fire.

"You want to go first?" Mark asked after a moment.

"I can't lose my job!" the man wailed.

"And why would you lose it?" Mark decided to discuss the topic that seemed most pressing to the suspect.

"Because I lied. I didn't want to, I had to."

"Lied about what?"

"You know. It's why you came after me."

"Yes, but sometimes it's good to say these things out loud. It helps put things in perspective."

"Perspective?" Randolph looked up. "Perspective!"

"Yes, perspective," Mark said, working to keep his voice level.

"How's this for perspective? I work harder than any other teacher on that campus!"

"And why is that?"

"Why do you think? Because when I don't work hard, people don't learn. I work hard for the kids. No one could ever know—" Randolph stopped abruptly and dropped his head back into his hands.

Out of the corner of his eye Mark could see officers approaching the door, getting ready to make a move. He held up his hand, and they paused.

"What is it that you don't want them to know?"

"I lied."

"Then tell the truth now. It might help."

"I don't have a doctorate. I never even finished my bachelor's," Randolph ended with a wail.

Mark blinked several times. This? This is what they were all wasting their time over while the killer still roamed free? He dropped his hand, and the officers entered and handcuffed Randolph, who sobbed uncontrollably.

Mark stood up as Paul entered the room. "Mr. Randolph, where do you keep your Shepherd's Cross?" Mark asked.

Randolph looked at him in confusion. "On top of my dresser."

Paul headed off and a moment later returned with the cross dangling from its chain. "We're fast running out of suspects."

"I know."

Cindy pulled her car into the driveway, and Jeremiah parked immediately behind her. She walked toward the house, trying not to let her fear get the better of her. She heard Jeremiah's car door close, and she tried not to jump as he came up behind her.

Taking a deep breath, she unlocked the door, and stepped inside. Everything seemed as it should be. She turned and nearly bumped into Jeremiah who had been right behind her.

"Sorry," he said. He moved toward the kitchen, which still showed the ravages of the intrusion.

"Sorry," she echoed. She walked in and scooped some books and papers off the floor and piled them on the table. It was stupid to be embarrassed, but she couldn't help it. Her mother had drummed into her that how clean you kept your house reflected on you as a person.

"You don't have to do this now," Jeremiah said.

"No, it's fine." She gritted her teeth and tried to sound cheerful.

She dropped another stack, and a few scraps of paper went fluttering through the air. Jeremiah caught one and looked at it. "Somebody doesn't like crossword puzzles," he said.

She glanced at the scrap of paper and then at the other ones scattered around the floor. It was the crossword puzzle she had been working on Monday. It was the only paper that had been torn up.

"That's really weird," she said.

"What?"

Her cell phone rang, and she jumped. She yanked it out of her pocket and flipped it open.

"Hello?"

"It's Detective Walters."

"Did you catch Jack Randolph?" she asked, turning toward Jeremiah.

"We did," Mark said. There was a pause. "I'm sorry, Cindy, but it's not him. The killer is still out there."

The phone started to slip out of her hand. Jeremiah stepped forward, caught it, and pressed it to his ear.

"Yes, this is Jeremiah. So, the killer is still out there?"

Cindy pulled out a chair at the kitchen table and sat down, shoving the pile of books and papers back onto the floor where it landed with a crash.

"No, nothing, just some books falling." Jeremiah took a step away.

She had hoped it was Randolph. She had wanted the nightmare to end. Of all the Shepherds, she had always liked him the least. She had almost been able to picture him as the killer.

She stared at Jeremiah as he continued to talk on the phone, hating herself for the doubts she still had about him. The mysterious stranger swoops in to save the day but later turns out to be the killer. She was sure she had seen that before in a movie. She told herself that was why it seemed to make so much sense.

She thought of the way he had appeared in the sanctuary that day. He had looked like some kind of devil. Maybe she had been right to think so. She took a deep breath and tried to calm her racing heart. Wild speculation wasn't helping any and only caused her to question the one person who seemed most willing to help.

"Yes, she'll be careful," Jeremiah said.

He said careful instead of safe. That's because I'm not safe, and no matter how careful I am I can't make myself safe.

"Yes, I'll be careful too," Jeremiah said.

Somehow, that made her feel a little bit better.

Jeremiah hung up and put her phone down on the table.

"Why don't you come with me tonight?" he asked.

She wanted to, desperately. But unreasonable as it sounded, suddenly, the idea of locking herself in her house seemed safer than going out. The killer had already been there, and what was it they said about lightning not striking in the same place twice?

She shook her head. "No, tonight's a special night, for your church, synagogue, family."

"Yes, but we're a family with a hundred Jewish mothers, which means, there's plenty of food for one more."

She forced herself to smile. "You know, I'm just really too tired to go. I think I need to get some sleep. It's been a long week, and it could get worse before it gets better."

He stared at her with doubt in his eyes. She knew she was going to win, though. He would have to leave soon, and he couldn't force her to go with him. *Not unless he's the killer.*

She shook her head and jumped up from the table. She got the orange juice out of the refrigerator and poured herself a glass to give her something to do so she wouldn't have to look him in the eyes.

"Thank you. Maybe next year."

It was lame, but it worked.

"Okay, call me if you need me," he said.

"I will."

"Lock the door behind me."

"I will."

He left.

She locked the door and then stood against it, shaking.

10

Finally, Cindy moved away from the door, chastising herself for being so suspicious. She hoped Jeremiah didn't know what she'd been thinking about him.

She glanced around the room in disgust. Evidence of the intrusion was still everywhere. Her mom would die if she saw the place looking like it did, and Cindy was positive no amount of excuses about killers and burglars would make up for the fact that it was in a shambles and that she had let somebody see it that way.

She started with the piles of books and papers in the kitchen. As order overtook the chaos, she felt a bit better. It terrified her to think of someone prowling around her house, going through her things. The harder she worked to undo the damage, though, the more her fear turned into anger.

At least I'm actually doing something. Unlike the police. Why can't they just do their job?

"Stop it!" she ordered herself out loud. It was unfair. The police were working as hard as they could, and if they hoped to catch the killer they didn't have time to post twenty officers to guard her around the clock just so she could feel safe.

When she was finally finished cleaning she grabbed a frozen dinner, popped it in the microwave, and then went into her bedroom to change into some sweats.

She checked her pockets, and her fingers brushed paper. Cindy pulled out the crumpled up program the homeless man had given her. She walked into the bathroom and tossed it in the trash. And suddenly, she remembered something. She remembered heading into the church Monday morning, seeing a crumpled piece of paper on the ground, and shoving it into her pocket to throw away in the office. But she never made it into the office.

She blinked. What had she done with that paper? Monday morning was a blur. She vaguely remembered washing her clothes, and she was pretty sure they were still in the dryer. She walked to the laundry room and stood there, trying to recall the events of Monday.

It came to her in a flash. She had removed her necklace and the piece of paper from her pocket and put them on the shelf right before the phone rang. She looked, and there it was.

Her heart began to race, and for a moment she wondered if she should call Mark. Odds were, though, that the piece of paper was just some bit of trash one of the youth group kids had dropped, and she would have pulled him away from the search for nothing.

Her hand closed around the paper, and she carried it back to the kitchen. She sat down at the table and slowly opened the piece of paper. A thick, dark scrawl covered it. She reached for her cell phone and a moment later heard Mark's voice as he answered.

"It's Cindy. I'm at home, and I found something. I think it's important. Yes, I'll be here. Hurry."

⸎

Sundown. Passover had just begun, and yet Jeremiah wished it were over. He sighed as he stood at the door to the hall and greeted families as they arrived. Most met him with broad smiles, and he had a feeling that having the responsibility of the Seder fall upon the Synagogue was a relief to many.

A small table had been set up at the front of the hall where he would preside. Then six long tables stretched toward the back of the room. Chairs lined the walls and provided a place for people to sit while they awaited table assignments.

Samuel walked in and clasped his hand. "Thank you, Rabbi. We told our neighbors what to expect tomorrow night, and they are still excited to join us."

"Great, Samuel. I'm sure it will be a blessing to your house to have them there."

The man beamed, fished a raffle ticket out of the bucket, and escorted his family inside. Fifteen minutes later everyone who had said they were coming had arrived. Jeremiah closed the door and then moved to the front of the room. He chose the table on the far left and then drew a raffle ticket.

"Ticket ending in 0082."

Samuel hurried his family forward, beaming broadly as they took their place at the top of the table. Jeremiah then proceeded to call several more numbers until the table was filled, and then he moved on to the next one.

Remarkably, his plan seemed to work. Some were excited, others were not, but no one blamed him for where they were seated. Belatedly, he had realized that drawing the tickets himself might not have been a smart move, but it seemed to have turned out well.

When everyone was seated, he moved to his table. The Seder plates were made of paper, with the pictures on them drawn by the children the week before. It had not been his first choice, but the Synagogue had not budgeted for buying Seder plates, which meant it was either convince a member to donate the money or allow the children to take part in that way. The teachers had told him that it ended up being an excellent learning tool, and he could see there was already a surreptitious game going on at the tables with children attempting to identify the plates they had decorated.

Jeremiah tried to hide his smile as he watched them. He picked up the first of his four cups of wine and gave the blessing:

"Barukh atah Adonai, Eloheinu, melekh ha-olam borei p'ri hagafen shehakol nih'yeh bid'varo Barukh atah Adonai, Eloheinu, melekh ha-olam asher bachar banu mikol am v'rom'manu mikol lashon v'kid'shanu b'mitz'votav vatiten lanu Adonai eloheinu b'ahavah mo'adim l'sim'chah chagim uz'manim l'sason et yom chag hasukot hazeh z'man sim'chateinu mik'ra kodesh zeikher litzi'at mitz'rayim ki vanu vachar'ta v'otanu kidash'ta mikol ha'amim umo'adei kad'shekha b'simchah u-v'sason hin'chal'tanu Barukh atah Adonai, m'kadeish Yis'ra'eil v'haz'manim."

He took a deep breath and repeated it in English, for the benefit of any who might be new to the Seder and its customs.

"Blessed are you, Lord, our God, sovereign of the universe who creates the fruit of the vine who made all things exist through His word. Blessed are you, Lord, our God, sovereign of the universe who has chosen us from among all people, and exalted us above every tongue and sanctified us with His commandments, and you gave us, Lord our God, with love appointed festivals for gladness, festivals, and times for joy this day of the festival of Sukkot, the time of our gladness a holy convocation, a memorial of the exodus from Egypt because You have chosen us and made us holy from all peoples and your holy festivals in gladness and in joy you have given us for an inheritance. Blessed are you, Lord, who sanctifies Israel and the seasons."

He drank the cup, and his congregation followed his lead.

Cindy stared in disbelief at the scrap of paper in her hand. *"Meet me at the church tomorrow night.* R.B." R.B. had to be Ryan Bellig. Ryan had known his killer and had requested the meeting to be at the church. *Why? What could he possibly hope to gain?*

Justice from the man who had killed his family? He should have stayed home and let the police handle it. She snorted in disgust and sympathized with Bellig's action. She was almost afraid to leave the murder case entirely to the police. Ryan probably felt too angry or *too frustrated* to let the system bring down his family's killer.

A couple of minutes later the detective knocked on her door. Mark came in quickly, eyes eager. "What do you have?"

She presented him with the paper. "I completely forgot about it until just now. I found this crumpled up outside the sanctuary Monday morning when I got to work. I put it in my pocket so I could throw it away in the office, and, well, I never made it there."

Mark read it over. "R.B."

"I figure that has to stand for Ryan Bellig," she said.

He shot her a disapproving glance, but he didn't argue. "It's not a lot, but every little bit helps," he said at last.

"Have you contacted all of the Shepherds yet?" Cindy asked. "If not, I can do some checking for you at work and see if we have alternate contact info for any of them."

"We've had at least a preliminary discussion with all of them."

"And?"

He shook his head. "At this point I don't want to risk leaking any information that could be crucial to the case."

"You haven't arrested anyone or you wouldn't have rushed over here."

"Unless we *have* arrested someone, and I hoped you had a piece of evidence that would make the case airtight."

She studied his face intently. "No, I don't think that's it. I think I had it right."

"Mind reader, Ms. Preston?"

"Your face is easy to read. That's funny. You'd think a detective could put on a better poker face."

"And you'd think a church secretary would be easier to read."

She smiled. "That's how much you know about working at a church."

He shook his head. "Is there anything else?"

"No," she said, feeling a little deflated that he didn't seem to find the paper as significant as she did.

"Call if you think of anything else. At this rate, just go ahead and put me in your speed dial."

She laughed, but as soon as she locked the door behind him she did exactly that. She added both his and Jeremiah's cell phones to speed dial on her cell. Now she wished she could curl up with a good movie and not think about what might be happening outside her door. She wished she could just let it go.

———⚬⚬⚬———

Jeremiah smiled as a small child, barely four, finished asking the final question of the first telling of the Passover story. Choosing him had been simple since the youngest child at a Seder was supposed to ask the questions, and he was the youngest child present who could *remember* the questions.

The second telling involved four older children, and to avoid the appearance of favoritism the teachers had chosen the four children who had had the most exemplary behavior in the preceding month.

He loved this part of Passover. He loved the ritual and the retelling of the story of God leading the Jewish people out of slavery in Egypt. It was a story no less powerful for the millennia that had inserted themselves in between that time and the present. He thought of those in his native country, who were a symbol of hope to Jewish people the world over. It was a land plagued by fear and terrorism. Yet it was indescribably beautiful because it was theirs. *Truly the promised land.*

As the second retelling began he allowed himself to relax, losing himself in the ancient ritual, living every breath in the moment and shutting out the future, the past, and the world outside the room.

———⚬⚬⚬———

No matter how much she wanted to, Cindy couldn't let the murders go. She sat down at her computer and meant to print out the latest crossword puzzle. Instead, she Googled *religiously themed murders.* The same references to the Raleigh murders came up. The Passion Week Killer had killed Ryan's family three years earlier, also during Easter week. The more she read about the murders, though, the more confused she became.

There had been the killing of the man on the donkey, the killing that represented money changers, and the killings of the woman washing a man's feet. The woman had been Ryan's wife. She had taken her daughter with her to work that morning, and the child had also been killed. *Probably because she saw the killer's face.* Then it had just stopped. No one knew why. And no one seemed to have been killed in a church.

Ryan's death had definitely broken the pattern. He must have searched for three years to find the killer and that search had led him to Pine Springs. To First Shepherd. She thought about a typical Sunday morning service and all the faces that she knew so well. Was one of them really a killer?

She stood up and grabbed a deck of cards from the closet and headed for the kitchen. She slid the cards out of the case and sucked in her breath. She could see her other deck of cards scattered around the body of Ryan Bellig, a man who had been trying to get justice for his murdered wife and daughter.

After taking a deep breath, Cindy forced herself to shuffle the deck and then start a game of solitaire while she thought about everything she had read. Evidently, Ryan had tracked the killer to Pine Springs, just in time to confront him after the first murder.

But why not go to the police? Maybe they wouldn't believe him. Or maybe he was looking for revenge. She had assumed the knife belonged to the killer, but it could just as easily have belonged to Ryan.

So why had the Passion Week killer only gotten halfway through Easter week before stopping? Had the police been closing in on him? Had killing the little girl somehow ruined his plan? As much as she couldn't imagine why somebody would kill innocent people, she really couldn't imagine what would make them stop.

The Passion Week killer had never been caught. And now, three years later, it looked like he had started up again across the country. Her game of solitaire ended, one of the worst hands she had ever played. She took it as a sign and headed back to her computer where she sat down and hesitated.

Leave it alone. The police will take care of this, the rational part of her brain whispered.

You're never going to feel safe again unless you can figure this all out, the other side countered.

Once again she typed *the Passion Week Killer* into her search engine. After a moment's thought she added the words *my wife's killer.* At the top of the list she found exactly what she was hoping to find—Ryan's blog.

She clicked on the link, and the page came up. It looked like he had created it right after his family was killed. She shivered as she read the last entry less than a week old.

I think I found him, the monster that killed Anna and Rachel. It's been three years, and I had started to lose faith. But I've found him, the man who was like a brother to me. I remember the times he came to our house for dinner, played with Rachel while we talked, and helped Anna in the kitchen. It makes me sick to think about it. How could I let a monster into my own home, under my very nose? But he will finally pay for his crimes. I will have justice one way or another.

Can you believe it? He's found another church to prey on. How many times evil walks among us, and we never know it! I have to hurry before he starts all over again. Just like I have often speculated but could never prove, this was not the first time he has done this. But I will make it the last.

Cindy reread it. Ryan couldn't have known when he wrote it that the post would be his last.

She scrolled down the page, clicking on different posts and checking out the comments. From what she could see Ryan had several hundred readers. Most of those who had posted seemed, like him, to be mourning loved ones whose killers had never been brought to justice.

JuliaN had lost her mother. *Bitter_and_angry* had lost his fiancée. *Nomoresmiling*'s son had been murdered. They and so many others posted again and again, sharing their own stories, their own struggles.

One person who had posted, *carlsbad10*, in particular seemed to have been egging Ryan on and encouraging him in his search. He had written, *I know you'll find the guy; I just wish I could be there when you do.*

"I wish you had been there, too, *carlsbad10*," she whispered out loud. It was painful to put a life and a voice to the face on the floor with the cold, dead eyes.

Then she saw a comment that had been posted by *bitter_and_angry* about two weeks earlier.

Dude, cops just arrested Shari's killer. This dude knows everything. See if he can't help you with your search: www.askgoliath.com.

Cindy clicked on the link. After a quick review of the site she learned that Goliath seemed to be some sort of forensics expert who knew something about any given topic. She was amazed at the ego the guy had and even more amazed at some of the questions people had asked him on the boards.

She found the link to email him directly. She took a deep breath and then typed: *I wanted to know if you helped a man named Ryan Bellig within the last few days whose wife was killed by the Passion Week Killer in Raleigh three years ago. Ryan's been murdered. I think he found the killer, but we're trying to figure out who it is.*

She added her name and email address and hit send. She glanced at the clock on her computer and realized it was getting late. There was probably no way she would get a response in time to help, but at least she had tried. She briefly considered posting a comment to the last entry, letting people know what had happened to Ryan. Her fingers hovered over the keyboard, but she couldn't do it. All these people were lost and searching for justice. To tell them about Ryan would make nothing better, only worse. No, when this was over and the police had caught the killer, then maybe she'd return and let them know.

"Sorry, everyone. Better luck in your own searches for closure," she whispered. She sent a quick prayer heavenward for all those lost and heartbroken people.

"Children, you know that at the end of the meal you have dessert, right?" Jeremiah asked.

Eager heads bobbed all around the room, several of them belonging to the adults. "The meal cannot be completed without it. We have hidden the afikomen somewhere in this room. Go and search for it!"

Children leaped up from the tables and scoured the room, looking under tables and chairs, searching corners for the piece of matzah set aside to eat at the end of the Seder meal. Several older children fidgeted nervously, unable to decide whether they were meant to look or to wait with the adults. Jeremiah walked by the tables. One more year as a child would not hurt any of them. He tapped each on the shoulder and sent them on the hunt, explaining that he thought the young ones needed "help."

When the children finally found the afikomen and scurried back to their tables, they each found a silver dollar on their chair as a reward. The children who had been coaxed were especially excited to see the money.

Jeremiah smiled. It was the small things, the simple things that mattered. It's what helped his people survive their adversity through the centuries.

<hr>

Cindy walked around the house, double-checking doors and windows before getting ready for bed. When there was nothing left to do, she checked her inbox.

Goliath had emailed.

She opened the message.

Yes, Ms. Preston. I had talked to Bellig. Sorry to hear he's dead. He wanted to know if there had been any other killings similar to the Passion Week killings. I told him yes, two years earlier in Boston and the year before that in Texas. I told him if the killer had changed hunting grounds again that in my opinion he would most likely have gone to the West Coast. Good luck.

11

GOOD LUCK. CINDY STARED AT THOSE TWO WORDS FOR A LONG TIME as she processed what Goliath had told her. He had added several links to the bottom of the email, and she clicked on the first one. It was a newspaper article about a politician who had been found dead on Palmer Street in Boston five years earlier. The second link produced an article about vandalism and murder at three different pawn shops two nights after the politician died. The next article told about a couple who was found dead in a fountain. The woman had drowned, and the man had been stabbed and was found with only his feet in the fountain.

The next was from a Texas newspaper. She clicked back to do a little more research on the Boston killings first. After thirty minutes surfing the Web, she was pretty sure the police hadn't connected any of the deaths, and none of the accounts even hinted at a religious theme, even though they occurred the week before Easter.

She reread the three articles and noticed only the most basic of similarities with the current string of murders. Finally, she clicked onto the articles linked to Texas. She read about a man found dead in The Palms Hotel, a currency exchange teller found dead, and another couple dead in a fountain. The final article was the most interesting, though. A friend and fellow church member of the couple had turned up missing the same night.

There was a grainy photo of the missing man who had long hair and a bushy beard. He looked fairly young, but it was hard to make out much from the picture. She did notice his eyes, though. They seemed to pierce right through her. There was something unsettling about them and almost familiar.

The phone rang, and she jumped. She got up and answered it with a sigh. Given the time of night, it could only be one person.

"Oh, honey. You're never going to believe what your brother did!" her mom gushed without greeting.

"Mom—"

"He was kayaking on one of those big rivers. The guide fell out, and Kyle saved his life using nothing but his paddle. His paddle! Can you imagine that?"

"Mom, I'm kind of in the middle of something."

"Don't tell me you're too busy to hear about your brother's act of heroism," her mom said with a sniff.

"Mom, there's still a killer on the loose. I've had my house ransacked."

There was a pause, and for a moment she thought she had gotten through to her mother. Then she heard, "You got it cleaned up, didn't you? A messy house reflects very badly on the people who live in it, regardless of how it got that way."

"Yes, Mom, I got it cleaned," she said, letting the sarcasm creep into her voice as she briefly considered kicking her filing cabinet.

"Then problem solved. Now, they were going down one of those dangerous rapids . . ."

Cindy wondered if her mom would notice if she put the phone down and walked away. She sighed and reached over to close out everything on her computer. Crime solving would have to wait. It was the job of the police to catch the killer, not hers. Apparently, her job in life was to listen to her mother brag about Kyle.

Jeremiah slept late. He checked his cell and felt relief that he hadn't missed any calls. He took it as a good sign that he had not heard from either Mark or Cindy in almost fifteen hours.

The synagogue was closed for the day, so he planned to get in some exercise and do a little reading. Then he would join Marie and her family for Seder at her house. He breathed deeply. It wasn't often he got a true day off, free from the responsibilities of being rabbi. It felt good, and he intended to make use of it.

After breakfast he headed to the park where he liked to jog early in the morning. But it was different with the sun high and far more people around. Lots of fellow joggers waved or greeted him. He saw some families from the synagogue playing together. He waved but kept moving. If he stopped to talk his day would cease to be his own.

He loved being a rabbi, more than he had imagined he would. But there were times when he still craved isolation, quiet. He often thought of his mother and brother back in Israel. He had friends who would check up on them for him—make sure they were okay. Sometimes it was hard being separated from them.

He jogged by the homeless guy he had met the day before, and the man waved. It had been unnerving for a long time, going out in public and being recognized nearly everywhere he went. His synagogue wasn't the largest, but it was one of the most well established in town, which made him a public figure as far as his congregation was concerned.

After jogging four miles he sprinted for one and then walked a final mile to cool off. He finished up with a couple of quick stretches and then left to avoid running into anyone else he knew.

Running always helped him focus, helped him think through problems. As he headed home he realized he had been thinking through a rather large problem. What to do about Cindy? Like it or not he was involved in the whole serial killer mess, and he had definitely not started out the week with the intention of making a new friend or being someone's Good Samaritan.

He shook his head as he thought of Mark. The detective was smart, he would give him that. Jeremiah would be happy when the killer was caught, and he could just fade back out of the spotlight. Being a rabbi was a tough enough job. He didn't need to stick his nose where it didn't belong.

He smiled. Besides, if he spent any more time with Cindy then Marie would force him to take a "nice Jewish girl" out on a date. She had already threatened. It didn't matter to his secretary that he was helping Cindy cope with death and was acting the part of a big brother. No, to Marie time spent was time spent and he needed to do some balancing out to make it all right. He'd thought about asking Detective Mark to explain the whole Good Samaritan thing to Marie but had decided it would get him too much attention from both of them.

When he got back to his house his answering machine was flashing to let him know he had a message. He hit play and heard Cindy's voice. "Hi, it's Cindy. Preston. From the church next door."

He smiled. He could tell from the tone of her voice that there was no immediate crisis and that she was feeling somewhat foolish. He would have to let her know that he only knew one Cindy so she didn't have to spend so long reminding him who she was.

The message continued. "Nothing's wrong. No dead bodies, at least, none that I know of. I was just calling to . . . I don't know, I was up late doing some research and it looks like this has happened other times in different parts of the country. I didn't want to call the detective, because he was already over at my house last night. I was just hoping to bounce a couple of ideas off of you. Nothing important. It's no big deal, I'll see you later. Maybe. Bye."

He reached for the phone and then stopped himself. Calling her back was what he shouldn't do, unless he wanted to get in deeper than he already was. *Just let it go. She admitted herself it wasn't important. She's not in danger. She doesn't need you to rescue her.* He took a deep breath and deleted the message.

On her lunch break Cindy checked her phone and was disappointed that Jeremiah hadn't called. Not that she should have expected him to. The murders weren't his problem.

She walked outside and realized there were no cars in the parking lot at the synagogue. She remembered he had told her Monday night that Thursday was a day off for everyone there.

Great. That meant she had called and disturbed him on his day off. It was hard. She felt like there was no one else she could really talk to about it. Geanie listened, but she was frantic with trying to get everything done for all of the extra services, especially the Easter pageant on Saturday night.

That wasn't it, though. On a deep level Geanie just didn't get it. She wasn't there; she didn't trip over the body. She only saw the aftermath. Her house hadn't been ransacked. Neither had Jeremiah's, but he had at least been there for her. He had seen her at her absolute worst. There was no need to be brave or paint a rosier picture. He knew the truth.

She had thought briefly that morning about calling Oliver when she couldn't reach Jeremiah. After all, he had helped her get up the courage to go back to her house. Until the police caught the killer, though, or officially cleared all the Shepherds, she didn't want to risk saying something she shouldn't. Besides, Oliver worked for the newspaper and she knew his editor really wanted him to get as much of the story as he could. It wasn't fair to ask him to keep yet another conversation confidential.

When she walked back inside the office, it was like being hit by a wall of sound. Phones were ringing, a dozen people were talking and running the copy and fax machines. Even the postage machine had been called into duty.

She couldn't deal with it. She had planned on just eating lunch at her desk, but she grabbed it and went back outside. She rolled down the windows of her car and just sat in it. She wished that she had remembered to stick her other deck of cards in her purse so that she could play a game of solitaire.

She had hoped that in the light of day her theories from the night before would seem crazy. Somehow, though, they just seemed more believable. Texas, Boston, even Raleigh. It was almost as though the murderer had been rehearsing, seeing what worked and what didn't. The first two had been failures since no one recognized that the murders were religiously themed.

How the egomaniac from askgoliath.com had known was a mystery, but it was one she was prepared to live with. In Raleigh things had changed. From what she'd read, though, the murders of the past few days had still been far more specific, more targeted.

He wants everyone to know exactly what he's doing. Well, maybe not everyone, she thought with a chill. That was the one thing that she hadn't been able to track down for the last three. There had been no single witness to all events in each place. No audience, at least as far as she could detect.

So why was this different? Why had he seemingly chosen her as his audience? Or had he not and she was just incredibly unlucky?

The timing was strange too. First Texas, then a year later Boston, then two years to Raleigh and now Pine Springs, three years later. Why was it taking longer each time to begin? Was it taking more planning on his part? Or was he choosing just the right place? And if the others had really only been dress rehearsals, what was the closing act?

She shivered. She still hoped that since none of the other places seemed to have a killing beyond the washing of the feet that it was over. Maybe in four years they would catch up with him someplace else.

She resolved there and then that even if the killings stopped she would share with Mark everything that she had learned, so hopefully, if the guy started up again somewhere else some poor church secretary wouldn't have to put the pieces together because the authorities hadn't linked them all.

She glanced at the clock on the dashboard. Lunch was over. She'd have to wait until after work to call Mark.

Cautiously, she walked back into the office. Things seemed a little quieter, and she suspected that many of the people who had been so busy flitting around had needed to return to their own jobs.

While the office was quieter Geanie seemed more frantic than usual. She hung up the phone with a groan and mimed pulling out her hair.

"Problem?"

"Yes, the woman at the Gazette can't find our ad for the Sunday paper."

"The one with the Easter message?"

"Yes. I gave it to her two weeks ago so that I could avoid taking the time out to go down there. And, of course, I can't email it since I use a design program they don't."

"What's your deadline?"

"ASAP!"

"Would it help if I dropped it off?" Cindy asked.

Geanie brightened instantly. "Really? That would be fantastic!"

"If it will help you, then it will help all of us."

"It's printing now. Angela is the one you need to see."

Cindy pulled her purse out of its drawer and then grabbed the flyer as it finished printing out. "It's quite stunning this year."

"Thanks, I was inspired." Geanie blushed.

"The boyfriend?"

"No . . ." She looked down.

"Everything okay there?"

"No, great, better than great. It's just, I found I was inspired by all the terrible things that have been happening. You know, the drama of it all. I kept wondering what it would have been like for those who knew and loved Jesus to watch everything that happened. Pain, fear, and yet, it was all so deeply meaningful."

"That's beautiful," Cindy said, feeling slightly choked up. She grabbed a large envelope, slid the flyer inside, and hurried from the office before Geanie could elaborate.

As she headed downtown, Cindy wished she hadn't volunteered. She kept a wary eye out for the yellow police tape and breathed a sigh of relief when she parked at the newspaper without having seen any.

As she walked inside, a bored receptionist glanced up.

Cindy waved the envelope in her hand. "I'm here to drop off something for Angela. I'm from First Shepherd."

"Her desk is in the back left. The one with the model airplane on it."

"Thanks."

She headed toward the back, noticing that all the desks seemed to be empty. She wondered if they took lunch later at the paper. The model airplane turned out to be easy to spot. Angela's desk, too, was deserted. She put the envelope down on the desk and then grabbed a Post-It for a quick note. She wrote the church's phone number on it and that questions should be directed to Geanie.

Finished, she stood up and turned to find Oliver staring at her with large eyes. "Hey, Cindy. What are you doing here?"

"Leaving an ad for the Sunday paper. Where is everybody?"

"Meeting."

She looked at him closely. He was pale, and his hands were shaking. "Why aren't you at the meeting?"

"Because I . . . I wanted to talk to you."

There was something wrong. He took a step forward, and she took a step back. She looked him in the eyes. "Oliver—"

Oliver.

Who had admitted to living in Texas when he got his first newspaper job.

Oliver.

Who had moved to Pine Springs the same time the killings stopped in Raleigh.

Oliver.

Who had come to her window Monday morning instead of her front door.

Oliver.

Who had talked to Mark but had not shown him his cross.

Oliver.

Who had the opportunity to steal the key to the sanctuary from Harold.

Oliver.

Who had questioned her so closely about what the police knew.

Oliver.

Who had different hair than the picture of the missing church member from the Texas church, *but had the same eyes!*

Cindy jumped backward and yanked out her cell phone. *Did I program Mark's number as 8 or 9? It has to be 9.*

"Cindy, listen to me, it's not what you think," he said, moving to follow her.

Her thumb slid on the keypad, and a moment later she heard a man's voice.

"Give me the phone, Cindy," Oliver said.

She ducked around a desk and frantically looked for something she could use as a weapon. "It's Oliver! We're at the newspaper!" she shouted in the direction of the phone.

He lunged forward, knocking the phone from her hand. She continued to move backward, her ankle slamming against the corner of a desk.

Something silver glimmered, and she snatched a letter opener off of the desk and brandished it in front of her.

"Cindy, no," he said, his voice laced with panic. "I don't want to hurt you."

"It's your fault! All those people died because of you. You're a murderer. How could you? People trusted you. They cared for you. I had dinner with you. I thought it was safe!"

He shuddered and then stopped advancing. She continued to move away, feeling with her feet and her free hand. She desperately tried to remember which way to the front of the building, but she was completely turned around and all she saw was a maze of desks.

"You're right. I am a killer. Dozens have died because of me." His voice sounded cold and hard. "Well done, Cindy.

Police in five cities are baffled. You've found the killer they couldn't."

Five? Where is the other one? "But why?" she asked, still holding the letter opener.

"Why not? It's a cruel world, and people don't get what they deserve. Someone needs to punish them."

"It's not for you to decide who lives and dies!"

"Somebody has to," he said with a smile.

Over his shoulder she saw Mark running toward them, gun drawn. Oliver must have heard him because he spun around, hands in the air. "Detective, I'd like to turn myself in. Cindy's right. I did it. I'm the killer."

"You confess to killing Ryan Bellig?"

"I confess to killing everyone."

"Here, Raleigh, Boston, Texas, and where else?" Cindy demanded.

Oliver laughed, and the sound made her blood run cold. "Maine."

Paul appeared a moment later and handcuffed Oliver while Mark kept his weapon trained on him.

"You have the right to an attorney," Mark began.

"I know my rights, and I'm willing to waive all of them," Oliver said.

He turned his head and stared at Cindy. His eyes seemed to sear her soul. "I'm sorry that you got caught up in all of this," he said softly before Paul led him away.

Shaking, Cindy sat down in a desk chair and dropped the letter opener.

"How did you figure it out?" Mark asked.

"He was the only one who fit the pattern."

"What was that about Boston and Texas and Maine?"

"Last night I found out that there were similar murders in both Boston and Texas, but none of them were ever recognized for their religious symbolism. He said five cities just a few minutes ago. So I asked him where the fifth was."

"And it was in Maine," Mark filled in. "We'll have to check it all out, but this is good. He's the only Shepherd who didn't produce a cross. I had planned to visit him at home tonight and arrest him if he couldn't show it to me."

"It does fit into a neat little package, doesn't it?" she asked.

"I never call murder neat. Messy, yes. Traumatic, yes. Neat, no."

"I just wish I knew why he did it."

"I'm sure that will come out eventually." Mark picked Cindy's cell phone off the floor.

"Thanks," she said as she reached for it. "I'm so glad you answered your phone. I thought maybe I should have called 9-1-1, but I wasn't sure I'd have enough time to give them all the information they'd need to find me."

"They can track cell phone location," he said. "You didn't call me, though. You called Jeremiah. He called me."

"I'm glad I picked up," a familiar voice said.

Cindy glanced up and saw Jeremiah striding toward them. "Thank you," she said.

"I'm just relieved it's all over," Jeremiah responded.

"You can say that again," Mark added. "If I ever see either of you at a crime scene again it will be too soon."

12

Half an hour later the staff of the newspaper returned from their meeting, and Cindy suddenly found herself the center of unwanted attention. The police were almost through questioning her, and she had hoped to escape without having to talk to anyone else.

It wasn't every day, though, that news happened in a newsroom instead of just being reported there. Finally, the police had to push them all outside the building so they could finish up.

Mark and Paul had taken off almost immediately with Oliver in handcuffs. Sometime after that Jeremiah seemed to disappear. Frustrated, Cindy felt like she had been abandoned to the mercy of the journalists who she could hear shouting questions to police officers outside.

She shuddered as she thought about the dinner she had shared with Oliver and how she had told him things she didn't tell people. She remembered how he had urged her not to be afraid to go home. All along he was the one who had broken into her house in the first place.

I guess you never really know people, she admitted to herself. She thought of the people outside. They had worked for three years with Oliver and had never suspected that the story to beat all stories was right under their noses.

"I have to get out of here," she said to the officer who was finishing taking down her statement.

"This will just take a couple of more minutes, ma'am, and then I'll help you get out of here," he said.

"Thank you."

She could feel the adrenaline draining from her body, and she knew that she would crash soon. She wished she could be certain of a good night's sleep. Even with Oliver in jail, though, she wasn't sure that would happen. The world seemed too dangerous still. Sure, a killer was off the street, but that killer was someone she knew, someone she let her guard down around. She wasn't sure how she could ever learn to trust people again.

Kyle's right, I do spend too much time in my own head, she realized in disgust. While she could never be as cavalier as her brother, she found herself really wishing she could have a small piece of his attitude to help her relax and take everything in stride. *Maybe I'll give him a call tonight, congratulate him on that whole rescue thing.*

"Okay, we're finally done here," the policeman said a few moments later.

"Great." Relief flooded through her. "How do we do this?"

"Out the side door to avoid the vultures," he said grimly, turning to lead the way.

"Sounds like a plan."

When they reached the exit she remembered in frustration that she had parked in the main lot. She would still have to face the gauntlet of reporters if she wanted to get home. The officer pushed the door open, and she followed him out.

There, parked next to the exit, was Jeremiah's car. He leaned casually against it, arms folded across his chest. "Need a ride?"

"Yes, please." Relief washed over her.

"I've got her, Officer," Jeremiah said.

The policeman snapped him a salute and hurried back inside. Cindy was amused at the exchange. She looked again at Jeremiah. There was something in his posture that did demand respect. Was it just because she knew he was a rabbi, or was he the kind of guy who got people's attention anyway?

"Hop in," Jeremiah said. He opened his door and slid into the driver's seat.

As soon as she had the door closed, he hit the gas. Cindy shrank back into the seat and fought the urge to duck her head like some kind of celebrity trying to evade the paparazzi. She glanced sheepishly at Jeremiah, who grinned at her.

"Go ahead and duck down if you want," he said, as though reading her mind. "We can come back for your car when they're all busy looking in another direction."

"When I couldn't find you inside I thought you had abandoned me," she confessed.

He smiled at her. "We've come this far together. I figured we might as well see it out together."

She leaned her head back and closed her eyes. "Thank you again, for everything."

"You're welcome. So, what shall it be, do you want me to take you home or to work?"

"Can I have a third option? I don't like the sound of either of those right now."

He chuckled. "Okay, how about a Seder tonight at my secretary's house?"

"Serious?" she asked, opening her eyes.

He shrugged. "Why not? It would be something completely different for you at any rate. And it fulfills your requirement of being neither at work nor at home."

"You're on. But I really should stop off at work and then at home before that."

"Acceptable."

A few minutes later he dropped her off in the church parking lot with a promise to pick her up in an hour. Cindy walked slowly toward the office, trying to catch her breath and remember what it was that she had to do there.

When she stepped into the office she found it crammed with people who saw her and burst into applause.

"What on earth?"

Geanie threw her arms around her. "We've been listening to the news on the radio. We heard everything about you and the newspaper. We're so excited that you caught the killer."

"Do you know who the killer is?" Cindy asked, wondering how much of their excitement would disappear once they knew that.

"Unfortunately, we do," Geanie said with a brief frown. "But what's important today is that you caught a murderer and helped us all feel safe again."

"I never realized anybody besides me felt unsafe," Cindy said quietly. It would have been nice to have known that she wasn't alone in that regard.

"Talking about that usually makes people feel worse," Geanie admitted.

"Well, I'm glad I could help," Cindy said.

"Are you going to the program tonight?"

"No."

"You're going to miss it?" Roy asked from across the room.

"I'll see the Saturday night program," Cindy called back. Roy nodded approval.

"What are you doing tonight to celebrate then?" Geanie asked.

"I'm going to a Seder."

"How cool! You'll have to tell me all about it tomorrow."

"I promise."

"Awesome."

The office door opened, and Gus carried in a massive bakery box. He struck a pose and hoisted the bakery box aloft. "I have cake!" he boomed in his best theater voice.

There was another round of applause. Somehow, Cindy found herself in charge of cutting the cake. There was excited chatter in the room as the pieces of cake were passed out. Cindy was glad to hear that there were also some more serious tones, though, as people considered the horror of having one of their own turn out to be a serial killer.

Maybe life does go on. She finally ate the first forkful of her own slice of cake. "This is delicious!"

"Chocolate, it's good for what ails you," Gus said. "Besides, nothing but the best today."

She had to smile. She wondered if this was what Kyle felt like all the time, a conquering hero who saved the day. For the first time she sort of envied her brother.

So much for leaving well enough alone, Jeremiah realized. For whatever reason, Adonai seemed determined to cross his path with Cindy's. He didn't know why or what the plan was, but when she had called his cell, screaming that it was Oliver, he had known he was meant to save her. And save her he did, if just from the newspaper reporters. He was amazed that she had single-handedly cornered Oliver and got him to confess. When he had seen her wielding the letter opener in the back of the building, it had been a far cry from the girl cowering on the floor of the church sanctuary.

Now it was over, though, and life could resume as normal. She would go back to her job, and he would go back to his, and they would wave as they passed each other in the parking lots. Somehow that didn't seem quite right, though. He had a feeling that Cindy Preston wasn't done with him just yet, although he couldn't say why.

Was it possible that she had something to teach him? Or maybe Adonai felt he needed to have more friends outside of his faith. Whatever the reason, she seemed destined to stay in his life, at least for a little while longer.

After dropping her off at the church he headed home to change his clothes for the Seder. Once that was done, he picked up the phone and called Marie.

"I heard they caught the guy, and he was one of their own," she said by way of greeting.

"Yes, Marie, they caught him. Cindy confronted him at his work, he confessed, and the police took him away."

"A blessing."

"Absolutely. Ready for another one?"

"What is it?" she asked.

"I invited Cindy to partake of the Seder tonight."

"I appreciate you inviting people into my home and feeling so free to do so," Marie said, sarcasm thick in her voice.

"I'm sorry. At least I gave you notice so that you can have the right number of place settings."

He realized it was the wrong thing to say almost as soon as it left his mouth. He winced, waiting for the backlash, but Marie gave no acknowledgment of it.

"She's your responsibility," Marie said darkly.

"I understand."

"It's no sin of mine if she taints the table," Marie continued.

"Absolutely not."

"Because I keep an immaculate house."

"I know you do," he reassured her. "I promise, she'll be properly attired and thoroughly purified before arrival."

"All right," she said grudgingly.

"Thank you, Marie."

He hung up the phone. The evening would either be a great success or a horrific disaster. All he could do was hope and pray that the two women would get along.

Be honest, it's not Cindy you're worried about, it's Marie. It was true. Marie was notoriously biased against Christians, and all the time he'd spent with Cindy didn't help.

Jeremiah glanced at the clock. He still had a while to go before he picked up Cindy. He grabbed a book and settled down in the living room to read for a few minutes.

He flipped open a book of Shakespearean sonnets, but couldn't focus. He had found that reading old English remarkably improved his vocabulary skills but was neither easy nor to be engaged in lightly. After rereading the same sonnet four times, he closed the book. He sat quietly for a few minutes before finally giving up and getting ready to leave the house.

He tried to blame his distraction on the earlier excitement or his apprehension about Marie's behavior at the Seder. The truth was, though, that something just wasn't right.

His day off was turning out nothing like he'd expected. He was relieved that the reign of the serial killer had come to an end, but at the same time something about the whole situation made him uneasy. Oliver didn't seem stupid to him. And the guy who had been able to perpetrate those crimes didn't seem like someone who would turn himself in so easily, confess, and happily go off to prison.

No, he would have tagged the killer as someone who would have gone down fighting, striving with his last breath to be smarter, quicker, deadlier than his opponents. It was hard for him to see Oliver as that type of individual, even without the afternoon's events.

Not everything has to be so complicated, he told himself. *Sometimes the bad guys do confess.* It happened all the time in his country, only with terrorists as opposed to serial killers. They were always proud to claim their work and would defend it at any cost.

Paranoid, that was what he was. He took a deep breath and decided that maybe it was time to pick up Cindy. He would be early, but the worst case scenario would have him shadowing some of her coworkers for a little while. That was preferable to figuring out ways to set a confessed killer free.

A handcuffed Oliver sat alone in one of the interrogation rooms. He looked tired, deflated, but also somewhat relieved. Paul and Mark had observed him for nearly five minutes through the one-way glass.

"Does it seem odd to you that he would just confess like that?" Mark asked. "After all the games, the elaborate setups? The man managed to keep every crime scene free of DNA evidence, and yet just sings like a bird with a little push from a church secretary?"

"Maybe it was the shock of being confronted with all of his crimes, especially by a church secretary."

"I don't buy it," Mark said.

Paul shook his head. "Stranger things have happened. Maybe his conscience is getting the best of him. Or maybe she really knew how to push his buttons."

"Maybe. Okay, it's showtime," Mark said. Moments later he entered the room that held Oliver.

Oliver stared at him as though he didn't quite see him. The man didn't look good. For a moment Mark wondered if he was ill.

"Oliver, I'm Detective Mark Walters," he said as he sat down across from Oliver.

"I know who you are."

"And now we know who you are," Mark said pointedly.

"Do you? Do you really?"

It was something in the tone of his voice that gave Mark pause. He stared at the other man, trying to figure out what it was that seemed so off about him, but couldn't quite put his finger on it. He looked ragged, like a man who hadn't slept for a while. Mark could relate.

"Yeah, you're the guy who's been running around town killing people," he said at last.

Oliver gave a noncommittal grunt.

"You confessed to that a little while ago. You also confessed to murders in several other states."

"Yes, I did," Oliver said.

"So, tell me about the murders this week," Mark said.

Oliver shrugged. "What's to tell? People are dead. I killed them. End of story."

"So you've said. Unfortunately, I'm going to need a little more than that from you."

"What do you want to know?" Oliver asked.

"I want to know why. Tell me why."

"People are basically evil. They need to be taught a lesson."

"And you think you're just the person to do that?" Mark asked. He had a hard time seeing this guy as a vigilante.

Oliver nodded.

"Tell me about the guy on the donkey."

"It's a representation of Christ's triumphal entry into Jerusalem just days before his betrayal and execution."

"No, I got that. Why did you choose Miguel Jesus Olivera?" Mark asked.

What little color was there drained from Oliver's face.

"Because, because his . . . middle name . . . was Jesus," Oliver stammered.

"And where did you get the donkey?"

"I, uh, stole it."

"What color was the donkey?" Mark asked.

"What?" Oliver asked.

"I want you to tell me what color the donkey was," Mark insisted, leaning forward.

"Brown, no grey. It was grey."

"You're sure?"

"Yeah, I think. It was dark."

It took all of Mark's self-control not to swear.

"Okay, let's talk about the money changer."

"Christ drove them from the temple."

"Yeah, I got that too. That's why you chose a check-cashing place that was next to a church, so you could make your point painfully obvious. What I don't get is why there was a sheep tied up in the back of the shop with blood poured over him."

"The sheep means . . ."

"Yes?"

"Uh, the sheep is significant because one of the things the money changers did was overcharge for sacrifices."

"Sacrifices?" Mark asked.

"Yes, to help atone for sin."

"So why did you leave the sheep alive instead of sacrificing it?"

"Because I'm not looking for forgiveness," Oliver said vehemently.

This wasn't good. The donkey had been ivory, and he was making up answers about a sheep that didn't exist. Either the guy was completely insane, or he was lying about being the killer.

Mark leaned back. "Tell me about the dead guy in the church."

"His name was Ryan. Ryan Bellig. He was from Raleigh. We were friends once."

"Really? What you did to him didn't look very friendly to me," Mark noted.

Tears sprang to Oliver's eyes. "He blamed me for the death of his wife and daughter. Somehow he found me. He demanded to meet with me in private before going to the police. I was hoping I'd have a chance to explain."

"Explain what?" Mark pressed.

"That I . . ." Oliver paused, thought quickening in his eyes. "That I never wanted to hurt them. And I certainly didn't want to hurt Ryan."

"So, why did you bring a knife with you then?"

"It wasn't mine. It was his. Turns out he didn't want an explanation. He wanted revenge."

"Can you blame him?"

"No," Oliver said, the tears now coursing down his cheeks. "He came after me. I grabbed for the knife. We scuffled. I got it away from him. I still hoped to talk. But he lunged at me, and the knife—"

He buried his face in his hands, and Mark watched him for a moment. "How did you get into the sanctuary?"

"I stole Harold's key at the Shepherd's meeting on Saturday."

"Tell me about the cross."

"I think the chain must have broken in the scuffle. I didn't realize I had lost it until the next day, but I'm still not sure where or how. There aren't many of those crosses, you know? They're special. They mean something. I went back to check the church, but police were everywhere. I learned that Cindy found the body, so I went over to her house, but I didn't see it. Then I went back later and broke into her house to see if she had it."

"How did you break into her house?"

"When I first moved to the area I rented a house from Harold. He always leaves a spare key hidden just in case. I found Cindy's and went through the front door."

"And then you left it open when you left," Mark said, trying to trip up Oliver's story.

"No! I relocked it. I was afraid a real thief might take advantage, and I didn't want that to happen."

"Okay, then what about the woman and the man?"

"What about them?" Oliver asked.

"Why them?"

"Isn't it obvious?"

"No, but what is obvious is that you're lying to me. What, are you in need of attention or something? Having a little dinner with Cindy, breaking into her house to be close to her, trying to flirt with her, get her attention? Then maybe confess to crimes you didn't commit just so she'll notice? That's stupid, because let me tell you, there are a lot more effective ways to get a woman's attention."

"But I *am* the killer!" Oliver protested.

"I don't buy it. Maybe you killed Ryan Bellig just like you said, but not the others."

The door opened, and Mark glanced up at Paul. His face was grim, but he didn't say a word, and he didn't look at Oliver. He handed Mark a sheet of paper before exiting the room.

Mark glanced at the paper. "So, I was right. You didn't kill all those people."

"But I did. They're dead because of me."

Mark shook his head. "No, because when the man and the woman were killed yesterday morning, you were already at work. In fact, you were in a meeting with your boss for over an hour. He's verified it."

"Maybe I have an accomplice," Oliver said.

"Look, I don't know what your problem is, but I'm glad it's not mine."

Mark stood up and headed for the door.

"Where are you going?" Oliver asked, his voice laced with panic.

"To find the real killer," Mark said.

He left the room, slamming the door behind him.

"Cut him loose?" Paul asked.

Mark nodded.

"What about the Bellig murder?"

"It's possible he's responsible for that one. If so, though, it sounds like it was self-defense."

"You don't want to hold him on it?"

"No, I want to put him back out there and see what our killer makes of that. Too many signs point to Oliver. I'm starting to think it's because someone wanted them to."

"I'll set up a team to follow him, see what we can flush out," Paul said.

"Just what I was thinking," Mark agreed.

"You know, I've been a cop for fifteen years, and I still don't get why some people confess to crimes they didn't commit."

"Guilt, fear, or gain. Those are the only three reasons anyone does anything."

"Nice," Paul answered with a roll of his eyes.

Mark shrugged. "It's not my fault it's the truth."

"No, but I can blame you for spreading your gospel of truth. I, for one, don't want to hear it."

"The question is," Mark said, "which one is motivating Oliver?"

"I rule out gain since I can't see anything he could possibly get from confessing."

"Then let's hope it's fear. Maybe the killer is targeting him and he knows it."

"If that's the case, isn't it risky putting him back out there where the killer can find him?"

"Yes, but it's Thursday, and right now it's a risk I'm willing to take," Mark said.

"Fair enough."

Mark headed for the door. There was still a killer on the loose, and the clock was ticking. Thanks to Oliver's little stunt he had lost a couple of hours when he might have been searching for the real killer. Hopefully, Oliver would still be of some use, and the day wouldn't be a total loss.

13

When Cindy slid into the passenger seat of Jeremiah's car for the second time that day, she was more exhausted than she had been earlier.

"Are you okay?" he asked.

She shook her head. "Long day."

"Long week."

"That too."

"I take it everyone heard the news?"

She nodded. "Yep. There was cake."

"One of your members was arrested and you celebrated? Here I thought you'd all be busy seeing who could deny knowing him the fastest. First one to three times wins?"

"Is that a joke? You can't possibly be comparing Oliver to Jesus, can you?"

He shrugged. "Apparently, a very poor joke. I'm sorry. I've been told my sense of humor can be a bit—"

"Twisted? Warped?"

"I was going to say 'dark,' but those will do just as well," he said with a smile.

"Ah."

"Do you want to risk trying to get your car?"

"No, I'm not in the mood to risk anything else today," she said. "It will be there tomorrow when the story's old news."

"True enough. Although we could swing by later tonight and see if the coast is clear."

"That would be awesome."

"It's okay to cry, you know."

She turned to look at him. "Why do you say that?"

"Because crying relieves tension, which is normal, especially when the situation is life threatening. And, you're pursing your lips. You tend to do that before you cry."

"Oh, my gosh, it is so not okay that you know that about me." She sounded horrified.

"Sorry."

Suddenly she laughed. "You're the first person to ever notice that. Wow. I guess you have really seen me at my worst."

"If this is your worst, then your best has to be spectacular."

"Thank you."

A few minutes later they pulled up in front of her house. Cindy sat in the car for a moment, just staring. "I guess I don't have to worry that someone is lurking inside."

"No, it should be safe, at least from that particular threat."

She cast him an uneasy look and wanted to say something sarcastic in response.

"Don't worry," he reassured her. "I'll go in with you just in case."

Together they approached the door. Her stomach twisted into knots, and Cindy tried in vain to quiet the pounding of her heart. *What's wrong with me? The police arrested Oliver.*

She opened her door and breathed a sigh of relief when everything looked to be in its proper place. Jeremiah followed her inside, walked to the back of the house, and quickly returned with a smile. "You're safe, no intruders."

"I guess I am safe," she said.

"You don't sound convinced."

"I'm not."

He cocked his head slightly. "Why?"

"I don't know, I just feel—" she paused, struggling to find a word that would describe it.

"Will you never feel safe here again because someone broke in once?" he asked.

"If I say yes will you think less of me?"

"No, of course not. Your home has been violated. That can take a long time to get over. Some people never do and eventually move someplace else."

"I can't afford to move, so I guess I better get over it," she said.

He stared intently at her. "That's not all of it."

"It's nothing."

"I can't help you if you won't tell me what the problem is."

"Speaking as my rabbi?" she joked.

"As your friend," he answered seriously.

"I think the real killer is still out there."

His dark eyes somehow darkened even more, and she stared in fascination. "Tell me why you think so." His voice thrummed with intensity.

She took a step back and wondered again if the real killer was staring her in the face. He reached out and grabbed her arms just above the elbows. Panic knifed through her, and she pulled backward. His grip only tightened.

"Cindy, tell me what you're thinking," he commanded.

"I think he only killed the guy in the church," she said, trying not to let the terror creep into her voice.

"Why do you think he didn't kill the others?"

"Because the murder of Ryan Bellig doesn't fit the rest of the pattern."

"Probably because he didn't plan on killing him."

"Yes, but given how thoughtful his murders have been, don't you think he would have found a way? I mean, he could have stashed the body somewhere and brought it out for one of his tableaus. Leaving him facedown like that was sloppy, not artistic. He could have just sat him up in a pew as a praying man and made more of a statement."

"So, if we're looking at two different murderers, what does that mean?" Jeremiah pressed.

"That one of them is still out there, and unfortunately, it's the crazy one. I'm not safe."

"If you're right, no one in this town is."

He let go of her abruptly and sat down at the kitchen table. Cindy's knees were trembling, but she forced herself to calmly pull out a chair and take her own seat.

"Actually," he said after a moment, "of everyone in town you're probably the safest. Since he's been performing for you it seems unlikely that he plans to kill you. At least not until this is over."

"Thank you, that is so comforting," she said sarcastically.

"Which brings us back to the original question of why he chose you in the first place."

"What if he didn't?" Cindy asked.

"What do you mean?"

"What if the killer is performing for someone, but it's not me. Who could he be targeting?"

"Is there any commonality between the victims?" Jeremiah asked, tapping his fingers on the table.

Cindy got up, grabbed paper and pen, and sat back down at the table. "The guy on the donkey was Miguel Jesus Olivera," she said, writing down his name. "Jason Schneider was the money changer. I don't know the names of the two from the salon." She glanced up.

"Mary Gomez was washing the feet of William Ollie Carruthers."

"How do you know that?"

"I asked."

"So how do we figure out a connection between these people when we don't know any of them?" She sighed.

"Internet?"

"I guess."

"Is it significant that Miguel's middle name is Jesus?" he asked.

"And he was playing the role of Jesus? It might be, but William was playing the role of Jesus as well, and he doesn't share a name with him."

Jeremiah suddenly grew still. His eyes focused intently on the list.

"What is it?" she asked.

"I see something those two men do have in common."

She looked down at the list. "Oh!"

"You see it?"

"Yes, both the men who were positioned as Jesus have as part of their name a variation on Oliver. Olivera and Ollie."

"I think you found the killer's real audience."

"He's doing this to get to Oliver," she whispered. "Oliver isn't the killer; he's the target."

175

Mark hung up with Cindy. The secretary and the rabbi seemed to have come to the same conclusion that he had. He rubbed his tired eyes and returned to the computer screen where a pattern was slowly emerging.

Both Miguel and Jason had been interviewed by Oliver in the past month. Miguel was a small businessman who was making news as having one of the only businesses in town that was expanding instead of shrinking. Jason had been the coach for a Little League team that had won its regional division.

As for the beauty salon, Oliver was one of Mary's special male customers who had early morning appointments. In fact, he had had one scheduled for that fateful morning. So, everyone was connected to him in some way. It stood to reason that the killer would continue to go after people who were somehow connected to Oliver.

Unfortunately, between his job as a reporter and his volunteer work with the church, that meant a lot of potential targets.

Paul appeared from the direction of the interrogation room where he had been taking his turn to get more information out of Oliver.

Exhausted, he sank down in the chair across from Mark. "Anything?"

"He won't budge an inch. He still insists on taking responsibility for all the murders."

"Did you explain to him that unless he helps us find out who's doing this that more people are going to die?"

"Yes. He swears that as long as he's in prison, though, there will be no more murders."

"What is his damage?"

"I don't know, but apparently it's extensive."

"Our hunch was right. All the victims were in some way connected to Oliver. Loosely connected, but connected," Mark said.

"Wonderful. You think the killer's keeping a close eye on our boy in there?"

"I don't know, but he's certainly done his homework."

"Just what I love, educated psychopaths. So what's the plan?" Paul asked.

"I figure we keep him another couple of hours, and then we cut him loose like we discussed."

"Even if he hasn't talked?"

"Yeah. We can try until then, though."

"Your turn. I need to sit down before I fall down."

"You are sitting down," Mark said.

"My point."

Jeremiah almost wished he didn't know there was a killer still on the loose. They said ignorance was bliss, and someday he'd like to find out for himself if it was true. He sat impatiently in Cindy's living room while she changed.

She emerged looking refreshed, and they were soon on their way. They were quiet for the drive, and Jeremiah thought about the coming Seder.

It still seemed strange to him. In Israel, the Seder was only on the first night of Passover. In America Seder dinners were celebrated the first two nights. He could tell Cindy was nervous as they parked outside Marie's house. Jeremiah gave her a reassuring smile and led the way to the front door.

Marie opened the door before he could knock. Her arms were crossed, and she gazed at him disapprovingly before turning and glaring daggers at Cindy.

Jeremiah felt his temper start to slip. He took a deep breath and regained control quickly.

Marie stepped back, allowed them to enter, and closed the door. "I would have thought this little alliance would be over now that the killer has been arrested."

"Didn't you hear?" Jeremiah asked. "Turns out it's the wrong man."

Marie's eyes opened wide, and she lost some of her aggressive posturing. She grabbed Cindy's arm. "Poor dear, you must be just terrified. You come in and tell me all about it."

Jeremiah barely restrained himself from smiling as he followed behind. They headed directly for the dining room where Marie introduced Cindy to her husband and three children. As Jeremiah took his seat, a feeling of peace washed over him. It was good to be celebrating Passover. It was even better to be a guest in the house instead of the rabbi presiding over everything.

***

Cindy was excited but also nervous. It didn't help that she could tell Marie did not approve of her presence. She just forced herself to keep smiling. She was tired, frightened, and completely unsure of herself. So, when she thought she might not be able to handle a rude hostess, she just pictured all the work Marie must have gone through to get her house ready to serve a Passover meal. It must have taken days' worth of effort. Cindy couldn't stop grinning.

That effort demanded some respect even if the woman annoyed Cindy. She had seriously thought about backing out of the dinner once they figured out the police had the wrong man. It seemed wrong to celebrate when there was a killer on the loose who could strike anywhere at any time.

Ultimately, that fact decided her evening. The last thing she needed was to sit alone at home worrying about who the killer was or what he was doing or whether or not he was really targeting Oliver or if it was somehow actually her after all.

Marie's home was expensively but tastefully furnished. They stepped into the dining room, and Cindy could feel the excitement in the air. A man and three children were already seated around the table, all looking eager to begin.

"Cindy, this is my husband, Eric," Marie said. "Eric, this is Cindy Preston."

Eric rose and shook her hand warmly. "The girl from the church next to the synagogue?"

"That's me," Cindy admitted.

He smiled at her. "I guess I've been rather misinformed. I was told you were a girl, but you are far more woman than child."

"Thank you, I think," she said, coloring slightly.

"These are our children: Josiah, our oldest; our oldest daughter, Erica; and Greta, the youngest," Marie said.

"It's nice to meet you all." Cindy smiled at them. She turned back toward Marie, "And thank you very much for inviting me."

Marie opened her mouth, but Eric cut her off. "Is this your first Seder meal, Cindy?"

"Yes, it is."

"Then we are honored that you are allowing us to share our traditions with you. Now, Cindy, Rabbi, if the two of you would take your seats then we can begin."

Cindy was relieved to find that she was sitting next to Jeremiah. She was reasonably sure that he, at least, wouldn't attempt to poison her food or stab her with a fork. She also planned on watching him like a hawk so that she could do what he did and not ruin the dinner through ignorance.

Each person had a plate with six different things carefully arranged on it. Four cups sat at each person's place. She glanced over at Jeremiah, wondering if it would be rude to come right out and ask him what it was all for.

Jeremiah smiled at her. "This is the Seder plate," he said, indicating the plate each person had before them that held a variety of things. "Every item is symbolic."

"What does it all mean?" Cindy asked.

"Starting at the top, that is Chazeret."

"It looks like Romaine lettuce," Cindy observed.

"It is. The root of the lettuce is bitter and is used as one of the bitter herbs that we are commanded to eat with the paschal lamb and the unleavened bread. It does not have to be the lettuce; it may be some other bitter herb such as a radish."

She nodded her understanding.

"Then we move clockwise," Jeremiah said. "This is the Zeroa, a roasted shank bone or chicken neck. Here it is a chicken neck as you can see."

"And what is it symbolic of?" Cindy asked.

"It is symbolic of the Paschal lamb offered as the sacrifice. It also serves to remind us of the might of Adonai."

"Next we have the Charoset which is a mixture of apples, nuts, wine, cinnamon, and sugar," Jeremiah said.

"It has an interesting texture."

"It's supposed to remind us of the mortar our ancestors used when building buildings for the Egyptians," the youngest daughter piped up.

"Thank you," Cindy said.

"Then we have the Maror, the other bitter herb," Jeremiah said. "Often it is horseradish root."

"And I'm guessing these bitter herbs also serve to remind you of the bitterness of captivity," Cindy said.

"Very good. That's exactly what they are for. Are you sure you're not Jewish?" Jeremiah teased.

Cindy smiled despite the fact that she was pretty sure she could feel Marie glaring at her.

"Next we have Karpas."

"Also called parsley," Cindy said.

"Parsley or celery is commonly used. This vegetable is dipped into salt water, which represents the tears of the Jewish slaves."

"Okay."

"And finally we have the Beitzah, a roasted egg. It is symbolic of sacrifice, mourning, and is also a symbol for spring."

"So, eggs are common to both Passover and Easter celebrations?" Cindy asked, surprised.

"Yes, and also it seems, to the secular chocolate bunny holiday," Jeremiah said with a smile.

Everyone at the table smiled at that one.

"I'm guessing you're a fan of the chocolate bunny holiday?" Cindy asked Greta.

"I'm a Peeps girl," she said with a toothy grin.

"Me too." Cindy gave her a conspiratorial wink.

"I'm a chocolate bunny girl," Erica said.

"Personally, I like jelly beans or those Cadbury eggs," her father added.

"Enough with talk of Easter candy," Marie said, unable to hide the irritation in her voice. "This is Passover, and that is what we are going to celebrate and discuss tonight." She took a deep breath and that seemed the cue for her husband and children to drop their eyes to their plates and look contemplative.

"Let's get started," Marie said.

Cindy listened in awe as Marie's husband recited a blessing. Following it, she did as the others and drank one of the four cups of wine sitting in front of her. Finished, Cindy put down her goblet and a moment later started to choke.

It couldn't have been more perfect if he had designed it himself. He stood outside the house, listening to the greetings. It was almost time. In the past he had never been able to implement this part of his plan. He saw now that it was as it should have been. Never before had he encountered such an opportunity.

Sacrifice was an important part of life. And this would be a great and terrible sacrifice. He had spent all day carefully mapping out and implementing his plan. At any moment the people inside the house would die.

Twenty minutes later when all sound had ceased from within, he entered through the kitchen door he had used earlier. He passed through the house and found his prey, dead as he had expected. It should have been perfect, but something was wrong. Someone was missing.

He refused to let it spoil the moment. He told himself the symbolism was even more appropriate this way. He smiled and went to work.

14

Mark watched as Oliver was released. He knew the two officers who had been assigned to shadow him. They were both good at their jobs. With any luck the whole case might be wrapped up in a few more hours. Not that he actually believed that.

With the confessions made by Oliver, and the strong possibility that he had killed Ryan in self-defense, the picture was becoming even fuzzier. He and Paul had speculated that the sanctuary killer could be a secondary killer, unrelated to or copying the first. Still, he didn't understand why Oliver kept insisting he had committed all the crimes.

He had spent half an hour on the phone with various friends and colleagues who all swore that Oliver had never shown any signs of mental illness. Still, it wasn't inconceivable that guilt over killing Ryan could have made him snap. That was especially true if they had once really been friends.

Following up on the information he had gotten from Cindy, Mark had faxed Oliver's picture to police and church officials in Austin, Boston, and Raleigh. Given the time difference and the holiday week for two major religions, he didn't expect to hear anything until the next morning. And even that seemed iffy.

As soon as Oliver left the building, Mark turned and walked back into the war room set up with pictures, charts, everything they had or guessed about the killings. He had spent half of his day staring at the wall hoping for something, anything.

And all he got for it was nothing.

If the killer was the same one who had left his stamp on those other cities, there was a good chance he was done. The feet washing had been the last murder every other time. Why? Was it as far as the killer was willing to go or had he just not found the right blend of theatrics and audience yet? One thing was for sure, he had finally nailed the theatrics of it.

Paul walked into the room with a fresh cup of coffee. "Think we're going to get lucky?"

"No. I think this is nowhere near over," Mark said.

"Where does that leave us?"

"Unfortunately, no better off than we were this morning. I think we can be guaranteed that if he's going to keep going, his next move is to recreate the Last Supper."

"Where do you think that's going to happen?"

"It could be at the Olive Garden for all I know," Mark said, gritting his teeth in frustration. "Although, it's probably going to happen in someone's house."

"What makes you say that? All the other scenes have been public. A street and two businesses."

"I don't know, just a feeling. The Last Supper should be an intimate thing. He'll also need time to set it up right."

Paul raised an eyebrow. "Should I ask you where you were yesterday morning?"

"Very funny. I was at the Intergalactic Circus of Sleep."

"Got somebody who saw you there?"

"The dancing bear can vouch for me."

"Nice."

"I thought so."

Paul sipped his coffee for a minute. "They doing anything like a Last Supper tonight at the church?" he asked.

Mark shook his head. "Nah. First Shepherd has some sort of drama tonight. The synagogue had a Passover Seder last night. I have a couple of officers attending the drama, just in case, but I'm not hopeful."

"There goes that theory."

"You got another one?"

"Not that's worth anything."

"Me either."

"So, we just wait for the next unhappy lot to bite it?"

"You're a real caring guy, Paul."

"So my wife tells me."

"Wait a minute," Mark said.

"What?"

"The Last Supper includes Jesus."

"So?"

"So, if the pattern is what we think it is, someone with Oliver in some part of their name will be there," Mark said. "Call the paper. Find out if Oliver has had any interviews, anything with anyone whose first, last, or middle name even slightly resembles Oliver. I'll call the church and see if any of the other members have Oliver in their names."

"Good idea," Paul said, already reaching for the phone in the room.

Mark pulled out his cell phone and called the church office. A minute later he hung up as he got the automatic recording stating that it was after hours.

Fortunately, Paul seemed to have reached someone at the paper. Mark tried dialing Cindy's phone, but it went straight to voicemail. He checked the board and dialed Harold's number. Harold Grey, head usher, First Shepherd to First Shepherd, must have a member directory.

"Hi, Harold, it's Detective Mark Walters."

"Detective, what can I do for you?" Harold asked.

"I need to know if you have a church directory."

"Yes, why?"

"Great, I'm coming over," Mark said, grabbing his coat and heading for the parking lot.

"Is there anything I can look up for you?" Harold asked, sounding perplexed.

"I need you to look and see if any one has a name that is some variation on Oliver. You know, like Ollie, Olivera, anything like that. Check for any middle initials of O as well."

"What's this all about?"

"I'm trying to stop the serial killer from striking again," Mark said, as he started his car. "Write down any names and addresses for me. I'm about five minutes away from you."

Mark looked at the clock on the dashboard and felt his chest tighten. It was just after six o'clock. The killer could strike at any moment.

"Well, there's Oliver, of course," Harold said.

"Yeah, I already know about him," Mark answered.

"Hold on a minute," Harold said, and Mark could hear him moving around. He waited, hoping the older gentleman found the directory before he got there.

"Does gender matter?" Harold asked suddenly.

"I, I don't know," Mark admitted. "Why?"

"Well, my wife's middle name is Olive."

"It is?"

"Yes. Detective, there's someone at the door. I'll have to call you right back."

"Don't answer it!" Mark screamed, but it was too late. Harold had already hung up.

Mark threw on the lights and slammed his foot down on the gas pedal, shooting through a red light and barely missing two cars. He grabbed the radio and called for police and ambulance to meet him at the house.

"No, no, no!" he shouted after he disconnected.

Two minutes later he drove up onto Harold's lawn. He could hear sirens in the distance as he leaped out of the car and raced toward the open front door.

"Are you all right?" Jeremiah asked.

Cindy nodded, still coughing. "Sorry, just swallowed wrong." The truth was she wasn't used to alcohol, and she had almost gagged on it. "I'm fine, really," she told the concerned faces around her.

Eric indicated a bowl and a pitcher. "It's time for the washing of the hands," he said, pouring a small amount of water over his hands into the bowl. Each person took their turn doing so with Cindy going last.

Eric picked up the Karpas and dipped it into a small bowl of salt water sitting nearby. Everyone did the same, including Cindy. She tried not to wrinkle up her nose as she did so. Parsley had never been her favorite thing, and adding salt did nothing to improve it for her.

After they had all eaten it in silent reflection, Eric picked up a plate that was covered with a towel. "Matzoth," Jeremiah said softly. "The unleavened bread. There are three on the plate."

Eric broke the middle one in half.

"Half will be hidden for later as the *afikomen*, the dessert," Jeremiah explained.

"This is the bread of affliction," Eric said as he completely uncovered the plate. As our ancestors were slaves, so are we. We know their enslavement, but we also hope for our freedom. Let any who are hungry or in need join us in this Seder dinner."

There was silence and for a moment Cindy wondered if as a guest she was expected to respond that she was hungry. She looked quickly to Jeremiah but he was looking contemplatively at the bread. She turned to look at the bread, and her stomach growled noisily.

Embarrassed she placed both hands over it. *Like that will actually help,* she scolded herself. And then suddenly, she had an insane urge to laugh. There was a serial killer running around loose. Her life could well be in danger every moment, and yet she was worried about a noisy stomach? It amazed her how she had been so caught up in the moment and the ritual that she could have forgotten for even a second the dangers lurking in the dark. She couldn't help but wonder if that was the secret of survival for the Jewish people. Did their ritual allow them escape from time to time from the horrors of the world they lived in?

She glanced at Jeremiah. He had grown up in a country where violence was a part of everyday life. And yet he seemed so serene most of the time. Was this somehow part of it, this idea that everything had a proper time, place, and way of being done? She glanced around at the others, each with the same contemplative look on their face.

"And now we will have the telling of the Passover story," Eric said.

"The story is told four different times, in four different ways," Jeremiah explained.

Cindy's stomach growled again. She smiled faintly. Apparently, she didn't need to worry about a serial killer. It was more likely that she would die of hunger first.

Greta stood up, her tiny face solemn. "The youngest child asks the four questions," Jeremiah explained.

"Mah nishtanah ha-lahylah ha-zeh mi-kol ha-layloht, mi-kol ha-layloht," Greta said.

"How different is this night from all other nights!" Jeremiah translated in a whisper.

"She-b'khol ha-layloht anu okhlin chameytz u-matzah, chameytz u-matzah. Ha-lahylah ha-zeh, ha-lahylah ha-zeh, kooloh matzah?" Greta asked.

"Why is it that on all other nights during the year we eat either bread or matzah, but on this night we eat only matzah?" Jeremiah whispered. "The answers are found in the Haggadah," Jeremiah said, indicating a book sitting next to Eric. "He will read from it."

Cindy struggled to pay attention as each of the child's four questions was answered. Finally Greta sat down and Cindy wanted to applaud her for being able to make it all the way through. A quick glance around the table convinced her, however, that it would not be appreciated.

"Now do we eat?" she whispered to Jeremiah as quietly as she could.

He smiled. "Not for a long, long time."

Mark raced into Harold Grey's home, gun drawn, expecting the worst. Instead, he saw Harold and his wife, laden down with grocery bags, heading toward the kitchen.

He quickly holstered his weapon as they turned to look at him. Sweat poured off of him, and his heart still pounded.

"I'm sorry, Detective," Harold said. "My wife forgot her key. It was her at the door. I was planning on calling back as soon as I finished helping her carry everything in."

"It's okay," Mark said, struggling to compose himself. He had thought for sure that he was going to find the couple dead and the killer gone. He wiped at the sweat that trickled into his eyes.

"The church directory's on the couch there if you want to look at it," Harold said.

"Thank you, I will," Mark said. He flipped open his phone and called in the false alarm. He sank down onto the couch and snatched up the directory. Just because the Greys were alive didn't mean everyone else was safe. He tried to go quickly, but he read every entry, afraid of missing the one that he would need.

When his phone rang, he grabbed it.

"They're still pulling up records at the paper, but it's looking less and less likely that there are any other Olivers to be found there," Paul said without preamble.

"I've got my hands on the church directory right now. I'll call you back as soon as I have something," Mark said.

The first telling of the Passover story was over, and the second one was just beginning. Jeremiah smiled encouragingly at Cindy, realizing that the distress she felt was his fault. He should have warned her to eat something before they came.

For the second telling, four "sons" were chosen to ask, each in a different way, about the meaning of the Seder. Josiah played the role of the wise son and had asked in length about the Seder and been given a response detailed enough and long enough that Jeremiah's stomach was also starting to growl. Erica then had the responsibility of asking as the simple son, a role that he could tell from the look on her face she did not appreciate.

"What is this?" she asked.

"With a strong hand the Almighty led us out from Egypt, from the house of bondage," her father answered.

Jeremiah had taken upon himself the task of asking as the evil son. "What is this cult of yours?"

Asking the question demonstrated isolation from the Jewish people and prompted the response, "It is because God acted for my sake when I left Egypt."

Finally, Greta was tasked as the son who was too young to ask. To her Eric responded, "It is because of what the Almighty did for me when I left Egypt."

He turned to Cindy. "The third telling will probably be most familiar to you as it is the story from the book of Exodus."

She smiled and sat up straighter, and he did his best not to laugh.

"And then comes the fourth telling?" she asked.

"Not exactly. Before we get to the fourth telling we will sing some praise songs including one called *Dayeinu*. It says that if Adonai had performed only one of the many deeds that it would have been enough."

"And *then* the fourth telling?" she asked.

"Yes."

Mark made it through the directory and felt sick. He couldn't find anyone else who might have a name similar to Oliver. That meant there was no way of telling where the killer would strike in the next few hours. Reluctantly, he called Paul.

"I've got nothing," Mark said after Paul had answered. "You?"

"More of the same."

Mark took a deep breath and closed his eyes. He was so tired. All he wanted to do was go home and go to bed, but somewhere not far from where he sat people could be dying at that very moment. He took a ragged breath.

"Then I guess we wait," he said.

"Yeah. Mark?"

"What?"

"Go home. I've had more sleep than you. I'll call you when something happens."

"Okay. Thanks."

Cindy felt bad about it, but her mind drifted during the fourth telling, which consisted of questions and answers about the customs of the Seder. The hungrier she became the more she felt uneasy. The outside world began to creep in again, and she couldn't help but wonder what the killer was doing while she sat there trying not to disrespect her hosts by going after the food early.

There was an invitation to see herself as being liberated from slavery and instead of being a beautiful moment, it angered her. She knew she was a slave to her own fears, but if she had to wait much longer she was going to be a slave to the needs of her body as well. The small amount of wine from her first glass was sitting in her stomach with only the parsley to keep it company. She felt slightly nauseous.

"And now we have completed the four tellings," Jeremiah said suddenly, turning to smile at her.

"Oh thank heavens," she said.

Eric raised his second cup and the others followed suit. "With the second cup of wine we celebrate our redemption!"

He drank it, and Cindy thought she might cry. She tipped the glass back and tried not to focus on the burning sensation in her throat.

She put the glass down and realized it was time for another ceremonial washing of the hands.

"Food next," Jeremiah whispered.

Thankfully, the blessing over the bread was shorter than she had imagined. Before they could eat it, though, they first had to eat some of the bitter herbs. Then they combined the herbs with the matzah to form a sandwich.

Cindy was pretty sure she had entered into her own personal nightmare. At least she was getting to eat, though. After that was finished they ate the rest of the meal. As the food hit her stomach she began to relax considerably.

When the time came for dessert she was enjoying herself again and laughed as she watched the children searching for the piece of matzah that Marie had hidden quite a while earlier. When it had been found and eaten, a blessing was said for the food they had consumed. Then Eric led them in the drinking of the third glass of wine.

"I had no idea Jewish children partook at such a young age," she confided to Jeremiah.

He began to laugh. Then Eric and the children did too. Marie just rolled her eyes.

"What?" Cindy asked.

"The children are drinking grape juice," Jeremiah said at last. "Although, whether they drink wine or grape juice is a choice left up to the parents."

"Grape juice? You mean I could have had grape juice instead?" Cindy asked.

"Only if you wanted to be treated as a child," Marie said.

Cindy decided right then and there that being friends with the other woman was never going to happen. Eric threw his wife a sharp glance, and Cindy bit her tongue and took a deep breath.

"Now we sing to welcome the prophet Elijah to the table whose coming would signify the coming of the Messiah," Jeremiah said.

"That's pointless," Cindy said, still glaring at Marie.

Silence.

Horrified, she realized what she had said. "I'm sorry," she blurted out, "I didn't mean that."

Eric smiled at her. "Of course you did. In your eyes, Messiah has already come, so what we are doing now is hollow for you. But, don't worry. I don't think you are used to the wine."

"I'm not," Cindy admitted, blushing furiously. "I did not mean to insult you or your traditions."

"We know that," Eric said. "Don't worry. After this song we then sing hymns of praise to Adonai."

"I can certainly get behind that," Cindy said, still feeling like a complete idiot.

"And then songs about freedom," Jeremiah said quietly.

"Wonderful," Cindy said.

"And then we drink the last cup of wine," Marie said, one eyebrow raised.

Cindy groaned.

When the call finally came it was close to midnight. Mark stood on the front steps, reluctant to enter the house. He knew what he was going to see inside, he had already been warned. Several officers on sight looked like they were going to be sick. One, barely more than a kid, sat on the curb, head in his hands with his body shaking. Five feet from him medical personnel administered care to a young woman who was clearly in shock.

Mark took a deep breath. He had seen his share of pain and horror. He knew the things people were capable of doing to each other. He stepped inside, turned toward the dining room and knew that everything he had seen could never have prepared him for that moment.

His stomach twisted, and he heard blood roaring in his ears. A casual glance around the table might have revealed a dinner party in full swing. But it took only a second to realize how horribly wrong it was.

The first thing he noticed was that everyone was seated on one side of the long table. The second thing that he noticed was they were all dead. There were twelve in total. Six sat on the right and six on the left with the seat in the exact center vacant.

The bodies had been posed to resemble the famous Last Supper painting. The young woman outside had been stuck in traffic or else she would have been the one in the center chair playing the part of Jesus.

15

Mark continued to stare at the dead man's version of the Last Supper. The people were clustered perfectly, if his memory served. Some were looking toward the center of the table; others were looking toward the ends. Unlike the other murders, though, the bodies were unmarked.

The table was set for Passover. The plates in front of each person were untouched.

"It looks like it was poison. They drank their first cup of wine, or grape juice in the case of the five kids, and it was over in minutes," Paul said.

"Then he just walked in and took his own sweet time."

"Except he was missing his centerpiece," Paul noted.

"What's the girl's name?"

"Olivia."

Mark nodded. He had been right, but he still had no way of knowing about these families. It was little comfort, though.

"Tell me everything we know about them," he said.

"Mom, Dad, two kids. Mom's sister, her husband, and their son were over. The other five are neighbors, Protestants."

"Jews and Christians sharing the Last Supper. Just like the first time, only it was the same people in each group," Mark said.

Paul stared at him hard. "I think you need to get more sleep."

"You're right, but this needs attention now. Go on."

"Timing of everything rules out Oliver as a suspect."

"I kind of figured that," Mark said. "If it turns out differently, though, I'd love to hear."

"As in, what if this Oliver guy is the killer but was clever enough to throw suspicion completely off himself with a fake confession?"

"Something like that," Mark said.

"Would love that. Unfortunately, I'm not buying it."

"Yeah, me either."

"Like before, we're not finding so much as a fingerprint from this guy."

"I'd be surprised if we did."

"So, what are we looking at next?" Paul asked.

"That's a good question," Mark said. "I'm not entirely sure. He might try to portray the whole trial thing or since it's technically now Friday he might just skip straight to the main point."

"The crucifixion?"

"Exactly."

"I don't want to be there for that one."

"I don't want to be here for this one," Mark said fervently. "But let's do everything we can to make this one the last one."

He waited in the shadows, like he always did. And he watched, like he always did. He saw Oliver come home. It had been a mistake, having the Last Supper while Oliver was in jail. But how could he have guessed that after so many years the devil would confess to anything? It wasn't part of the plan, and he had already spoiled far too many perfect plans. This time, the show would go on, and the final act would be performed. The curtain would fall, and Oliver would be there. And so would he.

He watched, unseen, while Oliver grabbed a suitcase and frantically threw a few possessions into it. He thought he was going to run again. Just like he always did. This time he was wrong. There was no running, not any more.

———

Jeremiah was uneasy in his bones. He couldn't shake the feeling, and so at three in the morning he got up. He and Cindy had successfully retrieved her car from the parking lot at the newspaper a few hours earlier. That meant he was off the hook for the morning as far as providing transportation. He was glad Cindy had managed to avoid the press of reporters, especially in light of Oliver's release.

The rest of the Seder had gone well with no more outbursts from Cindy. He didn't blame her. Marie had pushed her buttons from the start. He should have known better. Eric, at least, had maintained a sense of humor about the whole thing.

He realized there was no way he was going to get any sleep.

He decided to go for a jog and clear his head. He pulled on a T-shirt and sweat pants and twenty minutes later was in the park in the center of downtown.

Jogging there during the day was enjoyable, but at night it was almost magical. The city kept lights on all night, which gave just enough illumination to see by but not enough to ruin the beauty and serenity of the dark.

He started out at a nice easy jog, breathing in deeply of the cool night air, allowing it to fill up his lungs. As his muscles loosened, though, he lengthened his stride and began to run. Faster he went, enjoying the freedom, and the release from the physical effort. He ran completely around the perimeter of the park and then turned toward the interior, zigzagging around trees and hurdling benches. His pulse pounded, and the wind whistled by his ears.

He turned to take another bench, realized there were people sitting on it, swerved, and came to a halt as he saw the glint of a sword in the one man's hand. He spun to face them and realized that they were dead. Even in the dim glow from the nearest street light he could see them clearly. The shorter of the two men held a sword, and the taller of the two men had his right ear cut off.

Fifteen minutes later Mark arrived. He looked exhausted. His clothes were crumpled, and his hands shook from fatigue.

"I told you I didn't want to see you again at a crime scene. You know, for a rabbi you sure spend a lot of time at them," he said by way of greeting.

"Sorry to wake you." Jeremiah suppressed the urge to return the jab.

"I wasn't asleep." Given how bad the detective looked Jeremiah was pretty sure Mark hadn't slept in quite a while. The detective stifled a yawn and swayed slightly on his feet.

"And you saved me the trouble of having to wake you," Mark added after a moment.

Alarm bells went off in Jeremiah's mind. His first thought was for Cindy. He had checked her house out the night before when he dropped her off and had seen no sign of anything wrong. He shook his head. It couldn't be Cindy. He had not been on Mark's call list when she had been in trouble before, and it seemed unlikely that anything would have changed that in the last few hours. "I don't understand. Why were you going to wake me?"

"I just came from another crime scene. It was a party. The oldest daughter had car trouble, called home, and no one answered. When she was finally able to get home she found everyone murdered, seated around the dinner table posed just like in that da Vinci painting everyone makes such a fuss over."

"*The Last Supper*?"

"That's the one. A perfect tableau, except for one person. We figure the car trouble saved her life."

It was horrific news, yet did not explain why Mark would have called him in the middle of the night. A terrible suspicion dawned on him. "Last night was a Seder," he said.

"Yeah. The guests were neighbors, Protestants. But the hosts were Jewish. Rabbi, they were from your synagogue."

"Who?"

"Family's name was Schuller."

"Samuel Schuller?"

"Yeah, I hope you didn't know the family too well."

"I did know them well," Jeremiah admitted.

Inside him a fire began to burn. It was the same rage that had always filled him when he heard of the senseless death of someone he knew. In America it was easy to forget that such things happened every day. In America people died of cancer or in car accidents; they weren't brutally slaughtered.

He closed his eyes and for a moment he was back in Israel where everyone died and no one was ever safe. Images that always haunted him floated to the surface: a grandmother shot at the Wailing Wall, a six-year-old killed by a car bomb. Safe.

Cindy craved safety, and he had seen enough to know that no matter what she did, how hard she tried, she could never be completely safe. Some people could live with that truth and some couldn't.

Cindy had been right about a lot of things the last several days, and this time was no exception. Oliver, it turned out, was the audience, not the performer.

"Rabbi, are you all right?" Mark asked.

Jeremiah opened his eyes. "I will be."

"Okay. Let's see who we have here." Mark turned toward the two men on the bench. A moment later he made a strangled sound.

"What is it?"

"I know them. They're cops. They are … were … assigned to follow Oliver. They were keeping an eye on him while we tried to flush out the killer."

"Looks like the killer found them first."

Mark ran back to his car, and Jeremiah could hear him requesting officers be sent to Oliver's house.

Jeremiah had attended a Seder at Samuel's house the year before. Had he been there last night instead of at Marie's, would he have been able to save them?

Mark returned a moment later.

"How did they die?" Jeremiah asked.

"It looks like he poisoned the wine. He waited until it was over and then went in and posed them."

"Just the wine?" Jeremiah asked.

"No, the grape juice too," Mark said, his voice barely more than a whisper.

Jeremiah clenched his fists, his nails cutting into his palms until he could feel blood flow.

"I know, it's terrible," Mark said, bending down to take a closer look at the dead officers.

"And the one who escaped?"

"Oldest daughter, name's Ol—"

"Olivia," Jeremiah supplied.

"Tell me, why do bad things happen to good people?" Mark asked.

"Why are you asking me?"

"Because you're a rabbi. I figure if someone's going to know the answer it might as well be you."

"If I ever figure it out I'll let you know."

"Do the world a favor and let everybody know if you figure that one out."

More officers arrived on the scene and began to rope it off to collect evidence. Jeremiah waited, helpless and angry. There was nothing he could do but give his statement. He was eager to leave. He needed to be at the synagogue to help members cope as the news got out.

More than that, though, he wanted a chance to do some investigation of his own. The police might be doing their best to bring the killer to justice, but they would never succeed if he found the guy first.

As forensics took over the crime scene, Mark pulled Jeremiah to the side. "Let's compare notes."

"This is going to take awhile," Jeremiah said.

"I've got time."

All right, then, you first."

⧉

Cindy woke up still feeling embarrassed about some of the things she had said and done at the Seder. She realized there had been no excuse for losing it, no matter how much Marie annoyed her. At least her husband and kids had seemed nice.

She was too afraid to turn on the television or radio or even to check her email. She wanted the nightmare to be over, the killer to be dead or to have moved on. She knew she wasn't quite ready to cope with a reality that did not embrace one of those two theories.

She yawned. It was earlier than she usually got up, but with everything that had happened all week she was really behind. If there was any hope of things going well during the Saturday pageant or the Sunday services, then she needed to devote every hour of the day she could to work. Although she doubted she would have any uninterrupted workdays for a long time.

Happy Good Friday to me, she thought. She just hoped Geanie had managed to pull off her usual holiday miracle and would have her work wrapped up by ten in the morning so that Cindy would have a chance of recruiting her to help with her work.

It was still dark as Cindy drove to the church. She ran through the list of things she had to do that day. Like every Good Friday, the list was overwhelming. The fear that a killer was still loose only added to the sense of impossibility.

As she neared the church the sun burst over the horizon sending fiery tendrils of light across the sky. She gazed in awe as the light chased away the shadows, and she prayed that it might obliterate the shadows in her mind as well.

She pulled her attention back to the street and prepared to turn into the church parking lot. The light from the sun touched the middle of the three crosses and illuminated the face of the man hanging on it.

Cindy hit the brakes and yanked her steering wheel to the right, ramming her car into the curb. She came to a stop and flew from the car to the foot of the cross. She tripped on something in the grass and fell to her knees.

She looked up at Oliver's face contorted in pain, a gag in his mouth and a crown of thorns on his head. He looked down at her, and the agony and terror on his face overwhelmed her even as she watched blood trickle into his eyes.

She remembered standing on the lawn four days earlier when Ralph and Drake had said they were anchoring the crosses so that they could withstand a hurricane. She reached for her cell, realized she'd left it in the car with her purse, and ran back.

"9-1-1, please state the nature of your emergency."

"I'm at First Shepherd on the corner of Main and Lincoln in Pine Springs. A man has been hung on the cross on the lawn, and I can't get him down."

"Emergency services are on their way."

Cindy hung up and then dialed Mark. "It's Oliver!" she screamed when he picked up. "The killer found him. He's here, at the church, hanging on the cross."

"Did you call 9-1-1?"

"Yes. Hurry, we've got to help him."

"I'll be right there," he said, and hung up.

Cindy dropped her cell and grabbed her keys out of the ignition. She ran around to the gate, opened it, and then ran for the janitorial closet. Her hands shook so badly she could barely fit the key in the lock. Once inside, she grabbed a tall ladder and wrestled it from the room, knocking dozens of cleaning products off the shelves.

The metal squeaked and scraped, and she smashed two of her fingers between the ladder and the door. She bit her tongue to keep from screaming at the pain of it and continued to pull.

Once she had freed it from the room, she half dragged, half carried the ladder back around to the front of the church. As she passed the foot of one of the other crosses she glanced up and realized there was someone hanging on it as well. She gasped and dropped the ladder on her foot. She barely felt the pain as she stared up into the eyes. *Dead. Dead eyes.* She forced herself to turn and look at the third cross and saw another body there. And the eyes on it were also dead, so very, very dead.

She felt her chest constricting in pain and fear. *It's too late to help them, but you can help Oliver!*

Cindy grabbed the ladder and dragged it over to Oliver's cross, ignoring the stabbing pain in her foot. She stood it up and managed to open it. With shaking hands she began to climb. *Don't look down.* She glanced over at one of the dead men and felt dizzy. *Don't look at the eyes.* She continued to climb, but it felt like her throat had closed up and it was hard to breathe. *Breathe, don't stop.*

She heard the sound of squealing tires and the grinding crunch of metal. *Don't look back.* The pain in her foot was excruciating. *Don't think about it.* She forced herself to keep climbing and to look up at Oliver. *God, don't let him die.*

Finally, she neared the top of the ladder. Sweating, she felt as though she would fall backward. She reached out and grabbed Oliver's right arm. It didn't budge, and she used it to anchor herself for a moment. Once she had her balance, she took a good look at the arm nearest her, stretched out along the wood of the cross. It was flecked with blood and pulled tight.

A nail had been driven through his palm. A sermon she had heard as a kid flashed through her mind. The pastor had said that the nails would most likely have been driven through Christ's wrists because the hands wouldn't have been able to support so much weight without tearing. She remembered nearly fainting at the graphic description at the time. She screamed in anger and fear.

A hammer. She needed something to yank the nail out. But she was afraid that if she left to find one, she wouldn't be able to climb the ladder again. *I've got to find another way,* she thought frantically. *I could wait for the ambulance; they can get him down.*

She glanced at Oliver's slack face and realized he had passed out. His breath came in shallow little hisses. Crucifixion meant death by suffocation. The person would lose the ability to pull themselves up to get enough oxygen. Unconscious, Oliver would soon lose the battle to breathe. There was no time to wait for anyone to help. It was just her and what little strength she had.

Cindy grasped the head of the nail, prayed for strength, and pulled for all she was worth. It didn't budge. She tried again. Nothing. *Please, God, please!* She grabbed it a third time, and screaming, pulled with everything she had.

The nail came free, and Cindy started to fall backward. She dropped the nail and grabbed at the cross. She caught it. The wood cut into her hand, and she could feel a dozen tiny splinters embed themselves in the wound. She pulled her body forward until she was balanced again. Panting, she looked up, and realized in horror that Oliver's right arm was still affixed to the cross. It should have been hanging free since had pulled out the nail. She looked closely, trying to ignore the sweat pouring into her eyes, which caused them to blur and sting. It took a moment, but at last she saw the clear cable tie that had been wrapped around his wrist, and then around the wood, anchoring his arm firmly to the cross.

Her eyes flew to his other arm, and she saw that it also had been cable tied to the cross. She turned her eyes back to the one within her reach.

She sobbed in frustration as she tugged at it. *I need scissors, a knife, something.* She heard sirens in the distance. She took a breath and took a step down. Pain seared through her left foot, radiated upward, and her leg collapsed. She fell, screaming, fingers scraping on the ladder as she lost her grip. Her other ankle smacked a metal rung. She slammed into the ground, and blood filled her mouth.

Before she could move a shadow loomed over her. *Someone's come to help.* A moment later, her eyes focused on the face above her, and she knew she was going to die.

"You shouldn't have interfered," he scolded.

16

Mark drove his car halfway onto the lawn in front of the church, and he and Jeremiah jumped free. Jeremiah saw the three bodies on the crosses. At the foot of the cross were three other bodies. The man was dressed as a Roman centurion; the teenage boy was dressed in archaic clothing as well, probably representative of a disciple. Both were dead, necks twisted at impossible angles. The third was a woman wearing modern clothes, with the exception of an old-fashioned scarf wound around her head, prostrate on the ground as though praying. Next to her lay a pile of biblical looking clothes that it appeared the killer had not had time to change her into. She lay completely still.

Jeremiah knew without having to see her face that the woman was Cindy. He reached her before Mark did and gently rolled her over. Her face was swollen, and she had a ragged cut on her forehead. Relief surged through him when he realized that she was still breathing, even if it was shallow.

"She's alive, but she needs help immediately," Jeremiah said, looking up at Mark who stared slack jawed at Oliver.

Several feet above him Jeremiah could hear the crucified man's ragged breathing. "He doesn't have long," he added.

As he heard sirens blaring, he checked Cindy quickly for additional injuries. Moments later an ambulance and a fire truck arrived together. A paramedic dropped down next to Jeremiah.

"She's out cold—nasty blow to the head. Also check the broken bones in her foot. She's got lacerations on her hands, splinters in the one," Jeremiah said, standing up slowly and relinquishing Cindy to the other man's care.

A fireman had already ascended the ladder and was busy cutting Oliver down. Others were removing the bodies of the two dead men on either side.

There was nothing he could do for the living. He could only try and provide justice for the dead. Jeremiah took a deep breath and walked over to Mark.

"How is she?" the detective asked.

Jeremiah shook his head. "I'm not sure yet. She's alive, though, and I'm pretty certain she'll pull through."

"Thank God for small miracles, huh?"

"Given what we know this guy is capable of doing, I don't count it a 'small' miracle."

Mark grunted in the affirmative. "It looks like she interrupted him this morning."

"And so did we."

"He's probably long gone by now."

"Probably," Jeremiah said. "I'll check the rooms."

"I'll check the grounds and the surrounding area. Meet me back here in ten and call if you see anything," Mark instructed.

Jeremiah nodded and moved off. He glanced toward Cindy, who was being loaded onto a stretcher. The best thing he could do for her, he realized, was to catch the guy who had done this. She had complained about not feeling safe. All of them should have paid more attention to her.

He moved swiftly and silently toward the main gate which stood wide open. Inside he checked the doors one by one, starting with the sanctuary. It was locked, as were the next few. For a moment he wondered if the killer might have a key and if he should go get Cindy's keys so he could open all the rooms and make sure they were clear.

The next door he tried, the knob turned freely. He tensed, hand reaching for his cell. He stopped. There was no reason to call Mark off of his part of the hunt until he knew for sure he had something. He crouched down before throwing open the door.

Nothing. He waited a second and then another. Finally, he risked a quick glance into the room. He saw half a dozen beat-up couches and cushions scattered all over the floor. A window on the far side of the room let in the early morning sun. He stood and went inside, glancing around. He checked behind each of the sofas and realized it must be where the youth group met.

Suddenly, the door slammed shut and he spun, cursing himself for not having paid attention. He ran to the door and tried to open it. A doorstop had been jammed underneath it though. He turned and headed for the window on the other side of the room. He slid it open, pushed out the screen, and climbed through.

He hit the ground running, and pulled his cell free of his pocket.

"You got something?" Mark asked.

"Guy locked me in the youth room. He should be headed for the main gate."

"On it."

Jeremiah turned the corner and saw a man in black pants, jacket, and hat erupt through the gate and sprint into the parking lot. He turned and gave chase, wishing he hadn't spent so much energy that day running already. The muscles in his legs burned, but he pushed himself faster, ignoring the pain.

He heard footsteps behind him and realized they must belong to Mark. Ahead of him the killer vaulted the low wall that circled the parking lot. Jeremiah was a dozen steps behind him. He also jumped the wall and landed in someone's rose bushes.

He ignored the thorns as he plunged ahead. He saw the man disappear around the corner of the house, and a second later he heard a child's high-pitched scream. He slowed for a moment, and Mark caught up with him. Together they rounded the corner and saw a little girl lying crumpled in the path.

Jeremiah hesitated. He was the faster; he should go after the killer. Mark was armed, though and he was also a detective. He made a quick decision. "I'll take care of her, you stay on him."

Jeremiah stopped, and Mark surged forward. He knelt down next to the little girl and pulled his cell from his pocket. Her scalp was bloody where she had hit her head on the ground, probably when she had been thrown. He gritted his teeth as he called for help.

As he hung up the girl's mother came flying out of the house wearing a shirt and a slip.

"Help is on the way," Jeremiah said, in a soothing tone. "I've called for an ambulance."

"Who are you? What happened?"

"My name is Jeremiah. I'm a rabbi. The police are chasing a man, and it looks like he knocked your daughter down when he ran this way. She hit her head."

The woman collapsed next to her child, sobbing in fear.

"Wait until the paramedics look at her before moving her," Jeremiah advised.

He stood, itching to continue the chase, but the woman grabbed at him with trembling hands. "Help me, help me, please."

"I'm not a doctor," he said.

"Help me pray for her."

He stood, torn between his need to catch the guy who had hurt so many and this plea from a terrified mother. *You're not a policeman, you're a rabbi*, he told himself sternly. He knelt down, took the mother's hand, and placed his other one on the little girl's arm.

Ten minutes later an ambulance arrived, and a minute after that Mark returned.

"I lost him," he admitted as he and Jeremiah moved off a little ways, leaving the girl to her mother and the paramedics.

Jeremiah groaned in frustration. "Hopefully, either Cindy or the girl got a good look at him."

Mark nodded. "Why don't you head back to the church. I'll be back once I've covered things here."

"Okay," Jeremiah said.

He considered returning the way he'd came, but ultimately decided he didn't care for another run-in with the rose bushes. He walked the long way around and found himself again at the front of the church. In addition to the ambulance and fire personnel on the scene, police had cordoned off the area to keep back those who gawked in horror at the scene.

A uniformed officer moved to intercept Jeremiah, but Paul waved him through. "Any luck?"

Jeremiah shook his head. "He got away. There's a little girl who might be able to give us a description, though. Mark is with her and her mother now. What about Cindy? Is she okay? Has she said what happened?"

"She's still unconscious. I heard the paramedics say something about broken bones, but other than that, I don't know anything. Looks like they're getting ready to take her to the hospital, though."

Jeremiah turned and saw them loading Cindy's stretcher into the back of one of the ambulances. He jogged over.

"I want to go with her."

"We're full up back here. Follow us to County General," the paramedic said before closing the door and heading for the driver's seat.

Jeremiah gritted his teeth in anger. His car was still at the park. "But I don't have a car."

"Sorry guy, you need to find another ride."

How about I kill you and take your ride? Jeremiah turned, and his eyes fell on Cindy's car where it was half parked on the lawn. The door stood open. He walked over and discovered her purse and cell phone inside, but there was no sign of her keys. She probably had them with her, but it didn't hurt to check and see if she had left them in one of the doors.

He closed the car door and headed back to the main gate of the church. There were no keys in the lock. He didn't remember any keys in the youth room, but he went over to double check. He removed the door stop and swung the door wide, but didn't go in.

He turned and glanced at the other doors he had not tried earlier. One of them stood open, and he guessed it was where the killer had been hiding. He walked over and discovered that it was a janitor's closet. He checked the other side of the door and found her keys dangling from the lock. He removed them, careful not to touch anything else as he did so.

As he turned to leave his eyes fell on the soda machine. Just on the other side of it, hidden in the shadows, were the bodies of two women, dressed and ready to play their part in the crucifixion scene.

He returned to the front of the church and told Paul what he had seen. The detective looked sick. Jeremiah climbed into Cindy's car, started it up, and peeled out for the hospital.

His phone rang, and when he answered he wasn't surprised to hear Mark's voice. "Are you heading to the hospital?"

"Yes, why?" There was something in the detective's voice that Jeremiah didn't like.

"I saw the two women whose bodies you found."

"Yes, and?"

"And something really bothered me about the setup."

"What?" Jeremiah asked.

"I double checked with a couple of the pastors here. Traditionally, there are three named women at the crucifixion. Three women. Two bodies. And there were extra clothes for a third."

Realization hit Jeremiah hard. "He didn't use Cindy because she was in the wrong place at the wrong time."

"He meant for her to be the third woman," Mark said.

"How soon can you get to the hospital?"

"Not soon enough. You got it?"

"I got it," Jeremiah growled before hanging up.

He stepped on the gas and blew through a red light. He heard the squeal of tires around him, but he didn't care. If the killer wanted Cindy dead, it would be easy enough to accomplish. Since she might have seen his face, killing her would be that much more of a priority for him.

A minute later Jeremiah drove into the parking lot next to the emergency room, grabbed the first space he saw, and sprinted into the building. He ran up to the admissions nurse. "I'm here with Cindy Preston. She was just brought in by ambulance."

"Take a seat, sir, and someone will be with you in a moment," the nurse told him.

"I must be allowed to see her now," he insisted. "The ambulance driver told me to follow him over. It's very urgent."

"I'm sorry, sir, you will just have to wait. It won't be too long."

In a world with a serial killer, he had already been standing there discussing it with this woman for too long. His hand moved toward his phone as he considered having Mark tell her to let him in as part of the ongoing police investigation. "I have to get in there," he said.

The woman looked at him through narrowed eyes, her temper flaring. "I'm sorry, sir, but unless you're a blood relative, I can't let you in until a doctor clears it."

"I'm her husband."

"Can I see some identification?"

He pulled out his driver's license and handed it to her. "Mr. Silverman?" she questioned.

"Newlyweds, just back from our honeymoon. She hasn't gotten her name changed on everything yet."

The woman continued to stare at him skeptically. He set his jaw and met her eyes squarely. "If you don't believe me, call Detective Mark Walters, Pine Springs Police Department. He was the best man, and he'll verify it. I can give you his number if you'd like."

She backed down. "Okay."

She hit a button, and the door next to the counter unlocked. He was through it in a flash. "Follow me," she said, leading him past several beds until he saw Cindy.

"Thank you." Relieved, he sank down into a chair positioned next to the head of the bed.

"I hope your wife is okay," the nurse said, her voice softening.

"Me too."

After she left Jeremiah studied Cindy's face. They had hooked her up to an impressive array of machines. He prayed for her, specifically that she would wake up soon. The longer she lay unconscious following a blow to the head the worse her chances of survival.

Come on, Cindy. Wake up and tell me what this guy looks like. Tell me where I can find him. I'll rip him apart with my bare hands for you. Just tell me who he is.

In his mind he went over everything that had just happened. The Last Supper, the Garden of Gethsemane, and now the Crucifixion, all within a few hours of each other. The killer had missed a few steps, most notably the trial of

Jesus, and the crowd choosing for Jesus to die. Was he getting it right? He had studied the Christian scriptures once years earlier. He'd also seen that Mel Gibson movie, mostly because he'd wanted to hear the Aramaic.

He touched her hand and then leaned close to whisper. "Come on, Cindy. Wake up and tell me all about the Messiah and how he's already come. Then help me figure out what this mad man is going to do next."

"Let's take a look," a doctor said, drawing the privacy curtain partway around. "I'm Doctor Kim."

"Jeremiah," he said, shaking the man's hand.

"Tell me what happened to her."

"She was attacked. The man hit her on the head. I think she also broke her foot."

The doctor's eyes widened as he looked from Jeremiah to Cindy. His face hardened for a moment. "This *man* wouldn't happen to be you, would it?"

Jeremiah felt his self-control slipping. His voice was soft when he finally spoke. "A serial killer the police are tracking. Detective Mark Walters can vouch for that."

"I'd heard rumors," the doctor said, backing down.

"It's okay."

"Most times we see a young woman in here in this kind of condition it's either a car accident or spousal abuse."

The doctor examined her briefly. "You're right. Her foot is broken. She'll need a cast."

"What about the head injury?"

"We took some films. It appears to be a concussion. She should be okay as long as she wakes up in the next few hours. I'll schedule an MRI, just to make sure."

"Do whatever you have to do," Jeremiah said.

"Don't worry. She'll get the best care possible."

"Good. There's also a concern that the guy who did this might be back to finish what he started," Jeremiah said.

"I'll alert the staff to keep a close watch," the doctor said. "I'll be back shortly to put a cast on that foot."

A few minutes later Mark appeared, escorted by the same nurse who had let Jeremiah in. As soon as she had left Mark pulled up a second chair on the other side of the bed.

"Mazal tov."

"What?" Jeremiah asked.

"Next time I'm your best man, let me know. I'd like to make a toast or something. You know, maybe attend the wedding." Mark smirked.

"You're a jerk. Did you know that?" Jeremiah asked.

"Yes, I've been told it's one of my better qualities."

"Don't believe it."

"How is she?"

"It's mostly a waiting game at this point," Jeremiah said. "They'll run some tests, but as long as she wakes up in a few hours she'll probably be fine."

"I hate this whole mess. I'm so ready to be done with Easter," Mark said.

"Did I miss anything?"

"The two guys on the other crosses?"

"Yeah?"

"Thieves. Actual thieves. Can you believe it?"

"Anyone concerned that this guy seems to have skipped ahead a bit in the narrative of the story?"

"You noticed that too?" Mark asked. "I don't know what it means."

"How's Oliver?"

"He'll live. He's pretty messed up, though. I just stopped in to look at him. They have him so doped up he won't be worth anything in the foreseeable future."

"That's a shame, because there's something I'd like to ask him," Jeremiah said.

"What's that?"

"What did he do to this guy?"

Mark nodded. "Crazy is crazy, but I'm inclined to agree with you. I think you'd really have to hate a guy's guts to nail him up on a cross and leave him to die."

"Maybe not a couple of thousand years ago, but this seems very personal. I think things have been leading to this for some time."

"Makes you wonder what Cindy stumbled into, doesn't it?"

"You staying here for a while?" Jeremiah asked.

"Yeah, you need to get going?"

"I'll be needed at the synagogue as word spreads about the Schullers."

"Yeah, I would imagine. Go on, I'll watch her."

Jeremiah looked him over. "No offense, but I think you need to get some sleep instead."

"Probably a good idea. I have a feeling things will get worse before they get better. I'll have some uniforms come watch her."

Jeremiah hesitated.

"What is it?" Mark asked, yawning.

"I saw what happened to the last couple of officers you assigned to watch someone."

The detective grimaced.

17

Jᴇʀᴇᴍɪᴀʜ ᴄᴏɴsɪᴅᴇʀᴇᴅ ᴅʀɪᴠɪɴɢ ᴛᴏ ᴛʜᴇ ᴘᴀʀᴋ ᴀɴᴅ ᴛʀᴀᴅɪɴɢ ᴏᴜᴛ ᴄᴀʀs, but a glance at the clock on the dashboard convinced him he had no time to waste. He drove to the synagogue, doing his best to calm his mind so that he would be able to help others. He ran through a few breathing techniques and slowly brought his emotions under control.

It was a good thing. When he pulled into the parking lot, there were already more than a dozen cars there and Marie was calling his cell. "I'm here. I'll be inside in three minutes," he said, then hung up before she could respond.

Inside the office he found Paul questioning Marie about the Schullers. Jeremiah gave him a brief nod before walking into his office. He sat down in his chair, took a deep breath, and prepared for the onslaught. There was a soft knock on his door after a minute, and Jeremiah looked up to see Olivia Schuller standing there.

He jumped to his feet and crossed to her. He steered her inside and into a chair and then closed the door. "Olivia, you should be at—"

She looked up at him with pain-filled eyes, and he stopped speaking. He had been about to tell her she should be at home, but that was the last place she should be.

"Do you have other family members you should call?" he asked quietly, hoping there was someone who could be with her.

She nodded. "My cousin. She won't be here until tomorrow. Rabbi, why did this happen?"

Because bad things happen to good people. Because some crazy guy has a grudge to settle. Because police in four states couldn't put an end to a killing spree spanning nearly a decade. Because your parents were warm, generous people, and I gave them my blessing to invite the neighbors over. Because it was their time to go. Because suffering is common to the children of Israel. Because no one is ever truly safe.

He rejected every answer as they crowded his brain. None of them would help the young woman sitting in front of him. His words in the next few minutes and her experiences in the next few days would dictate whether or not she would ever again know happiness or peace or safety.

He reached out and took her hand and looked her in the eyes. "Olivia, I do not know why Adonai chose to let this happen. I do know this, there is a purpose for you on this earth, work for you to do, joy for you to own, and sorrows for you to share. If this were not true, you would have been allowed to go with them."

"You really believe that, Rabbi?" she asked.

He closed his eyes for a moment and saw the faces of everyone he had ever lost. Friends, family, colleagues. "I have to," he said, unable to fight the huskiness that crept into his voice. "The first duty of the living is to continue to live."

She nodded, and he knew that she understood. "You're going to be okay," he told her.

He prayed with her, using the moments to regain his composure. He would not have wished Olivia to be the first of his congregation to have to speak with that day, but he was glad that it had happened that way.

When they were finished talking he led her back into the main office. Paul had left, and Marie answered multiple phone lines. When she turned and saw Olivia her jaw dropped and she put her caller on hold. Jeremiah smiled. Somehow Olivia had walked past Marie unseen as evidenced by Marie's surprise at seeing her now. Good for her. Normally it was impossible to bypass his gatekeeper.

"Olivia has a cousin arriving in town tomorrow. Until then—"

"Say no more. Olivia, you'll stay with us. Let me just give Eric a call, and he can pick you up here."

Olivia looked questioningly at Jeremiah, and he nodded approval. "That's just what I had in mind," he said. Despite her flaws, there was no one better than Marie when someone was in trouble and needed a safe harbor. She and her family were always the first to respond in the face of tragedy with compassion and generosity that were overwhelming.

If only he had communicated Cindy's trauma and need more clearly, the Seder might have gone a lot smoother, he realized. A lesson learned.

A few minutes later he helped Olivia into Eric's car. Returning to the office he pulled a chair up next to Marie's desk. "How bad is it?" he asked.

She shook her head. "Everyone knows."

"And I'm assuming that really does mean everyone?"

She nodded. "I've had calls from at least one member of every family."

"And what have you been saying?"

"I've confirmed the deaths only. I've told them that for more information about what happened or services, they'll have to wait until tomorrow."

"So, they'll be expecting an announcement from me."

"Yes."

"Good enough. Couldn't do much better than that. Anyone stop by besides Olivia?"

"No, but the police just left, so I suspect they'll start coming out of the woodwork."

"I think you're right about that. Well, let's see what we can do to take control early."

"Fifteen minutes per person?"

"Yes."

"I know you hate that," Marie said earnestly, "but not everyone will respect the fact that there are others besides them that will need to talk."

"I know."

"If we get more than three waiting at a time, I'll cut that to ten-minute meetings," she warned.

"Sounds fair."

"Is there anything I can get for you?"

"Yes, can you have some food delivered? I ate a long time ago, and I need some fuel."

"Consider it done."

"Thanks, Marie. I'll be in the office."

———⊗∞⊗———

The hospital staff transferred Cindy to a room, and Mark went with her. He kept tabs on Oliver's condition and was pleased when he heard that the little girl had been released with only three stitches. Paul had a chance to talk to her and he had stopped by Cindy's room to let Mark know that she hadn't seen his face.

Cindy was still their best shot at identifying the killer. What Jeremiah had said about the officers who had been assigned to watch Oliver had struck a nerve, and Mark had decided that he would wait until Cindy woke up. He had already been over everything in the war room a dozen times and wasn't likely to come up with anything new there.

He dozed on and off as he waited. At noon he got a call from Jeremiah's secretary wanting an update on Cindy's status. He told her there was no change, and she informed him that he should call as soon as she woke up. He smiled as he hung up with her. Jeremiah's secretary sounded like someone he wouldn't want to cross.

A knock on the door made him look up. He recognized one of the staff members from First Shepherd. He was pretty sure it was the youth pastor. He carried a bouquet of flowers.

"Is it okay if I come in?" he asked.

Mark nodded. "Wildman, right?"

The pastor flushed. "Yeah, but you can call me Dave."

"Okay, Dave."

"You're Detective Walters, yeah?"

"Yeah, name's Mark."

"Cool. Is she going to be okay?" he said, looking at Cindy.

Mark had to admit that she didn't look good. She was white as a ghost, and the bandages on her head did nothing to bring any color to her cheeks. An array of tubes had been hooked up to her arms and pumped oxygen into her nose. A large and clunky cast dwarfed her broken foot. Bandages covered both hands and arms. She looked like half of a mummy.

"I sincerely hope so. The truth is the next few hours will tell us a lot. How are things at the church?"

"How do you think?" Dave said, rolling his eyes. "It's a madhouse, and the lunatics are running the place."

"By lunatics do you mean the head pastor and the music pastor?"

"How did you know?" Dave asked. He looked genuinely surprised.

"They struck me as not enjoying each other's company all that much."

"I'm not sure either of them actually went to kindergarten. They have no concept of what sharing is."

"Tell me how you really feel, Dave," Mark said.

It wasn't his most professional line of questioning, but he was so exhausted he couldn't even reach for his notepad. He also had a feeling that something official might scare off the youth pastor.

Dave sighed and sat in a chair. "You really want to know what I think?"

"I wouldn't have asked if I didn't want to know."

"I think that neither of them should have gone into ministry. Gus would be happier with a career in theater, and Roy would have been very well suited to a career that kept him away from people."

"Accountant?"

"Still too much interaction."

"Wow. Forest ranger?"

"Frankly, I think bears are probably too much like people."

Mark laughed. "That's funny."

"Thanks. It's either laugh or cry, you know?"

"Is that why everyone says you're bipolar?"

Anger flared in Dave's eyes and died out a moment later. "I guess. It's hard being a youth pastor, you know? It takes a level of energy and enthusiasm that is really difficult to maintain emotionally and physically. You've got to be up, up, up!"

"Until you can stop at which point you crash down, down, down," Mark guessed.

Dave sighed. "I don't get all depressed. I just enjoy being quiet and still. One person says bipolar, and shazam! You're stuck with a label."

"I can think of worse ones."

"Me, too. Like coma patient." Dave glanced at Cindy.

"Let me ask you something. I'm guessing you know at this point about the whole serial killer thing."

"That cat is well and truly out of the bag," Dave said with a snort.

"Yeah, not sure how long it was even in the bag," Mark said.

"Not your fault."

"Thanks."

"No problem."

"Okay, so, what would come after crucifixion?"

"Well, his followers put Jesus in the tomb and hid out in the upper room, hoping not to get busted by the cops themselves. Uh, no offense."

"None taken. Go on."

"Then the stone is rolled away, angels appear to the Roman guards, the women find the tomb empty, Jesus appears to them as individuals and then to the group altogether. Shazam! That's Easter."

"Yeah, that's Easter. So, what next then? The crucifixion is the biggie. Wouldn't it just stop there?"

"No, the biggie is the Resurrection. The death is necessary sacrifice, lamb of God, all that stuff. Very tied into Judaism, by the way. No, what makes Christ different than all other sacrifices is that he comes back to life. Good Friday is death. Easter Sunday is life."

"Okay, fine. So, what would you do next if you were a serial killer then?"

"Me?"

"Yes."

"Off the record?"

"I'm a cop, not a journalist."

"Sorry. Okay, let me think. If I were a serial killer, I think I'd go for the empty tomb and the guards."

"Yeah?"

"Yeah. That way I could kill a lot of Romans all at once and in a cemetery. Cool. Can you imagine how awesome that would look if you set the scene just right? You wouldn't need Jesus for that one, because the tomb is empty. For added effect you could even add an angel or two. Maybe have them pushing the stone."

"Okay, and that would be the end?"

"Not even," Dave said. "For my finale, I would wipe out the entire upper room."

"And the entire upper room would be what exactly?"

"The church," Dave said, leaning his head back against the wall. "I'd wipe out the entire church."

"The entire church?" Mark asked, sitting up straight.

"Sha-zam."

Cindy woke up screaming. Pain surged through her. When she opened her eyes, faces surrounded her. She looked for someone she knew and finally saw Mark standing in the corner watching her. He smiled weakly at her.

"What happened?" she croaked.

"You're in the hospital," he answered.

She glanced at a doctor and a few nurses. They were smiling at least. "Am I okay?"

"Yes, you're very lucky," the doctor said cheerfully. "You only suffered a few injuries."

She closed her eyes and began drifting off to sleep. But she didn't want to sleep. There was something she had to tell Mark. She shook herself awake and saw Mark sitting in a chair beside her bed. The rest had gone, and she had a feeling that a little time had passed.

"Oliver, you have to save him."

"It's okay. You saved him. We showed up in time. He's here, and they're taking good care of him. Now can you tell me what happened to you?"

She struggled to sit up.

"Where do you think you're going?" he asked.

"I've got a lot to do today."

"The only thing you have to do today is tell me what happened and then get some rest."

"I thought he was going to kill me."

"Fortunately, Jeremiah and I got there in time to keep that from happening."

"Jeremiah, but I didn't call him, did I?"

"No, he was with me."

"What was he doing with you?"

"We can get to that later. Right now, I need you to focus and tell me what happened to you," Mark said. "The more you can tell me, the better our chances of stopping this guy."

"He said his name was Karl."

"When he grabbed you?"

"No, when he showed up earlier this week at the church. He asked me to give a message to Oliver. He said his name was Karl. Tall, sandy hair, light eyes."

"So, it's someone Oliver knows."

"Yes. I think he's been stalking Oliver, killing people when he finds him. Trying to drive him crazy."

"What did I say about leaving the detective work to the professionals?" Mark asked.

"I don't remember. That's probably a good thing." She looked down at the cast on her foot. "What happened?"

"Hey, you still haven't finished telling me your part of it," Mark said.

"Please."

He took a deep breath. "You were unconscious at the foot of Oliver's cross. He put a cloth over your head. You and Oliver were still alive. The other six were dead, though."

"Six? There were only the two others on the crosses."

"When we arrived there was also a centurion, a disciple, and two more women waiting to be put into position. Jeremiah found them after we chased the killer and lost him."

"You said Oliver is okay?"

"Yes. You are too. Your foot's broken. They've put a cast on it already, but that's the worst of it."

"I dropped the ladder on it."

"Then that shouldn't have come as a surprise to you."

"No." Cindy took a deep breath and recounted the story to him from her arrival at the church. He listened quietly until she had finished telling it and then whistled low.

"You have been through it, haven't you?" he asked.

"What happens now?"

"We're putting you and Oliver under lock and key so that this Karl, whoever he is, can't finish what he started."

She lay for a moment, feeling the pain in her foot. She found the call button for the nurse and pushed it, hoping for some painkillers.

Under lock and key. Nice and safe. It's been ages since I felt safe. "But what if he keeps killing people?" she asked.

Mark cleared his throat. "Hopefully, with the two of you unavailable as witnesses or victims, he'll stop."

"Hopefully?"

He shrugged. "There are no guarantees, especially with something like this."

"I've got a better idea," she said, struggling to sit up again.

A nurse walked in. "What do you need?"

"Can I have some pain medication for my foot?" Cindy asked.

The nurse picked up her chart and flipped through it before checking her watch. "It's about five minutes early, but I think we can make that happen."

"Thank you."

When the nurse left Cindy turned back to Mark.

"So, what is this better idea you have?" he asked.

"I think you should use us as bait."

"Okay, now I know he hit you harder on the head than we thought. I'll get the doctor."

"No! This isn't going to stop until we stop him. If Oliver disappears so does Karl. That's what's happened every other time. Karl will just wait and then show up again later."

"Maybe we'll be better prepared."

"Maybe you won't be prepared at all. This has to end before anyone else dies."

"I'm not willing to gamble with your life," Mark said.

Cindy looked him straight in the eye, just like her grandfather had taught her when she was eight and learning to play poker. "I am."

He blinked first and dropped his eyes. She allowed herself a tiny smile. The nurse returned with her painkillers, and Cindy gratefully swallowed them.

"Did your husband have to go to work?" the nurse asked.

Cindy stared at her in complete bewilderment.

"Yes, unfortunately he did," Mark said hastily.

The nurse turned to him and gave him a once over. "And just who are you again?"

"I was the best man." Mark smiled.

The nurse nodded and left the room.

"Do I want to know?" Cindy asked.

"Probably not. But, for future reference if one of the nurses says something, you and Jeremiah are newlyweds."

"That's the last time I go to a Seder," Cindy vowed.

18

The afternoon had been interminable but Jeremiah was finally done meeting with and comforting members of the congregation. In the parking lot it took him a moment to remember that he had driven Cindy's car.

He fished her keys out of his pocket and a minute later had pointed the car toward the hospital. He was exhausted but he wouldn't be able to rest until he had checked in on Cindy.

When he reached the hospital it proved difficult to find out which room they had moved her to. The nurse on duty told him that she couldn't release that information but luckily the nurse from the morning walked by, recognized Jeremiah, and took charge of escorting him.

"Your wife is doing much better," she said.

"I'm so very glad to hear that."

"The police have kept a close watch on her, and we've restricted access to her area of the floor."

"Thank you, I appreciate the effort. I had this fear as I was driving over that something might have happened to her."

"I've personally acquainted the staff with the danger, and I can assure you we're all looking out for her."

They walked into Cindy's room. She was awake and smiled at him.

"Look who I found for you," the nurse said cheerfully.

"Hi, honey," Jeremiah said. He walked over and picked up Cindy's hand.

"You two behave," the nurse said, before leaving the room with a chuckle.

"I'm glad to see you awake," he said. "I've been worried about you."

"Thank you," she said. "It's not exactly how I planned to spend the day."

"How are you doing?" Jeremiah's glance took in the cast and bandages. She was pale, but her gaze was steady and her hand was warm to the touch.

"They won't let me go home." She frowned. "I tried arguing with one of the doctors, but he said tomorrow. Then he followed that up with a *maybe*."

He grinned. "You must be feeling better."

"Why?"

"Earlier this week wild horses couldn't drag you home and now you can't wait to get there."

She smiled. "I don't like hospitals."

"Most people don't."

"I hate the medicine smells and the beeping of machines, and the feeling of sickness and death. This time it's so much worse, though. I feel completely helpless and exposed."

"I'm pretty sure that's the standard hospital gown experience, although I could be wrong."

She made a frustrated sound in her throat. "It's like I've got a huge target painted on me."

"Perfectly understandable, given what you've gone through. I imagine Oliver must feel even worse."

"Speaking of Oliver, how is he?" Cindy asked, reaching for a cup of water on the table nearby.

Jeremiah let go of her hand and settled himself in the chair next to the bed. "I don't know," he admitted.

"I'd like to pay him a visit. Can you help me?"

"What is it you have in mind?"

"I have a lot of questions, and I don't intend to leave his room until I get some answers."

"Fair enough. You could be in for a long wait, though. I know he wasn't conscious earlier today and even when he comes to he's going to be on so much medication he might not be coherent for a while."

"It doesn't matter. They told me I couldn't leave the hospital but they didn't say anything about leaving my room."

He shook his head. "You've got your mind set on this, don't you?"

"Yes, now can you humor the helpless, exposed woman in the hospital gown?"

"It would be an honor to humor you," he said. "Let me find a wheelchair to make this easier."

"You don't want to see me try out my new crutches?" She pointed to the set leaning against the closet door.

"Actually, I didn't want the entire hospital to see just how helpless and . . . exposed . . . you are."

He left the room and returned with a battered wheelchair.

"That was quick."

"I just told the nurse my wife wanted to go for a little stroll."

"I've been meaning to talk to you about that," she said, blushing.

He couldn't help himself and he smirked. She noticed. "It's not funny!" she protested.

"It's a little funny," he said.

—◦◦◦◦◦—

Mark stood at the front of the room. Dozens of officers from Pine Springs and the neighboring communities sat in chairs, receiving handouts with physical descriptions and rough sketches of Karl as provided by Cindy. For the first time in days he felt like they had a fighting chance of putting an end to the bloodshed.

"We've alerted all the cemeteries in the area to watch for any suspicious activity. Thanks to the fact that Karl accelerated the crucifixion by at least six hours, we can't count on him waiting until late Saturday night or early Sunday morning to recreate the empty tomb and the Roman soldiers. There's also a chance that he'll skip the cemetery altogether, so we're exploring possibilities for other targets. However, odds are good he'll go for this one."

"If you see him, shoot first and ask questions later," Paul chimed in. "He's already killed dozens of people, and we can't risk letting him escape."

"Okay, you all have your assignments. Remember, watch one another's backs. This guy already took out two cops without a struggle. Let's catch this guy," Mark said.

With grim faces the officers left the room and headed for their cars. Paul edged closer to Mark. "Do you get the horrible feeling that we've just provided Karl with Roman soldiers?"

"I try not to think about that," Mark admitted. The fact that Karl had crucified real thieves was a detail no one had overlooked. The killer's grandiose crimes were becoming more detailed and specific. "I guess we should be grateful there are no army bases in town."

"Okay, partner, let's work on the next possible scenario."

"Right with you," Mark said. "I need to grab some more coffee first though."

He walked out of the room and made his way to the coffee maker. He had just finished pouring himself a cup when one of the dispatchers jogged over to him.

"What is it?" he asked.

"I just heard that a busload of tourists has been reported missing in Los Angeles a couple of hours ago."

Mark shook his head. "I'm sure they'll turn up. It's L.A. Odds are they had their tires stolen off the bus or they decided to spend an extra hour in front of the Chinese theater. Anyway, since when do those types of reports concern us?"

"Since this week. Since this one."

He looked at her intently. "Okay, tell me."

"The tourists are from Italy."

Oliver looked even worse than Cindy felt. He was awake and clearly suffering. His forehead and one eye had been bandaged. The other one was filled with pain. Bandages had been tightly wound around his chest, and his hands were thoroughly wrapped, but spots of blood stained the gauze. She winced as she looked at him. In her mind she still saw him hanging on the cross.

"How are you, Oliver?" she asked.

"Not so good," he admitted. "I remember seeing you get out of your car. You called the police?"

"Yes."

"Thank you. You saved my life."

"You're welcome."

"What happened to you?"

"Cindy was captured as she tried to cut you down, Jeremiah said. "Karl tried to make her a part of the story—one of the women at the cross."

"Is he dead?"

"No, he got away," Cindy said.

"I'm so sorry, Cindy. I never in a million years wanted you to get hurt."

"And yet you never warned her of the danger," Jeremiah said, his voice cold and unforgiving.

"I didn't think he would do anything to her. I mean, why would he hurt her?"

"Why would he hurt anybody?" Cindy countered. "And why would he want to kill you?"

Oliver shook his head slowly.

"Why is Karl targeting you? How do the two of you know each other?" Jeremiah asked.

"Oliver, remember everything you told me that night at dinner? You told me to face my problems. You encouraged me to talk about my past, about my sister. You were right. You gain nothing by staying silent, but you could save a lot of lives if you told us what Karl wants."

"Karl and I were in seminary together," Oliver said, his voice barely a whisper.

"You went to seminary?" Cindy questioned.

He nodded. "I graduated too."

"And you didn't go into ministry?" Jeremiah asked.

"I couldn't. Not after what happened."

"What happened?" Cindy pressed.

"We were best friends. We both had very religious upbringings and felt a call to ministry when we were young. People always made fun because Karl was so shy and had a hard time speaking to people. His parents were very legalistic, and they never spared the rod. Next to him I looked like a fun-loving extrovert, even though I wasn't.

"We had another friend, Abby. We were the Three Musketeers. Her family was incredibly strict and controlling. They sent Abby to seminary because they wanted her to marry a pastor, not because they ever expected her to do anything with the education."

Cindy realized that Abby was probably the loved one Oliver had once told her he had lost. When he paused, she nodded, encouraging him to continue with the story.

"But Abby was special. She had big plans to change the world. She wanted so much to help people."

"What happened to Abby?" Jeremiah asked.

"Exactly what her parents had hoped. She fell in love."

"With you?" Cindy asked.

"With both of us, actually. And we fell in love with her. Karl was too shy to ever let her know how he felt, though."

"But you weren't," Cindy guessed.

"No. We were young and we were stupid and for a short while it seemed like the world smiled upon us. We were involved with the theater ministry group. Karl was always too terrified to actually go onstage and talk, but he loved building sets and helping out backstage.

"It was Easter, and our professor had written a new play telling the story of Easter in modern day with language and situations that would be understandable to those who had grown up in the inner cities. He hoped to use it as a real ministry tool. We were debuting it the night before Easter, and most of the school came. Our parents were there. It was meant to be a great night."

Oliver drew a deep breath. "Then, two hours before the play was supposed to start, Abby found me. I could tell by her face that something was really wrong."

"She was pregnant?" Cindy guessed.

Oliver nodded. "Nothing I said helped, but then I was terrified, looking out for myself. I begged her not to tell anyone. I was a coward."

"What happened to Abby?" Jeremiah asked when Oliver stopped talking. The reporter's eyes stared into space as though he were reliving that moment.

"She killed herself. In our play there was a stage gun with blanks. She switched the blanks for real bullets. Then she left a note apologizing, explaining everything, and saying that in the end she didn't have the courage to shoot herself."

"If she didn't shoot herself . . . ?" Cindy let the question trail off.

"Like I said, it was a big night. The role of the mugger was a very small one. No speaking lines. It had taken us four weeks to convince Karl that he could do it. So, when act three started he aimed the gun at Abby, just like he had in all those rehearsals. He fired."

"And shot her to death," Jeremiah finished.

"Yes," Oliver said, sobbing openly.

"He had to know it wasn't his fault," Cindy said.

"The note explained everything. I was so terrified. I was afraid of my parents, of her parents, of being kicked out of seminary. I destroyed the note."

"Without a suicide letter, people thought he meant to kill her?" Cindy asked.

"He was this shy, awkward guy with some really oppressive beliefs. Everyone knew he was crazy about her. And, after she died, they quickly discovered she was pregnant."

"How terrible," Cindy said.

"I never dreamed they would think it was anything more than some crazy accident. I ran away, took a two-month sabbatical from school. Everyone thought I couldn't live with the horror of what had happened. They were only partially right. When I came back I discovered that the drama professor had been fired and that Karl had been convicted of murder."

"Why didn't you speak up?" Jeremiah asked.

"I was still too afraid. I lost my best friend, the woman I loved, and my unborn child. And even to save my soul I couldn't tell people the truth. Because of me she died. Because of me Karl went to prison for ten years, a sweet shy boy falsely accused and locked up with murderers and rapists because I couldn't confess the truth. I violated the most important principle."

"Which is?" Jeremiah asked.

"Do unto others as you would have them do unto you."

"It's not too late," Cindy said. "Maybe if you confessed publicly Karl would stop."

"It's my fault he became a killer, and I would give anything to change that, but it's not going to work."

"How do you know unless you try?" she insisted. "You have the power to stop this."

"You know how I stop it? I run. That's what I do. When I'm not here to witness his performances he stops."

"You can't know that for sure," Cindy protested.

"Especially not now that he's taken such an interest in Cindy," Jeremiah pointed out.

"It's always about me," Oliver said. "He watches me, taunts me. He even broke into the newspaper and swapped out the online crossword puzzle just to taunt me, because he knew what I'd done to Ryan. He knows I love crossword puzzles. He knew I'd see it. No, the only way anyone is safe is if I disappear."

That was one mystery solved. It also explained why Oliver had shredded the puzzle in Cindy's kitchen.

"Why does he keep putting people with names similar to yours in the position of Jesus?" Cindy asked, hoping to at least keep him talking so that she could try and convince him to help.

"Because at seminary I was voted 'Most Christlike'. Ironic, huh? And in the play, I was supposed to be Jesus." He pushed the button for the nurse, and turned his face to the wall.

"You should get back to bed," the nurse said sternly when she walked through the doorway and saw Cindy.

Jeremiah wheeled Cindy back to her room, and she couldn't control her frustration. "Why won't he help us?"

"He's afraid," Jeremiah said.

"That's no excuse for letting people die."

"I know, but you can't force the man to help."

"You sound like a truly frustrated cop," Mark said, popping his head into the room.

"What are you doing back here?" Cindy asked.

"The hospital called to tell me Oliver is awake. However, that looks to have been a temporary condition. A little bird did tell me, though, that the two of you were in there talking to him. Tell me everything."

Unlike most weeks there was no Friday night service at the synagogue, so Jeremiah stayed at the hospital until visiting hours were over and the nurses kicked him out. When he finally got home he sat down at his computer and attempted to organize his thoughts for the morning service.

There was so much to say about Passover itself, and now he had to incorporate what had happened to the Schullers in a way that answered people's questions but didn't create panic or hinder the efforts of the police.

He thought about the things he had told Olivia earlier. He truly did believe them, and he could do worse than sharing some of those thoughts with the congregation. He jotted down a few notes, but tried to keep it open. He often found that when he only gave himself a basic framework there was greater opportunity for inspiration, and people often found the least scripted sermons to be the most moving.

He thought about the two people in the hospital who had survived the latest attack. One was an innocent victim, guilty only of repeatedly being in the wrong place at the wrong time. The other was a guilty victim whose actions had started a chain reaction that resulted in the deaths of dozens, perhaps more. They were a perfect illustration of the fickle and tempestuous nature of fate that gave to each not as they deserved but as it willed.

There was a sermon in there somewhere. He felt it. He also knew that he was too tired and too close to the events to truly see it. The best thing he could do for Cindy, his congregation, and himself was to get some rest. Like most things in life, though, it was easier said than done.

19

Jeremiah had not gotten as much rest as he would have liked. He stood before his congregation and tried to bring comfort for the loss of the Schuller family. He spoke some words from the Psalms and then asked people to reflect on the meaning of Passover. In light of all the death in the community it seemed a poignant reminder. He wondered if the more superstitious among them would consider it a good time to mark their doors with lamb's blood.

After services some of the elders approached him. He could tell by the looks on their faces that they had something in mind, and it would be difficult to talk them out of it.

Malachi was the apparent spokesman for the group, and he plunged in without preamble. "We intend to hold a vigil tonight for those who have lost their lives in the recent tragedies."

Jeremiah didn't like it. With the end of Easter week in sight the last thing he wanted was for members of his congregation to gather together and make a target of themselves.

Before he could protest, Malachi continued. "We've spoken to a few of the elders next door and have decided that a joint vigil would be a good idea, especially in light of what happened to Samuel's family and their guests. These deaths are a blow to the religious community as a whole."

Any other day and Jeremiah would have been pleased at such thoughtfulness. It was just asking for trouble, though, and the involvement of members of First Shepherd would just make disaster all the more likely to strike.

"We understand that you may have some concerns, Rabbi, but we feel that it is crucial for us to make this effort. We will not be hunted into our homes like rabbits hiding from dogs."

He looked into their eyes, and he understood. Never again would they go quietly into that good night, or do the safe thing instead of the right thing. He could respect that. It was one of the things that had made it easier for him to bond with the congregation. Like those in Israel they had not forgotten that being God's chosen people came with a price. They never stuck their heads in the sand but always responded with courage and passion.

He smiled at them. "You have made it impossible for me to say no," he admitted.

"That was the plan," Malachi assured him. "We will hold the vigil tonight at ten o'clock here. That's right after the Easter play ends at First Shepherd."

"I will be here," he said.

"Thank you, Rabbi. We appreciate your understanding and support."

"And I appreciate yours," he answered.

Meeting over, they were eager to be on their way with their own families. Jeremiah successfully avoided getting pulled into any other discussions, and made his way toward the hospital.

⧫

Karl smiled as he drove past Fairhaven Cemetery. The police were so predictable. This cemetery actually had a squad car parked out front. That was okay. What he had in mind would surprise them all. This time he would finish what had been started so long ago.

Oliver would pay for what he had done, and no one would stop his hand of justice. The bus bounced over a pothole, and he eased up a little more on the gas. No hurry. He had plenty of time.

In the back he could hear someone whimpering, a pathetic sound, weak and helpless. Good soldiers shouldn't whimper. He sighed. He'd just have to turn them into good soldiers.

Karl turned off the main road onto the access road and smiled. Soon, all the good little disciples would discover that Oliver wasn't where they had left him. Oh how they would run around and scream and fret. That was okay, because they would all be reunited soon enough.

⧫

Jeremiah was pleased to see that Cindy looked much better than the day before. Color had returned to her cheeks.

"You look like a woman ready to get out of here," he said by way of greeting.

"I am. I'm desperate to get out of here."

"Food terrible?"

"I've had worse. The situation here is intolerable."

245

Before he could ask what was wrong a young nurse bustled in and asked cheerfully, "How are we doing, Mrs. Silverman?"

Cindy glared at him, and it was all he could do not to laugh out loud. "I'm ready to go home," Cindy told the nurse.

"We'll have to see what the doctor says once he gets a chance to look you over," the nurse replied.

She checked Cindy's chart, made a few notes, and then went on her way, leaving Cindy to glare at her retreating back.

"You see?" Cindy asked.

"I do." Jeremiah struggled not to laugh. "Still, it could have been much worse."

"How do you figure?"

"You could have been Mrs. Walters."

"That's not funny," Mark said as he walked in the room. "That would make me a polygamist."

"Can you get me out of here?" Cindy asked.

"Only if the doctor clears it."

"Any news?" Jeremiah asked.

Mark shook his head. "So far all's been quiet. Frankly, I don't like it."

Neither did Jeremiah. After accelerating the pace of the murders sudden inaction by the killer was suspicious. It made him wonder if the next murder had already taken place, and they just hadn't found it yet.

Mark's phone rang, and he flipped it open, his voice anxious as he answered, "What?"

Jeremiah strained so he could hear the voice on the other end. It was Paul, and he sounded grim. "We got a possible hit on Karl and the missing tourists."

"Which cemetery? Who do we have on-site?" Mark glanced at Cindy.

"None of them, and no one."

"What do you mean?"

"It looks like he's reenacting the empty tomb, but he's way ahead of us."

"Just tell me where he is," Mark said, moving into the hall.

Jeremiah followed.

"I'm on my way," Mark said.

"I'm coming with you," Jeremiah informed him.

"No, you're not," Mark snapped, breaking into a jog.

Jeremiah easily kept up with him. "I need to see this through, and it sounds like you need all the manpower you can get."

"This is not a job for a rabbi."

"Yeah, but if you need one, you'll call. Skip it, I'm coming. This guy has done too much damage to the community, and I intend to see that he gets taken down."

"Short of handcuffing you I can't stop you from following me," Mark said grudgingly.

"Great, we'll carpool. It will save gas."

"For a rabbi you sure like to stick your nose into other people's business," Mark said.

"Professional hazard." Jeremiah picked up the pace.

Moments later they were flying down the road, cars scattering as they came up behind them with lights and sirens.

"Which cemetery?" Jeremiah asked.

"A private one. A few of the really old mansions in the area have them. I should have seen it coming. This one belongs to a First Shepherd member named Joseph."

Clearly, that was meant to be significant, but Jeremiah was at a loss. "Okay, you'll have to explain that one for the rabbi in the car."

"When they took Christ off the cross, one of his followers, a rich man named Joseph of Arimathea, gave them his tomb to lay the body in."

"That is clever. It's like he finally picked the right community that had everything he needed," Jeremiah said.

They turned off the street and onto an access road and pulled up behind four patrol cars. Another couple pulled in behind them. Together they wound up the narrow road to the top of a plateau.

It didn't feel right to Jeremiah. It felt too private. For the most part Karl had chosen bigger and flashier. This was wrong somehow.

They parked a short distance from the first gravestones and leaped out of the car. One man dressed like a Roman guard sat on the ground. Another man dressed in normal clothes stood beside him, looking in surprise at all the police cars.

Police officers fanned out as Mark and Jeremiah headed straight for the two men.

"Are you Joseph?" Mark asked.

"Yes."

"Detective Mark Walters. Tell us what happened."

"Well, I came outside this morning to walk a little bit, and I happened to glance over here and saw something moving on the ground. I came over, thinking it was somebody's dog who had gotten loose or something, and I found this guy. He was dressed just like that but his hands were tied behind his back, and he was gagged. I called the police immediately and then I untied and ungagged him."

Jeremiah saw the rope and the bandana on the ground that the killer had used.

"He must have interrupted him during his work," Mark said. "Spread out people. Find Karl and those tourists!"

"I don't think so," Jeremiah said quietly. He crouched down next to the man and spoke a few words of rusty Italian. The man responded with a torrent, and after Jeremiah asked him to slow down he did.

"He's been here for hours," Jeremiah said. "I'm pretty sure he's a decoy. He said that he is the only one in his tour group who doesn't speak any English whatsoever."

"Karl counted on us not being able to talk to him," Mark said, gritting his teeth.

"I think he lured everyone away while he did his work in another cemetery," Jeremiah said.

"What are you talking about?" Joseph asked.

"A serial killer is mimicking the events of Passion Week. We thought since you were Joseph of Arimathea that he was going to use your tomb," Mark said.

Joseph stared at him for a moment. "If he was going to use my tomb, it wouldn't be here."

"What do you mean?" Mark glanced around at the small graveyard.

"I've always found this place pretty creepy. That's why several years ago I bought my family a crypt in Fairhaven."

"Thank you for stopping by and letting me borrow your laptop," Cindy said.

"No problem," Geanie told her with a shrug. "I don't need it back until Monday."

"I'd better be out of here by then," Cindy said.

"Surely, they'll let you go by then."

"What did I miss at work yesterday?"

"Chaos. Fortunately, I think everything got straightened out. The Easter pageant is on for seven o'clock tonight as planned."

"I really want to see it," Cindy said.

"Well, you've still got about six hours. It could happen."

Six hours. Cindy hadn't heard anything yet from Mark or Jeremiah. Had they caught Karl or would people at the pageant need to worry about when he would strike next? How gruesome.

"Anything else I should know about?"

"There's a prayer vigil afterward at the synagogue."

"Whose idea was that?"

"Theirs. Pastor Roy called me this morning to fire up the prayer chain so everyone would know in advance. We'll also make an announcement at the pageant that anyone who wants to join can."

"And the prayer vigil is for . . ."

"Everything that's happened, everyone who's been killed. I think it's mostly for the Schullers and the Jensens."

"I'll be there if I can," Cindy said. "I'm still waiting for a doctor to sign off on me."

"You want me find one for you? I can be really annoying when I want."

Cindy smiled. She had been on the receiving side of Geanie's annoyance. "Let's give them another couple of hours, and then I'll turn you loose."

"You got it. I need to print off some things at church for the prayer vigil, but give me a call if you need a ride or if I can crack some heads."

"I will," Cindy said.

Geanie left, and Cindy fired up the laptop, keeping her fingers crossed that she'd find a wireless signal. She breathed a sigh of relief as she got online.

Armed with more information, it only took her five minutes to find articles relating to the death of Abby and the imprisonment of Karl. She read the original articles about the death. The first one called it a tragic accident.

So when did they start calling it murder?

She scrolled through the initial articles, then found others about the trial. If only Oliver had spoken up, so many lives could have been saved, including Karl's.

Still she searched for that moment—that news article—when it shifted from an accident to a murder in the public eye. If everyone had been willing to accept it as an accident, then it would have been incredibly tragic. Karl might have been scarred for life, but he wouldn't have gone to prison and things would have probably turned out differently. She took a deep breath and continued to search on.

Finally, she found an intriguing link: "Prayer Vigil Turns Ugly." She clicked on the article and skimmed through it. As she read deeper into the piece she realized the true horror of what had happened. The night after the shooting, seminary students held a vigil for Abby. It was still considered an accident.

At the vigil Abby's roommate came forward and revealed Abby's pregnancy and that she was afraid it might have had something to do with her death.

Instead of setting the record straight, Oliver had come right out and accused Karl. The police arrested his former best friend, and the rest was history.

"Oliver, how could you?" she whispered. Photos showed a younger version of Oliver. His face looked innocent, but his eyes might as well have been dead.

You didn't just keep silent, you accused him.

Rage filled Cindy as she thought about what Oliver had done. She surfed the Web for a few more minutes but didn't find anything else of interest. She shut down the laptop, put it away in a drawer, and then swung her legs over the edge of the bed.

Her crutches leaned against the closet. If she could reach them, then she could make it to Oliver's room and give him a piece of her mind. Maybe she could brain him with one of her crutches.

"And just where do you think you're going?" a doctor asked in surprise as he walked into her room.

"Home?" she asked hopefully.

"Well, let's see about that." He picked up her chart and flipped through it.

She briefly considered making a break for it while he was distracted but figured that in the long run it would be less than useless. She waited in frustrated silence as he took his own sweet time.

"How do you feel?" he asked.

"I feel like going home."

"What's your pain number?" he asked.

"Two," she lied. The throbbing in her foot was more like a five, but she wanted to leave.

"Has someone taught you how to use the crutches yet?"

She wanted to lie about that, too, but she figured if she tried them and then face planted they would definitely keep her longer. "Not yet."

"Okay, I'll send a therapist down to help you practice. I tell you what, if he checks you out then you can go home today. If not, you can go home tomorrow."

"That's fair, send him in," Cindy said.

He smiled. "You really are eager to get out of here, aren't you? Is the food that bad?"

She shrugged. *No, there's a killer stalking me, and I'm not safe here. Then again, I'm not sure I'll be safe anywhere.*

Mark cursed himself as he drove through the gates of Fairhaven Cemetery at eighty miles an hour—lights only, no sound. He didn't want to alert Karl yet.

"We've spotted the bus on the northeast corner," someone reported in on the radio.

"You stay here. I don't know what we're up against, and the last thing I need is to worry about you," Mark told Jeremiah.

Not waiting for an answer, Mark exited the car and slipped silently through the grave stones, trying not to dwell on their symbols of death or the death that he was likely to discover.

Movement flashed in the corner of his eye, and he turned his head to see a police officer, weapon drawn, also advancing toward the northeast corner. Northeast. That was where Joseph had said his crypt was. Northeast was where they had found the bus.

A tall structure came into view, and something told him it was Joseph's crypt. He paused, not sure he wanted to see what waited there. He pushed himself on. Even a second's delay could cost someone their life.

He realized he was approaching the crypt from behind. He moved quickly, silently, and circled around.

The scene burst into view. A man dressed as an angel sat atop a small boulder in front of the crypt. Lying on the ground were "Roman soldiers."

Silently, officers converged on the latest crime scene. *We're too late, he's finished his work.* He turned in a slow circle, and then a flash of light several yards away caught his attention.

A second flash told him it was a camera. He took off running, vaulting a low-lying headstone. He twisted in and around the graves and then spotted a man in a dark hoodie and jeans running from him.

Mark shouted, and two other officers joined the chase.

The man ran, then tumbled down a steep slope. Mark struggled to keep his footing. He was almost within reach when he hit the bottom. The guy twisted and ducked behind a large stone angel just as one of the other officers fired his weapon. Shards from the angel dusted Mark's shirt.

The guy ran and zigzagged in and around monuments, making it impossible to get a clean shot. Other officers fired their weapons, and Mark ground his teeth in frustration as more monuments and headstones caught the lead meant for the man they were chasing.

Hindered by the headstones, the man pulled away from them until they hit a long, straight section of land. Mark nearly screamed as he saw the guy put on a fresh burst of speed, which would take him hopelessly out of reach.

Just then, another man stepped out from behind a tall monument right into the runner's path and popped him in the face. The runner dropped, and the interceptor fell on top of him, pinning him to the ground.

Mark didn't slow until he reached the two of them. "Thanks," he said to Jeremiah, his breath ragged.

The rabbi just nodded and continued to pin the man's arms. A digital camera hung on a cord around the guy's neck. Mark bent down and pulled back the hood covering the face. Disappointment washed over him. It wasn't Karl. It was a teenager with wide, terrified eyes and an acne problem.

"Who are you?" Mark shouted.

"Chip."

"What are you doing here?"

"Some guy gave me a hundred bucks and said he needed a picture for a newspaper article. He said not to let the cops catch me because they might take the camera away and use it for evidence."

The other officers groaned. For a brief moment Mark reflected on how Chip owed his life to the gravestones that interfered with every shot. Somebody upstairs was looking out for this kid. Jeremiah stood up slowly, and the sweating teen sat up, rubbing his jaw.

"Were those guys actors or what? It's illegal for them to do what they're doing, is that why they're in trouble? Is it some kind of protest?" Chip asked.

"No, it's a crime scene," Mark said. "Now give me that camera."

20

"Did you catch him?" Cindy asked as Jeremiah walked into her hospital room.

He shook his head.

"Then you're just in time to help me," she said.

"Help you do what?"

"Give Oliver a piece of my mind."

"Is that such a good idea?"

"I don't care. It's what needs to be done," she said, perching on the edge of the bed. "Now hand me those crutches."

He retrieved them for her and she pulled herself up, balancing precariously. Her foot throbbed and she felt like she could topple over, but she set her jaw and started on her way. Jeremiah walked quietly beside her.

When they reached Oliver's room Cindy braced herself and then walked in. The room was empty. She exchanged a puzzled glance with Jeremiah who turned and grabbed a nurse passing in the hallway.

"Where is Oliver, the patient who was in this room?"

"He checked out early this morning," the woman said.

"He got to check out!" Cindy said, brandishing the crutch.

"Is your wife okay?" the nurse asked Jeremiah.

Cindy wasn't sure whether she wanted to laugh or hit the woman with her crutch. Fortunately, Jeremiah intervened. "It's been a long day, and she just wants to go home."

Cindy walked out into the hall and saw her doctor at the far end. "You! Doctor!" she shouted.

He looked up startled.

"See, just fine with the crutches. Now check me out of here immediately!"

Jeremiah stared at her like she had gone crazy. Maybe she had, but she wasn't staying another hour. Not when there was a killer on the loose. Not when Oliver had managed to get out.

Half an hour later she sat in a wheelchair as Jeremiah pushed her out the exit.

"Where's your car?" she asked.

"At the park actually. Fortunately, yours is here."

"Do I want to know?" she asked.

"Probably not."

Soon, they backed out of a parking stall and drove away. She breathed a sigh of relief.

"Are you okay?" he asked.

"Not really. I think I'm about two seconds away from a complete breakdown."

"I think you're entitled," Jeremiah said.

"Not until this is over. Tell me what happened earlier."

"I don't think you want to know."

"Maybe not, but I need to know. It's important. I can't help if I don't know what I'm up against."

"All you really need to do is go home," Jeremiah said.

"No, not until it's all over."

"Seriously, Cindy, I admire your courage, but what do you really think you can do that the police can't? You're a civilian with a broken foot and a deep seated fear of being unsafe."

"I've also been more up close and personal with this guy than anyone else but Oliver," she said. "And I know more about what he might do than anyone else."

"I'm not going to ask you what makes you think that," he said.

"Good. Now take me to Oliver's house."

"Okay, you're going to have to direct me, I've never been there."

"Neither have I," she said. She pulled out her cell phone.

"Who are you calling?"

"Mark. He's been there. He can tell me what I need to know."

She dialed the phone, and a moment later Mark answered. He sounded near his breaking point too.

"Mark, it's Cindy."

"Please tell me you're safe at the hospital. I put Jeremiah into the cab back there to keep an eye on you."

"He's here," Cindy said, "but we're not exactly at the hospital."

"Where are you, home? I'm not sure that's such a great idea right now."

"Then it's a good thing I'm not home."

"I'm not going to like this, am I?" he asked.

"Probably not. I need you to tell us how to get to Oliver's house. He checked himself out of the hospital this morning."

"And you think Karl's headed there?"

"I have no idea, but I am. Just tell me where to go."

Cindy handed the phone to Jeremiah who handed it back after getting directions. "Got it?" she asked him.

He nodded and turned left at the light.

"Thanks, Mark," Cindy said. "I'll call you when I know something."

"Forget that. I'm meeting you there. Paul can finish up here."

Cindy hung up the phone. "Mark's meeting us there."

"I'm not surprised," Jeremiah said.

They pulled up outside Oliver's house in time to see him getting into his car.

"Block him in!" Cindy said.

"It's your car," Jeremiah said. He pulled up behind the other car.

Oliver honked, but Cindy just got out of the car and limped on her crutches over to the driver's side window.

"Oliver, we need to talk."

"I have nothing more to say to you or anyone," he said, his jaw set.

"Yes you do."

She heard another car pull up and assumed it was Mark. "You know, it seemed like everyone saw Abby's death as an accident. In fact, it looked like from those old newspaper articles like there wasn't really an intense investigation. In fact, no one was even talking about prosecuting Karl."

"I don't want to talk about it!" Oliver shouted.

"I do. Tell me what happened next?" Mark asked quietly.

"A prayer vigil for Abby. Everyone got together to pray, remember, mourn. And then her roommate started to talk.

It turned out she was suspicious. She had figured out that Abby was pregnant when she died. She thought someone might have killed Abby. She hadn't thought that Abby might have killed herself.

"But you couldn't risk her hitting on that idea," Cindy said. "So you accused Karl of killing her. And suddenly what everyone thought was an accident turned into murder. You ruined Karl's life at that prayer vigil."

"Stop, just stop!" Oliver begged her.

"No, I won't stop because it's time the truth was told. And you're going to tell the truth, tonight at the new prayer vigil."

"No, you can't make me!" Oliver said.

"I might not be able to force you to do it," she said, "but it's the right thing. The man who looked me in the eye and told me he understood pain would do the right thing. He would help dozens of people get closure and save dozens more from being killed. How many more times can you run from Karl? How many more times before he kills you? It's time to put an end to this. Help us catch Karl. All you have to do is go to that prayer vigil and tell people what really happened. Karl will come. He'll hear your confession, and we'll catch him. It's the right thing to do. It's the only thing to do. If you ever hope to be a true shepherd you'll act like one now."

She could feel Jeremiah's hand in the small of her back. Beside her Mark stood, arms crossed.

"Cindy," Mark said softly. "I get what you're trying to do, but we've already figured out that he's going to hit the Easter pageant at First Shepherd. It's the upper room. He's looking for a way to symbolically wipe out the early church."

"No, it was the Easter pageant. But now it's changed. Now it's the prayer vigil."

"How do you know?" Mark asked.

"Because the play is where Abby died, but the prayer vigil is where Oliver betrayed Karl. It's the terrible irony. Oliver was the one voted most Christlike by his peers, and yet he was Judas. He gave the kiss of death and betrayed an innocent man to the authorities. It has to be the prayer vigil. We've come full circle. I'm right, aren't I, Oliver?"

Oliver nodded slowly. "Yes, you're right about everything."

"Everything?"

"Yes. It's time to stop running. It's time to tell the truth and stop being Judas."

She turned away so that Oliver wouldn't see the look on her face. She breathed deeply, trying to regain control of herself. She hadn't believed until that moment that he would do what she asked. She looked at Jeremiah and smiled weakly.

"Are you okay?" he mouthed.

She nodded her head.

∞

Mark was amazed. He wasn't entirely sure what he had just witnessed, but he was grateful he had been there. His team was set to catch Karl at the Easter pageant, but Cindy had given him a viable alternative. It was still up to him to decide where to concentrate his forces. The church and the synagogue were next door to each other, and the events were back-to-back so he could overlap some of his coverage.

"Rabbi, I'll need some help from you prepping at the synagogue," he said.

"Of course." He glanced apprehensively at Cindy.

"I also need you to baby-sit her. I'll take care of Oliver."

"Fair enough."

"All right, let's go catch a killer."

—⚬⚬⚬—

A few hours later Cindy sat with Jeremiah in his office at the synagogue. She was exhausted, and the painkillers had stopped working.

Mark had offered to take her home, to surround her with half a dozen officers and let her ride it all out in relative safety. She had refused. She knew she wouldn't feel any safer there. As much as this was all about Oliver, she couldn't deny that Karl had set his sights on her too.

She worried that Oliver would change his mind. She wanted to be there in case she needed to talk him into it again. And, as much as she didn't want to admit it, she had come this far and she needed to see it play out.

"The Easter pageant should almost be over," she said, glancing at her watch.

"I'm sorry you missed it," Jeremiah said.

"It's okay. I can see it next year."

"It's not too late to go home. I can take you."

"No, I have to do this," she said.

Someone knocked on the door. She held her breath as Jeremiah opened it. Mark stood there, looking intently at them both. "It's time."

Cindy got up and followed Jeremiah and Mark on her crutches out into the hall, where the Seder had been held. Since the prayer vigil would include a mixed group of Jews and Protestants, it had been decided that the hall would be the more appropriate venue.

An impromptu stage had been set up, and Jeremiah helped her to her seat. On the far side of the stage a trio of officers escorted Oliver to his chair before disappearing into the woodwork. It was important that the police be present but practically invisible.

Jeremiah wrapped his hand around hers and leaned close to her. "I have to be honest, this is going to be dangerous," he said. "We're risking our lives."

She threw her arm around him and hugged him hard. "Thank you."

"For what?" he asked, looking startled.

"For telling the truth. I know we could die. It's just so nice to hear someone else admit it. Usually people try to tell me I worry too much. This . . . this is better."

"You just needed the danger to be acknowledged?"

"Yes."

"What happened to your sister, Cindy?"

"It's not important," she said, shaking her head.

"All evidence to the contrary. Come on, who can you tell if not your rabbi?" he said, voice teasing.

"Oh, you're my rabbi now. Here I thought you were my husband."

"I suppose you'd like an explanation about that?"

"Oh, no, it's so much preferable to have you and Mark teasing me and the hospital staff calling me Mrs. Silverman."

He chuckled.

"You see, there you go again!"

"You're right, I'm sorry. When we arrived at the emergency room, they wouldn't let me in unless I was blood family. I couldn't risk leaving you alone with the killer on the loose after he had already made an attempt on your life. So there you have it."

"Wow, somehow the truth is more boring than I anticipated."

He shrugged, and then his expression turned serious. "What happened to your sister?"

"She died when I was a kid. It was terrible, and stupid, and didn't have to happen. Maybe someday I'll tell you the whole story, but that's all I've got right now for my husband and my rabbi."

He smiled at her, and it was tinged with sadness. "'From childhood's hour I have not been / As others were; I have not seen / As others saw; I could not bring / My passions from a common spring. / From the same source I have not taken / My sorrow; I could not awaken / My heart to joy at the same tone / And all I loved, I loved alone,'" he quoted.

"That's from one of Edgar Allan Poe's poems."

"Yes."

"I thought those poetry books didn't belong to you," she accused.

He shrugged. "I said I didn't own them. I never said I didn't read them."

She shook her head in amazement. "I read that poem a lot when I was a kid."

"I'm not surprised."

"I am. You're just full of surprises."

The lights flared on in the hall, and Cindy took a deep breath. "Here we go."

People poured in quietly and sat in the rows of folding chairs that had been set up. Cindy found she couldn't look at them. She knew friends and fellow church members were in the group, and she felt that looking at them would somehow make everything that much more frightening.

The police had debated about warning people so that they might want to stay home, but the enormous task of reaching everyone and the certainty that if they tried the killer would also hear had eventually meant that they said nothing.

Jeremiah had told her that since the truth about the serial killer was out, the people attending the vigil should already be aware of at least a modicum of danger, but it didn't make her feel any better.

The room filled up quickly, a hush on the crowd. Jeremiah stood up, and all eyes focused on him.

"Welcome friends and neighbors. We are here tonight to reflect on the lives of those we have lost and to pray for the family and friends who must carry on despite this great loss. I am pleased to welcome members of First Shepherd here. I only wish that it could have been under happier circumstances.

"First, let us bow our heads in a moment of silent prayer."

Cindy didn't bow her head or close her eyes, though she prayed. She could see Oliver's eyes glinting in the dim light that filled the hall. Jeremiah's head moved slowly from side to side.

She didn't realize that she held her breath until Jeremiah spoke again. "We have with us tonight two survivors from yesterday morning's crucifixion," he said, turning to indicate first Cindy, then Oliver. "Join me in a moment of silent prayer for them."

Now. *He's going to come after us now*, Cindy thought, her heart pounding out of control.

The silence stretched on, and there was a roaring in her ears. Her breath quickened, and she could feel panic rising up in her.

"They have asked if they could say a few words," Jeremiah said. His voice was so loud that she jumped. "Oliver?"

Jeremiah sat down, and Oliver stood up. He shook from head to toe, and his face seemed ash white. "My name is Oliver. I was the one on the middle cross yesterday. I just wanted to say I'm not Christ. In fact, I can't think of anyone more un-Christlike than me. I'd just like to say I'm—"

The power went out, plunging the entire room into darkness. A murmur of concern rose from the crowd, and Cindy lunged to her feet, wincing as pain shot through her broken foot and up her leg. She heard a thud from the other side of the stage.

Jeremiah pulled a flashlight from his pocket and trained it on the space where Oliver had been standing. He was gone. Jeremiah ran forward, and Cindy worked her crutches to thump right behind him.

They heard a muffled grunt behind the stage. Jeremiah turned and his flashlight played over the body of Paul, who lay unmoving on the floor.

Cindy screamed. Jeremiah paused to scoop up Paul's gun, and Cindy saw him tuck it into the back of his waistband before heading out the back door.

She followed, too terrified to be left alone. She hit the crash door and was outside in a moment. The cold night air hit her face full-on.

She glanced around. There were a few lights on outside, but they were weak and far between. "Oliver!" she shouted, praying he could hear her and make some sound that would help them find him.

She stopped and realized she couldn't see anyone. She fought the urge to turn around and head back into the hall. She could hear shouting from inside, though, and realized the police had their hands full maintaining crowd control.

She heard a noise like a whimper to her left. She took a few steps, trying to let her eyes adjust to the dark. "Oliver?"

Where was he? Where was Jeremiah, or Mark? Where was Karl? Her heart pounded faster and faster. She shuffled a few more steps.

Suddenly, someone grabbed her from behind, and an iron arm wrapped around her neck. The tip of a knife pressed against her throat. She twisted and kicked, her crutches flailing uselessly before clattering to the ground, but he was too strong. She tried to drive her elbow into his stomach, but he twisted in such a way that her blows only glanced off of him.

I'm going to die! I'm going to die! I don't want to die!

She tried to stomp on his insole but failed. In response he tightened his grip, cutting off her air supply. Fresh panic surged through her, and she struggled harder, even though she could feel the knife cutting into her neck.

He laughed in her ear. "Sad little Cindy. So afraid, so alone. No one can save you."

She looked around wildly, and then saw a grim-faced Mark standing nearby. He had drawn his gun. She tried to fight loose, terrified that Mark would shoot her accidentally.

She looked up again, and her eyes found Jeremiah. He stood a few feet away from Mark, his hands hanging loosely at his sides, his whole body still.

Out of the corner of her eye she could see Mark slowly lowering his gun. She kept her eyes focused on Jeremiah, though. If anyone could save her, it was him. It had always been him. Gently, he smiled at her.

Then his hand moved so fast she couldn't see what he had done. She heard a gunshot, and Karl fell straight to the ground, the knife he held falling with him. She jumped toward Jeremiah who stood with empty hands. He reached for her and she fell into his arms.

As Jeremiah held her up, she turned and saw Karl on the ground, a gaping hole where his left eye had been. Mark snatched up his gun from the ground and moved toward the killer.

Jeremiah tried to turn her head away, but she needed to look. She needed to see his other eye, so very dead, before she could completely relax.

"It's over. He's dead," Jeremiah whispered.

She shuddered in relief and turned back to look at Jeremiah. His eyes were cold and hard, but he smiled at her—the same smile he had given her just before he shot Karl.

"I thought you said you were excused from military service in Israel," Cindy said.

"I said it was possible to be excused from service. I never said I didn't serve."

"Thank God for that," she said.

"Yes," he agreed.

It was over, truly over. Other officers arrived and swarmed around Mark and the body. They left Jeremiah and her alone, though. She saw Paul stagger out of the hall, rubbing the back of his head.

Lights flooded on around the area. She jumped and screamed as her eyes met Oliver's. He was dead, hanging from a rope tied around a tree limb.

They all stared in horror. "Karl's last victim," Cindy said quietly.

Paul shook his head. "When the lights went out, Oliver rushed me and knocked me out."

"Do you think he killed himself?" Jeremiah asked quietly.

Cindy looked at the slack face. "I don't know whose hand was on the rope, but I think it's safe to say that he did this to himself."

Jeremiah kept his arms around her, and she put hers around him before leaning her head against his chest. She thought she might cry, but she didn't. The relief was too great, too complete, and there had been enough tears shed.

"Hey," he said softly.

"What?" she asked, tilting her head up to look at him.

"There's been something I've wanted to say to you all week."

"What is it?"

"Happy Easter, Cindy."

She smiled. "Happy Passover, Jeremiah."

21

Several hours later, Jeremiah and Cindy stood quietly and watched the sun rise. She hadn't watched the sun rise on Easter Sunday since she was a little girl. It was magnificent, and she could feel the warmth as though it were the love of God, wrapping her in His arms, comforting her.

Jeremiah put an arm around her back, and she leaned her head briefly on his shoulder. They had made it; they had survived.

"I couldn't have done this without you," she said quietly.

"I think you could have, but I'm glad you didn't have to."

"Can you imagine? Last Sunday we didn't know each other at all."

"It does seem strange," he admitted.

"You know what else?"

"What?"

"Today, right now, I feel safe. Completely safe."

He smiled at her. "Glad I could be part of that moment."

Mark walked up and watched the sun rise with them. "It's a good day."

"Yes, it is," Cindy agreed.

"There are some reporters here who'd like to talk with you. Do you want me to chase them off?"

"No, I'll talk to them now. Might as well get it over with."

"You want me to go hide some chocolate bunnies for you for afterward?" Jeremiah teased.

Cindy punched him lightly in the arm. "You aren't going anywhere. But you totally owe me chocolate bunnies later."

Jeremiah looked uncomfortable as the reporters approached. As they answered questions he did his best to downplay his role in the events. She gave the reporters the information they wanted and was glad when they left.

As she looked at Jeremiah she thought about the smile he had given her right before he had killed Karl. She wondered how he was dealing with that, but didn't want to ask. She figured if he wanted to talk about it he would. She was just grateful he'd had the skill and the resolve to save her life.

"Can I buy you breakfast?" she asked.

"I thought I was buying you chocolate bunnies?"

"Don't be silly. That's not breakfast, that's dessert."

"Okay, you twisted my arm."

Her foot still hurt but she would live. She walked slowly out to the car on her crutches, and he stayed next to her, a hand on her back as though ready to spring into action if she should need him. It was nice.

In the parking lot they again ran into Mark who gave Jeremiah a thoughtful look.

"Do you need anything else from us?" Cindy asked.

"No, we're good to go," Mark said. "The two of you okay?"

"Yes," Jeremiah said.

"Good call about the prayer vigil," Mark told her.

"Thanks."

"You've got an eye for this sort of thing."

Cindy blushed. "Call it persistence fueled by motivated self-interest."

"Whatever it was, thank you. And don't ever do it again."

"Don't worry, I won't," she laughed. "Care to join us for breakfast?"

"No. Soon as I'm finished here I'm headed home to my wife."

"Happy Easter, Detective."

"You, too, Cindy."

After breakfast she helped Jeremiah retrieve his car at the park. He followed her to her house, made sure she was comfortable on the couch with her leg up, and finally said good-bye. She was sad to see him go, but it was nice to be home and to feel completely safe there.

Minutes later the phone rang, and it was Geanie. She came over to collect her laptop an hour later and ended up staying all day to watch movies with Cindy.

After she left Cindy went online to their local newspaper. The headline read: "Church Secretary Stops Killer!" She flushed with pleasure but felt bad that the title said nothing about Jeremiah. Included with the article was a picture of her and Jeremiah taken early that morning.

"Not bad," she said with a smile. For a woman who had been terrified, held at knifepoint, been up all night, and was suffering from a broken foot, she looked pretty good.

She captured the article as a PDF and then emailed it to her parents and her brother with a feeling of satisfaction. "Top that one, Kyle," she said as she hit send.

Next, she went to Ryan's blog. There, under his last post, she posted a comment letting everyone know that while Ryan had been killed by the same man who took the lives of his family, that killer was now dead. She hoped that it helped the people who visited the site believe that there was hope for closure for themselves. It was sad, but at least she felt like it was a small thing she could do for the man she had tripped over.

She slept better than she could ever remember sleeping in her life. When she woke up in the morning she took her time getting dressed. Then she picked up the phone and called her mother.

"Hello?"

"Mom, did you get the newspaper article I sent?" Cindy asked.

"Yes, dear, it was very nice."

Nice? That was it?

"I was very sorry, though," her mom said.

"That so many people died? That I had to go through so much?" Cindy prompted.

"No, that the nice young man is Jewish. It's too bad, really. He's quite handsome."

Cindy stared in disbelief at the phone. "That's it? That's what you got from the article, that it was too bad Jeremiah's Jewish?"

"Yes, I'm sure he'll make someone a wonderful husband."

"What about the rest of it, Mom? My life was in danger from a serial killer. And I stopped that serial killer. I saved lots of lives."

"I'm sure you did your part."

My part? There weren't words for what she was feeling.

"Well, dear, I won't keep you from your work. Kyle sends his love."

She hung up on her mom and pounded the ground with a crutch before she burst out laughing. Some things never changed.

I've changed, she thought proudly. She grabbed some breakfast and then headed for the church. She had thought about calling in sick, but she had missed most of the previous week. Besides, she would have to deal with the gauntlet sooner or later. She might as well get it over with.

Everything seemed different as she drove to work. Colors seemed brighter, crisper. She finally pulled into the parking lot and realized she was the first one there. For a brief moment she remembered the Monday before. So much had changed since then. Even still she felt a moment's hesitation wondering what waited for her on the church property.

Jeremiah noticed that Cindy's car was already in the parking lot when he drove up. Marie's car was also there. Jeremiah got out of his car, slammed the door, and then noticed Marie standing a few feet away with her arms crossed, glaring at him.

"What is it?" he asked. "Things went really well the other night. The police caught the killer . . ." His voice drifted off as he realized that wasn't what she was angry about.

"The hospital called a few minutes ago looking for you."

"Yes?" he asked, still not sure what she was so mad about.

"They wanted to check up and see how Mrs. Silverman was doing."

"I can explain," he said.

"I don't want to—"

Suddenly, there was a scream from next door, and Jeremiah recognized Cindy's voice. He turned and vaulted the hedge between the two parking lots and raced toward the church buildings.

Not again!

The sanctuary door stood open, and he flew through the door, skidding to a stop as he took in the scene.

Cindy hands were pressed to her mouth. A few dozen people stood in the sanctuary decorated with balloons and streamers. A huge banner read, "Thank you, Cindy!"

She turned to stare at him with wide eyes.

Jeremiah burst out laughing. "I take it you're not in distress."

"I am, but not the bad kind!"

"Surprise," Geanie said with a smile, handing Cindy a deck of cards. "To replace the deck you lost."

"Thank you," she said.

"Thank you," several people chorused.

She turned and looked at him. "Thank you, Jeremiah," she said softly.

He thought about the wild week that had ensued after he answered her first scream. He thought of everything that had happened and the lecture that he would get from Marie when he returned to the synagogue.

"You're welcome," he said, giving her a wink.

Discussion Questions

1. At the heart of this book is the question of what is safe. In the first chapter Cindy thinks "no one is ever safe." Has anything happened to you that robbed you of your ability to feel safe? What did you do about it?

2. At their first meeting (chapter 2) and throughout the book, the detective refers to Jeremiah as a Good Samaritan. What was the story of the Good Samaritan and why does Jeremiah object to the title?

3. Was there a time when you were a Good Samaritan? Was there a time when someone else was one for you? How did you feel either time?

4. There is the reality of being a Christian and there is the perception of the outside world to being a Christian. How do these two differ in your life? Are there things you do like Cindy's card playing (chapter 1) that some people wouldn't expect of a Christian? How do you educate nonbelievers about the reality of being a Christian as opposed to the stereotype?

5. In the opening moments of the first chapter, it is revealed that while Cindy is a Christian and works at a church she still struggles with understanding her place in the church and even what is and isn't church-like behavior. Have you ever felt you didn't fit into a church because people worshiped differently or had different expectations of church than you? What did you do?

6. Two of Cindy's coworkers, the pastor and the music director, can't get along, and their squabbles hurt the

rest of the staff (chapter 8). Are you involved in a dispute with a coworker or fellow church member that is hurting other people? If so, what can you do about it?

7. What is Passover? How does it relate to Christianity? What part of the Jewish Seders did you find most intriguing or relate to most strongly?

8. In chapter 7, Cindy reveals that her sister died when she was younger. It clearly has a great impact on her. Have you experienced the death of a loved one that changed how you interacted with life and other people?

9. In chapter 7, Samuel struggles with whether or not to invite his neighbors to a Seder at his house even though they have expressed interest. Do you know someone who has expressed interest in your faith that you have not followed up with?

10. If there is someone you haven't followed up with regarding faith, what is standing in your way?

11. Like Oliver is there some truth from your past that you've been hiding from and that has been slowly destroying you (chapter 19)? What can you do to let the past go and to move on?

12. Cindy feels like she is constantly being overshadowed by her brother, Kyle, and that her mother favors him. Do you also struggle withaz the feeling that a relative, friend, or coworker overshadows you? If so, what can you do to focus more on your own talents than on wishing you had theirs?

I Shall Not Want

⸻⸻⸻

1

CINDY PRESTON LOVED FRIDAYS. ANYTHING-CAN-HAPPEN FRIDAYS WAS how she liked to think of them. As First Shepherd Church neared the holidays, Fridays became even more deserving of their names. Being a secretary at a church was a far more chaotic life than most people imagined.

For Cindy, the job had gotten even more exciting a few months earlier when she had stumbled across a dead body in the church sanctuary. The week that followed had seen several people murdered by a serial killer. Along with Jeremiah, the rabbi at the synagogue next door, Cindy had been an important key in halting the killing spree.

For a couple of months afterward the church had seen a swell in attendance as people came to gawk at the woman who survived an attack by the Passion Week Killer and helped the police turn the tables on him.

Their interest had gradually waned, and aside from three new members who actually joined the church, things had pretty much returned to normal. That was just how Cindy liked it.

The one unfortunate downside was that her friendship with the rabbi—forged in shared danger—had slowly faded as well. They still exchanged pleasantries over the hedge that separated the parking lots of the church and the synagogue, but not much else. It made sense, really. They had nothing in common.

But Cindy had grown increasingly restless. She blamed it on the fact that the spice of her friendship with Jeremiah had deflated like a birthday balloon. She, Cindy, who had always walked on the safe side of life, had actually been considering doing something a little daring for once.

Of course, participating in a speed-dating event would rank low on most people's danger scales. It wasn't exactly bungee jumping. To Cindy, though, it was bold and risky. She was always so selective about the men she dated, thoroughly getting to know a guy before spending time alone with him. People had told her she was paranoid, but it wasn't like she didn't have reason. After all, the last man she had eaten dinner alone with had turned out to be the same one who had killed the man whose body she had tripped over in the sanctuary. A girl didn't get over that quickly.

No, anything-can-happen Fridays were her idea of excitement. Even showing up at work on a Friday was a big risk. It was the week before Thanksgiving, and people were starting to get that crazed look in their eyes that said Christmas was coming.

Poor Thanksgiving. It had been relegated to the lone Thursday holiday that heralded the biggest day of the year—Black Friday—when every mall was packed with Christmas shoppers. It was a shame, really. It was such an American custom, and in a world that seemed like it was on the verge of constant chaos, people needed that oasis of time to contemplate what had gone before and to be grateful for having survived it one more year.

Geanie, the church's graphic artist, flopped down in the chair at her desk. Her red leather mini-skirt and black silk blouse might have looked odd on someone else, but on Geanie it was almost elegant. By contrast, Cindy's long black skirt, white sweater, and sensible shoes felt boring.

Just then, the front door to the church opened, and Joseph, one of the church's most prominent members and Pine Spring's most eligible bachelor, walked in. One of his dogs, a large white poodle, paced beside him. Joseph walked right up to her desk without hesitation and sank into the chair across from her. The dog lay down next to her master.

"How's it going?" she asked.

He smiled that bone-tired smile people gave when the answer was "crappy" but they were too polite to say so.

"Fine."

"Are you all set for the big event?" Cindy asked.

He nodded and closed his eyes. "You're still coming tonight, right?"

"Of course, I wouldn't miss it. This is huge, and I want to support it," Cindy said.

"I knew you wouldn't let me down."

In addition to all of his church activities and running his own media empire, Joseph was constantly involved with charity work. His latest project, targeted at helping the homeless to improve their lives and find the inspiration and help to get back on their feet, was ambitious. Many critics said he was crazy, but Cindy believed in what he was doing. The church, along with all the others in the area, supported a local homeless shelter, and Cindy dealt with several of its regulars. After weeks of preparation, a new program would be launched that evening on the lawn outside of Joseph's family mansion.

"How's it going, Clarice?" Cindy asked, addressing the dog. "I haven't seen you since you had your puppies."

Clarice looked at her and gave a slight shake of the head.

"She needed a break so I brought her with me. Seven poodle puppies is enough to drive anyone insane. They're fast and clever. She and I have been chasing them all over the house this morning, trying to get them corralled into one room."

Cindy laughed out loud at the image, and Joseph grinned.

"Six o'clock, right?" she asked.

"It starts at six. Please tell me you'll be there before that."

"I'll head straight to your house from work. It should only take me about ten minutes."

"You are an angel," he said.

"Do you need me to bring anything?"

"Your sense of humor. Without it, this might get really depressing."

She smiled. "I'll do the best I can."

He stood abruptly. "That's all anyone can ask of us. Thanks, Cindy."

"You're welcome."

He waved to Genie and then left the office.

"You should totally go out with him," Genie said.

"Not my type."

"Yes, because tall, dark, and rich is sooo unattractive," Genie said.

"Why don't you go out with him? You're not seeing anyone right now, are you?"

Genie made a face. The younger woman was once again between boyfriends and didn't like it one bit.

When five o'clock rolled around, Cindy chased everyone out of the office, locked the door, and headed for her car. Ten minutes later she was driving up the hill to Joseph's house. She made it to the designated parking area and wedged her car in between a Humane Society vehicle and a news van.

Joseph directed the chaos from the center of the lawn, with Clarice beside him. Half a dozen large tents had been set up with outdoor lights to illuminate them. Several small paddocks had been created with little portable fences. Inside each, a variety of dogs napped, ate, or played with each other.

When Joseph saw her, he hugged her impulsively. Surprised, Cindy hugged him back but pulled away when she saw a flash go off from someone's camera.

"What do you need?" she asked.

"If you could go inside and tell my assistant, Derek, to bring out Buford Augustus Reginald the Third that would be great."

"Who?" Cindy asked.

"It's a puppy."

"Oh, Buford . . . August—"

Joseph stopped her with a raised hand. "Just ask him to bring out Buff."

"Okay, I think I can handle that," Cindy said with a smile. "Any idea where Derek will be?"

"No, I've called his cell twice, but he's not picking up. His car's here, though, and he's not outside, so he must be in the house. Try my office first—second floor, third door on the right."

"Got it." Cindy turned and headed for the house.

The massive mansion had been built by Joseph's grandparents. She had been in it only twice before, and that was for church functions. When she entered the foyer, she left the noise of setting-up outside. The house seemed empty.

"Derek!" Cindy shouted. So it wasn't dignified to yell, but it would be a lot faster than searching the house. She listened before heading for the stairs.

"Derek!" she called again as she reached the upstairs landing.

Suddenly, she heard the sound of smashing glass, like someone had dropped a water goblet. She noticed the third door on the left was ajar. She moved toward it.

"Sorry to startle you, Derek," she said, swinging the door open.

There was no one in the room. "Derek!" she called again.

She saw a cell phone on the desk and wondered if it was Derek's. She had seen Joseph's on his belt, and he had said he'd been trying to call his assistant. She moved toward the desk, picked it up, and then turned. Her shoe crunched on something, and she looked down. Broken glass littered the floor on the left side of the desk, and some shards seemed to have flown several feet in all directions.

Behind the desk, sheers that covered the French doors, leading to a large balcony, fluttered in the breeze, and she walked around the right of the desk. As soon as she did, she saw him—Derek—lying on his back with blood pooling underneath his head. His eyes were fixed in a death stare at the ceiling. In his fist, he clutched a dog's leash.

Cindy screamed and leaped backward. She dropped the cell phone on the floor, dug through her purse, and found her own cell. She hit the speed-dial button for Detective Mark Walters, the investigating officer on the Passion Week Killer case.

"It's Cindy Preston," she said as he answered the phone.

"Cindy?" he asked, sounding bewildered. "Why are you calling me?"

"I'm at Joseph's house—the guy who lives on the hill. Someone's been murdered."

"On my way. I'll call it in. Make sure nobody touches anything."

"I will," she promised, and then hung up the phone.

She heard footsteps racing up the stairs and down the hall. "Are you okay?" a familiar voice asked behind her.

She spun around and stared at Jeremiah in shock. "What are you doing here?"

"The charity event. The synagogue is supporting it. What are you doing here?"

"So is First Shepherd. Joseph asked me to come."

Jeremiah moved slowly into the room, his eyes checking out every inch. "Did you scream?"

"Yes."

"What happened?"

"It seems you've come to my rescue again," she said, her voice quivering.

"I don't follow."

She took a step to the side, and he saw the body. He blinked rapidly several times and then looked at her. "You just found him?"

She nodded.

"You've got to be kidding me."

She shrugged as tears spilled down her cheeks. "It's any-thing-can-happen Friday."